The Immortelles

The Immortelles

Gilbert Morris
&
Lynn Morris

WestBow
Press
A Division of Thomas Nelson Publishers
Since 1798

visit us at www.westbowpress.com

Published in Nashville, Tennessee, by WestBow Press, a division of Thomas Nelson, Inc.

Scripture quotations are from the King James Version.

Publisher's Note: This novel is a work of fiction. All characters, plot, and events are the product of the author's imagination. All characters are fictional, and any resemblance to persons living or dead is strictly coincidental.

ISBN 0-7852-6806-5

Printed in the United States of America
04 05 06 07 PHX 5 4 3 2

I dedicate this book to my children—
Lynn, Stacy, and Alan.
All so different—but all so loved.

The Creole Heritage

In the early nineteenth century, the culture of New Orleans was as rich and wildly varied as the citizens' complexions. Pure Spanish families, descended from haughty dons, still dwelt in the city, and some pure French families resided there, but many were already mingled with both Spaniards and Africans. Acadians—or "Cajuns," as they came to be called—lived outside of the city. This small pocket of Frenchmen had wandered far from home, but, like many groups in New Orleans, they stubbornly kept much of their eighteenth-century heritage intact and ingrained.

Of course, there were many slaves, but there were also the *gen de couleur libres*, or free men and women of color. Some of these were pure Africans, but most of them were the mulattoes, griffes, quadroons, and octoroons who were the result of French and Spanish blending with slaves. There were Americans, too, though they were strictly confined to the "American district." And there were Creoles, people of French and Spanish blood who were born outside of their native countries. Creoles born in New Orleans were Louisianians, but they were not considered Americans.

All well-born Creole families sent their children to receive a classical education at the Ursuline Convent or the Jesuit schools, and both institutions accepted charity children.

This series of novels traces the history of four young women who were fellow students at the Ursuline Convent School:

- *The Exiles:* Chantel
- *The Immortelles:* Damita
- *The Alchemy:* Simone
- *The Tapestry:* Leonie

PART ONE

· May–November 1831 ·

Chapter one

New Orleans, Louisiana, May 1831

"One thing I'm sure of: I'll never be a nun!"

Assumpta Damita de Salvedo y Madariaga stared at herself in the mirror she kept hidden behind a wall hanging. The sisters felt that mirrors led to vanity and forbade them in the rooms of the students at the Ursuline Convent. Sister Agnes, the sternest of them all, had said at least a thousand times, "It is the beauty on the inside, *not* vain painting on the outside, that makes a person."

Damita studied her features: large, well-shaped, dark eyes, a wealth of glossy, jet-black hair, a complexion like a healthy baby's—rosy and smoother than silk. The chin showed firm determination, and full lips hinted at a willful disposition.

Damita turned around and shook her head, muttering, "A girl might as well not have a figure if she has to wear this hideous dress!" The dress was, indeed, a model of economy. The pupils at the Ursuline Convent were mostly young ladies from wealthy families, but the strict rules at the convent permitted wearing only the plainest of sober, dark dresses. Despite this, at the age of seventeen, Damita could see that the ugly dress clearly outlined her figure, and she laughed aloud. *I'm going out to buy a new dress,* she thought, *a bright, elegant one. I'll wear it back from the shop and give the sisters a shock.*

The thought pleased her, and she pirouetted around the room, a wicked light dancing in her eyes. She had not been a model pupil at the convent, but her father had prestige enough, and had given money enough to the sisters' work, that Damita had never been a candidate for expulsion.

Damita looked around her and thought with satisfaction, *Another two weeks, and I'll never have to look at this old room again.* Indeed, graduation was coming on May fifteenth, and Damita had longed for emancipation from the place for years. Her spirit was not conducive to discipline, and her educational process had been hard both on her and on the Ursuline sisters.

The door opened, and a young woman entered, wearing the same style of dress Damita wore. She scolded Damita, "You're going to be late for chapel. We've got to hurry!"

"I'm not going to chapel, Chantel, and neither are you."

Chantel Fontaine stared at Damita. The two had been best friends for years, but Chantel had learned to be cautious about joining Damita's schemes. "We've got to go to chapel!" she exclaimed. Anxiety showed in her green eyes, in a pretty face framed by auburn hair. She asked with trepidation, "What are you going to do?"

"I'm going down to get a new dress."

"You can't do that!"

"Yes, I can, and you're going with me. What can they do to us—throw us out? You know we're only going through the motions anyhow. In two weeks, we'll be out of here. Let's go."

Chantel began to protest, but the force of her friend overwhelmed her. Indeed, Damita Madariaga overwhelmed most people. She was domineering, and once she made up her mind, no one could stop her. Her eyes were sparkling as she grabbed her reticule with one hand and Chantel's hand with the other. "I can't stand another one of those boring chapels."

Chantel, despite her protest, was caught up in Damita's excitement. The two tiptoed out of the room and down the long corridor, and then stepped outside into the garden. They could hear the singing beginning in the convent, and Chantel made one more effort to dissuade Damita."They'll tell our parents. They might even expel us. You know how Sister Agnes is."

"They can't do anything to us. The school year is nearly over.

Come on, now! It'll be fun. You can help me pick out my new dress."

As always, Damita grew excited as she dragged Chantel into the city of New Orleans. The air in the city was heavy with the ultrasweet odor of molasses and the pungency of mixed spices. Wisps of cotton floated off the bales piled on the levy. The Port of New Orleans competed with New York as the nation's biggest, and the land along the river was always packed with people—the population had doubled in the past decade. The mighty Mississippi made them rich. Merchandise from a hundred river ports arrived there, and the saying went "Kick a barrel of flour in Minneapolis, and it will roll to the gulf."

The sight of vessels of all sizes, shapes, and colors, crowded in from everywhere, awed the two girls. The most impressive were the steam packets, white and arrogant, at their landing along Canal Street. Oceangoing ships, gray sails furled, were giving up their sailors, who were attired in the garbs of a dozen nations, on the gangplanks. Much closer to the American sector, flatboats, keelboats, and small river crafts huddled together; floating stores that the Kaintocks presided over, regardless of their place of origin.

The two girls passed through the stacks of tobacco, hemp, animal skins, salted meats, kegs of pork, barrels full of pickled food, rum, tar, coffee with its unmistakable rich scent, and—always—cotton. The bales, some of them spoiled, towered on the open wharves.

The city was crowded as the two girls made their way through the French Quarter. They had become accustomed to the din. Stevedores scurried with their loads, and men ran to clear the ships. Tin-roof shanties lined the passageways with stores that sold sailors' trinkets. Grogshops were everywhere, and new arrivals from the ships waited in long lines. Damita and Chantel passed an oyster stand, where a native forked his delectable wares from their shells. A blind man played a fiddle, and children juggled for pennies. Dark-faced Spaniards sold flowers, and black women waddled by, bearing coffeepots in their baskets, ready to pour a cup for any who wished.

"There's the shop I want. I saw that dress in the window the day before yesterday," Damita said. "I've got to have it."

Chantel had no choice but to follow, and they entered the shop. A woman stepped forward and asked, "May I help you ladies?" She was a tall woman, obviously of Creole blood, and she waited expectantly.

"I want to try on that dress in the window."

"Oh, that is an exquisite dress! A little expensive, I'm afraid."

Damita gave the woman an arrogant look. "I'll try it on, and if it fits, I'll buy it."

"*Certainement,* mademoiselle."

At the woman's direction, Damita and Chantel walked back to a small fitting room. When the owner brought the dress, Chantel gasped. "It's so—it's so bright!"

The dress was indeed bright: an emerald green sheen with sequins around the neck, the sleeves, and the hem. As the store owner assisted Damita in putting on the dress, she exclaimed to Damita, "It might have been made for you! It's a beautiful fit!"

Damita turned around and around, admiring herself. "What do you think, Chantel?"

"It's a lovely dress, and it does just fit you."

Damita studied herself in a mirror. The dress had a low-cut, square neckline with an inset of a gray, shimmering material encircling the neck and the tight-fitting sleeves that ended at the wrists in a small ruffle. Its empire waist let the fabric drape loosely to the floor, where embroidered and brocaded trim formed the hem.

"I have other dresses, if you would care to try them on."

"No, I'll take this one, and I'll wear it. Wrap up my other dress, if you please."

The dressmaker stared at her. "You have not asked the price."

"My father will pay for it. Send the bill to him."

"And who is your father?"

"Alfredo Madariaga."

"Oh, you are Señor Madariaga's daughter!" A pleased smile spread over the woman's face. "You have made a wise choice. Are you certain you want to wear it now?"

"Yes, I am."

Ten minutes later, the two girls emerged. Chantel's face wore a worried expression. "Won't your papa be shocked at the price of the dress?"

"He promised I could have a new dress for my birthday, and he said I could pick it out. I'm just saving him the trouble of going shopping with me. Chantel, he promised me something else too."

"What is that?"

"He said I could have a maid of my very own." Damita laughed at Chantel's shocked expression. "Well, I *need* one. Monica can't take care of Mother and me both, can she? So, Papa said I could have one."

"Are you going to hire someone?"

"No, we're going to buy one. That will be good economy in the long run. We'll buy a young girl, one who will bring a high price when we decide to sell her."

Chantel bit her lower lip thoughtfully, and then commented, "I never liked the idea of buying human beings."

Damita stared at her friend. "What are you talking about?"

"It just doesn't seem right, Damita, for one human being to own another one."

"Of course it's all right! They're not like we are, Chantel. They're inferior."

This was, of course, the standard position of Southerners and some Northerners, too, at the time. Some in the country were beginning to protest. The Abolition movement was picking up steam, but, in New Orleans, an abolitionist would not last very long!

At Chantel's silence, Damita said, "Come on. Let's go get something to eat."

"All right, but I didn't bring much money."

"I've got plenty."

The two girls stepped quickly up the street. Damita was well aware of the glances she drew as they made their progress along the crowded walkways. She enjoyed the women's glares. Many of them, she knew, envied her beauty and her figure. This amused her, and she met their glances with a self-satisfied smile.

She was also aware of the men, both young and old, who turned to watch her stroll by. Damita de Salvedo y Madariaga was accustomed to the admiration of men. In some respects, she had led a sheltered life, being confined in the convent classrooms, but she had also been able to participate in the social life of New Orleans. The Creole gentry had a world of its own there, and she had found it exciting to flirt with the dashing young men who sought her out eagerly at the balls and parties that took place regularly in the city.

Damita suddenly stopped. "There's the auction!"

Chantel stopped and looked at the red-brick building to her right. Men were coming and going, but she saw no women. "I've never been in there," she said nervously.

"Neither have I, but I'm going now."

"Damita, we can't go in there! Women never go unescorted into a place like that."

"Well, I'm going. Papa said I could have a maid, and I want to see what's available. Come along."

Against her better judgment, Chantel accompanied Damita up the steps and entered through the door. She murmured, "I don't like this, Damita."

"We won't stay long. I just want to look over what they have for sale."

The main room of the auction was a large, spacious area with a high ceiling. Cigar smoke created a purple haze, and a hum of talk sounded as the prospective buyers mingled. They studied the black people who were up on a slightly raised platform.

Damita ran her eyes around the room, and for one moment, she was almost tempted to fall in with Chantel's mood. It was somehow a place that deadened the spirit. Despite the loud talk and laughter of the buyers, the black men, women, and young people who lined the platform along the wall gave her a start. She was accustomed to slaves, of course; her father owned many who operated the family's cotton plantation just outside of New Orleans. There were house slaves also, but Damita was used to them. Something was different about those who stood against the wall.

"Miss Madariaga, what a pleasure to see you."

Damita turned to face Lewis Depard, a slender young man dressed in the latest fashion. Bright brown eyes shone from a friendly, olive-complected face. He bowed and said, "I don't believe you've met my friend Philip Moreau. Philip, may I introduce you to Miss Damita Madariaga."

"I am happy to know you," Moreau said with a smile. He was a larger man than Lewis, somewhat overweight, and well-dressed.

"This is my friend, Miss Fontaine."

"A pleasure, Miss Fontaine," the young man greeted her.

"Have you fought any duels today, Lewis?" Damita asked, arching her eyebrows.

"Not yet, but the day is young."

"Mr. Depard is a famous duelist, Chantel," Damita said. "If a man wears a coat that doesn't suit him, he challenges him."

"Oh, come now! It's not that bad, Miss Madariaga." Lewis Depard had indeed fought in two duels and had won both of them easily. He was an expert swordsman, as well as an expert shot with dueling pistols. Dueling was so common among the young Creole gentlemen of New Orleans that it had become something of a fine art. Men fought duels over the most inconsequential of affairs.

"Are you here to make a purchase, Miss Madariaga?" Lewis asked curiously.

"My father promised me a maid for my graduation. I thought I'd look over the wares."

"There doesn't seem to be much along that line," Depard said, shrugging. "Except for a few strong-looking young slaves, this group happens to be pretty well picked over. Look, the auctioneer is starting the action. His name is Saul Lebeaux. He's made a fortune selling slaves."

Damita turned and watched with the others. The auctioneer, a short, muscular man wearing a dark brown suit, had stepped up beside an elderly dark woman. He said, "Now, then, we have a fine specimen here. This is Irene. She's a clever house servant and an excellent cook." He winked and added, "She does have one fault: she's always pretending to be sick. Nothing wrong with her, I assure you. She's healthy."

"She doesn't look well at all, does she?" Chantel whispered.

"But the man says she's faking."

"I don't think so. She looks sick to me."

Damita watched as several prospective buyers approached. One of them put his hand under the old woman's chin and raised her head.

"Open your mouth," he said, then looked inside. "Not many teeth left."

"No," another buyer said. "Nothing but skin and bones."

Lebeaux tried to work up some interest. "Gentlemen, who'll bid a hundred?"

"Why, she'll be in the ground in a week."

"No, I tell you, she's fooling you. Just full of humbug. You give her a touch or two of the cowhide, and you can get plenty of work out of her." Despite all his efforts, the auctioneer could arouse no bids, and finally a voice said, "Let's get on with some of the better stock, Saul."

The auctioneer shrugged and moved along to a large and powerful-looking black man. "Now, here is just what you're looking for." He poked the man in the ribs with the stick he carried and said, "Look at those muscles. Why, he can work eighteen hours a day in the fields."

Damita listened, and her eyes went to the face of the black man. He appeared to be in his mid-thirties. He was black as a human being could be, and she saw that his eyes were dull. An air of hopelessness hung about him. He sold for $450, and his purchaser led him away.

"Do we have to stay, Damita?" Chantel whispered.

Damita hesitated. At that instant, a woman holding a baby was brought forward, and the auctioneer began his pitch. "We've got a fine house slave here, and a picaninny. Two for the price of one."

"I'll bid on the woman but not the picaninny," a voice called.

The auctioneer argued, but a burly man with a shock of coarse, black hair finally bought the woman. He stepped up to pay the fee and take possession forward. He ordered the woman, "Get rid of that baby. You won't be needing her to pick cotton."

Damita and Chantel watched as the woman clung to the baby and shook her head, but the auctioneer pulled the child from her arms. "Go along, now," he said.

The woman cried out something in a language that was not

French and not English. She reached for the baby, but her new owner grabbed her by the arm and said roughly, "None of that! You'll have plenty to do without taking care of a baby." He led the woman away crying, and the auctioneer handed the baby to one of his helpers.

"That's awful!" Chantel whispered.

Damita had not liked the scene herself. "I don't see why he couldn't have let the slave take the baby." She started to say more, but, at that moment, the auctioneer said, "I've got something very special for you gentlemen." He called, "Bring that girl out, Al."

Damita turned to see, emerging from the door, a young woman being pushed forward by a white man. The girl was apparently in her teens and looked as different from the rest of the slaves as was possible. As Al brought her to the front, a buzz of talk sounded, and Lewis exclaimed, "By heaven, there's a different sort of property!"

Despite the plain dress she wore, the young woman was a beauty in every way. She had raven-black hair, and her skin was smooth and of a faint olive tint. She kept her eyes down, for the most part, but when she lifted them, Chantel saw they were a pale green, large, and striking.

"She'll fetch a pretty penny," Lewis whispered to his friend. "I wouldn't mind owning her myself."

The auctioneer let the audience peer at the woman for a moment, then said, "This is a prize, gentlemen. Only sixteen years old. Make a perfect house servant. She's healthy, and she'll dress out fine. Come, look her over."

Damita watched as a number of men moved closer. One at a time, they squeezed the girl's arms and looked at her teeth.

"That's shameful," Chantel hissed.

Damita was staring at the girl. She was an impulsive young woman, and in that instant, she made up her mind. "That's the girl I want for my maid."

"You can't mean it!" Chantel exclaimed.

"She's pretty enough. I can dress her up. And she looks strong and healthy. I'm going to bid on her."

"You can't do that!"

Damita loved a challenge, and when the bidding started, she did not speak until the price rose to eight hundred dollars. Then Lebeaux cried, "Come along, gentlemen! Any more bids?" He waited expectantly and said, "If there are no more bids—"

"Nine hundred dollars!"

Every man's eyes turned to Damita. Lewis's face showed shock. "Miss Madariaga, you can't mean that!"

The auctioneer also was nonplussed. It was uncommon for a woman even to attend the auction. But he was there for profit. "The bid is nine hundred dollars. Do I hear another?"

A hum filled the room, and the bidding rose to twelve hundred dollars. Damita calmly raised it to thirteen.

One of the men asked, "Lebeaux, how do you know she's got the money to pay for that girl?"

The auctioneer swallowed hard. He was in a difficult position. He needed to make the money, but indeed, no young girl like this had ever bid on a slave. "May I ask how you intend to pay for this, mademoiselle?"

"My father is Señor Alfredo Madariaga. He will pay the money."

The auctioneer obviously knew Damita's father. Still he said, "Your father is not here."

"No, but he's buying me a maid, and that's the one I want."

For a moment the auctioneer wavered, then nodded. He tried to get the bid raised, but no one was willing, for it was clear that the young woman was going to pay whatever was necessary. "Mademoiselle, your bid is accepted. Come forward and take your property!"

Lewis stayed close beside Damita while she looked the slave girl over carefully. "Your father's very generous," he commented.

A man slid some papers over a small table to Damita.

"He always has been," Damita said. She signed the papers, turned to the young woman, and asked, "What's your name, girl?"

The woman stood straight as an arrow. She faced Damita and said in an even tone, "My name is Charissa Desjardin."

"That's some name. We'll just call you Rissa. You belong to me now. If you do as you're told, you'll be well treated." Damita waited for the girl to answer. When she only stood silently, Damita added, "If you misbehave, you'll be whipped."

A light blazed in the girl's green eyes. "I've been whipped before!" she said defiantly.

"I believe you've got a rebellious servant on your hands," Lewis said. "She may require a touch of the stick."

"Get your things," Damita said.

The girl said in the same tone, "I don't have any things."

"Come with me, then."

"I hope she turns out well," Lewis said.

"Thank you, I'm sure she will. Come along, Rissa."

Damita turned and left the auction, aware that every eye was upon her. As soon as she stepped outside, she turned to Chantel and said, "I'm going to take my new maid home. Do you want to go with me?"

"No, I think I'd better go back." Chantel had had enough adventure for one afternoon.

"All right. If the sisters ask about me, tell them I won't be back for the rest of the day. I'll be there tomorrow."

Chantel left hurriedly, and Damita turned to the girl, who still stood without speaking, and said, "Rissa, I won't put up with sullen behavior." She waited for the girl to say something. When she got no response, she said, "Answer me when I speak to you."

The words came reluctantly. "Yes, ma'am."

Damita looked into the eyes of the young woman and shook her head. "This is a bad beginning, but we'll do better, I'm sure. You just have to learn some manners, and I'll teach you. Come along." As they walked toward the Madariaga home, she was already thinking about how to approach her father. He was lenient and had spoiled her, but she had taken a big step. She began to feel nervous. She wondered if she had done the right thing.

It will be all right, she reassured herself. *I'll smooth it over somehow.*

Chapter two

Charissa walked quickly down the street, holding a basket in her right hand and a wrapped parcel in the other. The afternoon sunlight of New Orleans illuminated the houses on both sides. Smooth plaster covered most of them, and the Madariaga house had been painted a warm peach shade. It was one of a line of similar structures rising directly from the *banquettes,* as dwellers of the city called the sidewalks. Other homes were blue, some a faint purple, each fitted to the desire and artistic temperament of the owner.

She paused a moment before the house, thinking of the two weeks that had passed since she had come to live there. One of her memories was of the argument between Alfredo Madariaga and his daughter on the day she had arrived. Damita had ordered Charissa to wait in the kitchen, but she could hear the master of the house, his voice rising in anger, and had felt certain she would be taken back to the auction and sold again.

As she stood remembering that day, she thought, *Well, this is better than it might have been at some other place. I just have to put up with that selfish, demanding girl.* She glanced up now at the facade of the house, three stories dominated by three tall galleries, and she admired the delicate ironwork that sketched a lacelike outline of leaves and flowers on the stucco. Waist-high railings and scrolled panels of filigree marked the balcony, and on the second level, dozens of containers held geraniums, wax flowers, ferns; on the first one, a big birdcage contained a brilliantly colored, screeching parrot.

With a sigh, Charissa, wearing a simple brown dress and her long hair pinned up in a coil, passed through a large patio with a gate big enough to admit the carriage that was kept in the rear. Charissa turned to enter the door, but someone grasped her from behind so suddenly that she dropped the basket and the parcel, hearing something crack in one. She fought fiercely, but the arms were strong, and she heard a rough voice saying, "Stop fightin'! You know you like it, girl."

Charissa managed to free one of her arms, but even as the man she knew to be Garr Odom, the carriage driver, tried to grab it back, she pulled a long pin from her hair. Without a moment's hesitation, she stabbed the hairy arm that went around her breast and was rewarded by a loud screech. She was free. Turning quickly, she held up the pin like a dagger and glared at the big man, saying, "You keep your hands off me, Odom, or I'll put your eye out."

"You she-devil!" Garr Odom was not tall, but he was broad and strong. His hazel eyes burned, and the battle had loosed his long hair from its tie. He held his hand over the wound, his mouth twisted in a murderous expression. "You stabbed me!" he gasped.

"Yes, I stabbed you, and I'll do worse if you don't keep your hands off of me!"

"Well, ain't you somethin' now! You've had a man's hands on you before."

"I won't have yours. You heard what I said. If you ever touch me again, I'll make you regret it." She leaned forward and swiped the pin in front of Odom's face.

"Hey, watch out!" he yelled—the pin had passed within a few inches of his eyes. He stumbled backward and then glared at Charissa, muttering, "You won't always have that hat pin." He turned and stomped away, disappearing through the carriage gate.

Charissa took a deep breath, standing still until the fear dissipated. It was not the first time that Garr Odom had tried to attack her. He had come once to her bedroom, and only her threats to scream and raise the house had prevented his assault. Charissa replaced the hat pin, then reached down and picked up the basket, replacing the vegetables that had rolled out of it. She saw that liquid was dripping from the parcel. She picked it up as well as she could and stepped quickly through the door. She hurried through the corridor to the kitchen at the very back of the house. A heavyset woman with skin the color of ebony was standing over a stove, and she turned at once to ask, "Where you been so long? Miss Damita's havin' a fit."

"It took me a long time to get all the things you wanted, Ernestine." Charissa put the basket and paper bag on a counter and said, "I dropped this bag. I broke whatever's in it."

"You busted it!" Ernestine, who had been with the Madariaga family for years, heaved her bulky body over to where Charissa stood. She was almost as broad as she was tall. She began pulling items out of the sack. "How'd you smash this?" she asked, holding up pieces of a broken bottle.

"Garr grabbed me from behind."

"He botherin' you again? Why don't you tell the master about him?"

"It wouldn't do any good," Charissa said coldly.

Ernestine stopped removing items from the sack and turned to Charissa. Her eyes were compassionate. "That man is no good. He may be a good carriage driver, but he ain't no good in no other ways. Did he hurt you?"

Charissa laughed. "No, but I hurt him." She pulled the pin out of her hair. "I used this like a sword and ran it right into his arm. I'm surprised you didn't hear him holler."

Ernestine Brown grinned broadly and chuckled deep in her chest. "That's good! You know how to take care of yourself. But you'd better get on up now. Miss Damita's plumb fit to be tied. I told her I had to send you to the market. She got mad and raved at me. She say you don't work for nobody but her."

"She doesn't care a pin for anybody in this world."

"Oh, she's spoiled and selfish, but I reckon she's got a good heart."

Charissa glared at Ernestine. "A good heart? She hasn't done anything but mistreat me since I got here. She slapped me in the face just two days ago, when I couldn't find her hat quick enough to suit her."

Ernestine put her big arm around the girl. "You could be lots worse off, honey. Out in the plantation I've seen Claude Napier, the manager, whip men and women both until their backs was cut all to pieces. You just be glad he ain't been turned loose on you yet."

"I'd run away if he ever did that to me."

"And then they'd catch you. Ain't nobody can get out of bein' what she is."

Charissa stared at the big woman, who had proven to be her closest friend in the household. "Don't you ever wonder what it would be like to be free, Ernestine?"

"There ain't no sense thinkin' about what can't happen," Ernestine said. "You just make the best of what you got. We got plenty to eat. We got warm clothes. We don't have to go out in the fields. The master and Miss Elena, they ain't cruel folks at all."

"Damita is."

"She's young. She'll outgrow that by the time she has a few knocks herself."

"She has everything," Charissa said bitterly. "Why is it some people in this world have everything, and some of us have nothing?"

"I don't know, but that's the way it's always been, and that's the way it's always gonna be. Now you go on up, and don't give Miss Damita any of your sass. No matter what she says, you just smile and say, 'Yes, ma'am.'"

"I'll do what she says, but she can't make me like it. I'll come back and help you cook when she gets through with me."

"She ain't likely to get through with you today. She's gettin' ready for that graduation of hers. Go on, and you be sweet like me."

Charissa could never resist Ernestine. She hugged her and said, "All right. I'll be sweet like you—to you, but never to Damita."

Juanita Mendez sat on the balcony, watching the passersby below her. She had seen Charissa come down the street and enter the gate, and now she commented, "That new slave you bought for Damita is a rebellious girl."

"Yes, she is," Elena Madariaga agreed, turning to her husband.

She was a small woman, shapely, and at the age of forty-five, she still had traces of her youthful beauty. "You spoil Damita, Alfredo. You shouldn't have paid that much for another maid. We could have gotten by with Monica. She's already paid for, and she can wait on both of us."

Alfredo was a trim man of fifty-one. As he sat with his chair tilted back, looking at his wife and his sister, he shrugged. "I promised her a maid, and the girl will probably be a good investment. Always a good market for beautiful young mulattoes."

"Mulatto! What are you talking about?" Juanita exclaimed. "She's no more mulatto than I am." A mulatto was a person half-black and half-white. "She's not even a quadroon. She looks like an octoroon to me." These two terms were well known to refer to the mixture of black and white blood—quadroon being one-quarter black and an octoroon only one-eighth black.

"So much the better for a sale. You know how the young bucks like the Creole girls, with their lighter skin."

"I know it very well, but Rissa will never be one of those," Elena said.

"She may be, if we have to sell her. I expect her mother was mostly white. The town's full of octoroon Creole girls, and most of them wind up as mistresses to wealthy white men."

Indeed, men in New Orleans often maintained two families. The white one society accepted, the dark one no one did. Many men divided their time between the two households, rearing two sets of children. The white wives had no choice but to accept the situation, and almost everyone attended the sumptuous quadroon balls, where tawny-skinned women displayed their charms in what amounted to a bazaar for prospective men of wealth. Among the well-to-do Creoles, the marriage of convenience was common, but often the couple had not even met, and when a young man did not get a beauty, he was quick to go to the quadroon balls and find himself a mistress.

"The girl could pass for white easily enough," Alfredo remarked. "We won't have any trouble selling her."

The two women stared at Alfredo; the subject was usually taboo. But Elena was not finished and repeated harshly, "You spoil Damita terribly. Her husband's going to have an awful time with her."

As a matter of fact, Alfredo Madariaga was himself still somewhat angry over Damita's buying the slave without his permission. "I'm going to whip that girl," he said loudly.

Both women smiled at each other grimly. They were well aware that he had never struck Damita in his life and never would. "Well," Juanita said, "I think you'd better sell the girl quickly. She's not a good maid."

"No," Elena agreed. "She's headstrong."

"So is Damita," Alfredo murmured. A gloomy look crossed his face, and he shook his head. "I may have to sell Charissa and some others from the plantation as well. I've got a payment coming due on the loan, and the crop was terrible this year. The drought nearly ruined us."

Neither his wife nor his sister paid much attention to this statement. It was a common enough plaint from Alfredo. Most of the plantation owners lived on credit, and no one considered owing money a sin in any way.

Changing the subject, Juanita said, "I want you to let Damita go with me when I make my visit to Savannah."

"I don't have any objection. Does she want to go?"

"I haven't asked her about it yet, but the trip isn't until November. I think she'd enjoy it. Besides, there may be some suitable young men there for her."

"That's very important," Elena said with a nod.

"Indeed it is." For once, Alfredo agreed with his wife and sister. "She needs to marry someone with a bank full of money. Somebody who could help pay these debts off."

"She's a beautiful girl, and she won't have any trouble marrying," Juanita said. She had other nieces in Savannah, but she had made a pet out of Damita. "It's essential that she not only marry money but that she marry someone socially acceptable."

"What do you expect her to do—marry a monkey?" Alfredo laughed. "Of course he'll be acceptable."

"I don't know. Young girls are willful these days," Elena said. "When Fannie Metlous married that awful American, it nearly killed her parents."

"It certainly did," Juanita agreed. "He was like all of the other Kaintocks: little more than a beast."

The white men who came down to New Orleans from the west, mostly on the Mississippi, were known as *Kaintocks.* They had reputations for fighting and drinking and were coarse to the genteel members of New Orleans.

"Damita's got more sense than that," her father said firmly.

"Yes, she has," Juanita said quickly. "I'd better go see if she's dressed. We don't want to be late for the graduation."

Damita stepped out of the brass tub and stood while Charissa dried her off with large, fluffy towels. This was an everyday ceremony and one that took up a great deal of Charissa's energy. She had to heat the water in the kitchen, then bring it up, two heavy pails at a time, to fill the tub. It was one of the tasks she hated, and now, as she dried Damita off and powdered her, she thought, *She's never paid me a single compliment. Not once has she said a simple thank-you.*

"Hurry up, Rissa, I'm going to be late."

Charissa had learned never to respond to such useless comments. She was working as quickly as she could, and it did no good to protest. All she would get was a sharp word or sometimes, even a slap. She helped Damita into her undergarments, then slipped the snow-white dress, the color all the girls were wearing for graduation, over her head. She buttoned it up, and Damita said sharply, "Go down and get me some wine. Make sure it's been cooled."

"Yes, ma'am," Charissa muttered, turned, and went downstairs. She found the wine, poured a glass, and carried it carefully back up the stairs. Entering the room, she walked over to where Damita was standing before the mirror. "Here's the—"

She had no time to finish the sentence. Damita suddenly turned, and her hand struck the glass that Charissa was holding out to her. The dark red liquid splashed onto Damita's bosom, and for one moment, she just stood with a shocked look on her face.

Charissa's heart sank when she saw the hideous red blot. She had no time to speak, however, because Damita screamed, "You've *ruined* my dress!"

"It wasn't my fault. You're the one who hit the glass!"

"Don't you talk back to me! It was your fault!"

Ordinarily, Charissa would have had sense enough to keep quiet and let Damita have her fit, but she could not always control her quick temper. She responded loudly, "You're the clumsy one, not me! You knocked the glass right out of my hand and spilled the wine all over yourself!"

Damita's face turned pale. She slapped Charissa and said, "You come with me. I'm going to break you of this habit of talking back!" She whirled and stormed out of the room.

Charissa followed her mistress through the hall, down the stairs, and out the side door. As soon as she stepped outside, Damita saw Garr Odom, leaning against the iron gate. "Garr," she said, "come here."

"Yes, ma'am. What is it?"

"I want you to take this girl and whip her."

A chill ran through Charissa. Garr's brutal face broke into a smile. "You mean really whip her with a stick?"

"Yes, and make sure you're harsh. She's a clumsy, insolent girl, and I want her broken. You hear me?"

"Yes, Miss Damita. I'll do what you say."

Damita glanced at Charissa and said with satisfaction, "A beating is just what you need." She turned and rushed into the house without another word.

Charissa stared at Garr Odom.

"Well, well," he said. He grabbed her by the arm. "You come on back. You and me got a little business." He was a strong man, and although Charissa struggled, she had no chance against him as he dragged her back and entered the darkness of the barn.

~

The faculty of the Ursuline Convent had gathered on a small platform erected in the courtyard. The black robes of the priest and the nuns, highlighted by blinding white collars and hats, and the graduates in their white dresses made a startling contrast to the colorful and stylish dress of the family and friends.

The date was May 15, 1831, and as Damita moved forward in the line, she felt a fierce sense of exultation. She heard Chantel's name called out, followed by the words "*summa cum laude.*" She felt no jealousy for the applause because Chantel was, by far, the best scholar in the class. She reached out and accepted her diploma from Sister Agnes, who did not smile. "You never thought I'd get it, did you, Sister?" Damita whispered. The nun gasped and Damita giggled, then turned and flashed a smile at her family.

She strode back to her seat, thinking, *This is the last day I'll have to spend in this place.* She watched as her classmates received their diplomas, and when the ceremonies came to an end, she stood to her feet with all the others while the bishop said a brief prayer. As soon as he spoke the amen, the graduates broke ranks and joined their families.

Damita's father was waiting for her, and when he put his arms out, she threw her arms around his neck and kissed him soundly on the cheek. He smiled at her and said, "I'm proud of you, daughter. There were times I thought you'd never make it."

Damita smiled and said, "I don't think I could have, if it had gone on another day. But now I feel as if I've been let out of prison." She turned and embraced her mother and aunt, then walked over to Chantel. The two girls hugged, and Damita said, "You're the best in the class!"

Chantel smiled. "You could have been, if you had tried."

"I can't waste my time learning useless things. Have you asked your parents if you could make the trip to Savannah with us in November?"

"We're going to be out of the country. I can't go."

"That's too bad. You're going to miss seeing a lot of good-looking men, from what I hear."

They mingled for the last time with their other classmates, especially with Simone d'Or, with her long, blond hair and dark-blue eyes, and Leonie Dousett, who was smaller than the other girls and the poorest of them all. She was a charity student, and perhaps this was the reason she was the humblest of the four.

"We're the Four Musketeers, and we've got to stay in touch,"

Damita said. "I'll tell you what. Let's get together early this week and go to a party."

"What party?" Simone asked.

"I don't know, but there's bound to be one somewhere."

Simone commented, "That's not the dress you bought to graduate in."

"No, that stupid maid of mine spilled wine all over it, but she won't do it again. I had her punished."

"She didn't do it on purpose, did she?" Leonie asked quietly.

"I have no doubt she did. She never did like me. I've been as nice as I can be, but she's a stubborn, rebellious girl. We may have to sell her. It would do her good to go out in the cotton fields and put in some time there. Maybe she'd appreciate me then."

At that moment Juanita appeared and said, "Come along, dear, it's time to go."

The girls embraced, and each felt the poignancy of the moment. They had spent many years together at the convent, and now each girl knew that a new life lay before her. They made their promises to stay together and to keep in touch, but knowing how things change, all four of them felt that this was the end of something.

Damita chattered all the way to the house, filled with excitement. As soon as the family entered the front door, Charles Devere, the butler, appeared and said, "I must speak to you, sir, if you don't mind."

"Why, what is it, Charles?"

"I'd better tell you alone."

The two men left, and Elena looked at her daughter. "What was that all about, do you suppose?"

"Oh, some problem with the household, I suppose. You know Charles. He's a worrier."

Damita went to her room and started to change out of the white dress, but a loud knock on the door sounded and she said, "Come in."

Her father stepped inside, and Damita saw that he was upset. "What is it, Papa? What's wrong? Somebody sick?"

"Damita, come with me." Her father's tone was cold, and the look in his eye chilled her. She had seen him angry at others, but never had he looked at her with this expression. "What is it, Papa?" she asked again.

Alfredo turned and walked out of the room. Damita followed, and he led her up the staircase to the third floor, where the servants' rooms were. He opened one door, stepped inside, and Damita followed him. She stopped dead still. "This is Rissa's room."

"I know whose room it is. Come in here."

Again his voice was cold, and fear grabbed Damita. She stepped inside and saw that Rissa was in bed, but she was lying facedown. Her black hair had come down loosely, and her arms lay outside the sheet covering the rest of her body.

"What's wrong?" Damita whispered.

"This is wrong." Her father reached out and lifted the sheet. For a moment, Damita could not speak. Charissa's back was crisscrossed with welts, all of them blue, and some of them oozing blood.

"Did you order this done, daughter?"

"I . . . I told Garr to punish her, but I didn't mean this."

"You're a fool to let that man beat this girl! Don't you know his reputation?"

Indeed, Garr was known as a cruel man, and that was why her father took him out of overseer's work and restricted him to the barn and carriages. But in her fury at having her dress soiled, Damita had forgotten that. "I didn't intend this."

"I could shoot that man! In addition to being barbaric, he was just stupid to mark up a valuable girl like this. And you should have known better."

Damita could not bear to look at the lacerated back. She saw Charissa glaring up at her and met her eyes. Hatred flared in them. Damita could not speak anymore and turned away, sickened by the sight.

"I'll have to send for Dr. Morton. Ernestine has done what she could and given her something that will ease the pain." Turning to the figure on the bed, he said, "I'm sorry this happened, Rissa."

The beaten girl made no sound, and Alfredo left the sheet off of her back. He stepped outside the door, saying roughly, "Come out of there, Damita."

As soon as they were outside, he grabbed her arm and led her down the hall, where he stopped and faced her. "You're a fool, Damita, and inhumane besides! I know you're not kind to underlings. You never have been, but I never expected anything like this. I'm so ashamed of you, I can't speak."

Her father whirled and left the hall, and Damita began to tremble. Tears came to her eyes, and she pulled her handkerchief out of her reticule and held it over her face. She stood there for what seemed like a long time, then turned and looked at the door. *I've got to go back and tell her I'm sorry.*

She walked to Charissa's room and entered. The young woman had not moved. Damita could not face those eyes that seemed to bore into her, nor could she bear the look of the bloody back. "I'm—I didn't mean for this to happen," she whispered.

Charissa merely responded, her voice like steel, "Yes, you did."

Damita turned and fled the room. She ran down the two flights of stairs and found her mother in the hall near the kitchen. Elena said, "Your father's told me what happened."

"It wasn't my fault. I didn't tell him to beat her that savagely."

Elena knew her daughter very well, and she put her hands on her shoulders. "You must learn to be kind, Damita," she said. She turned and walked away, leaving Damita alone in the hallway.

Chapter three

Although it was only slightly past nine o'clock in the morning, the streets of the French Market were already crowded. Damita and Charissa had to thread their way through the throngs of customers who, like them, had come to buy food and supplies. A babble of languages broke the morning air: English, French, German, and Spanish. The streets were lined with shops of all sorts, but selling was not confined to them; many individuals stood next to their wares and advertised loudly. A black woman with a large bowl on her head called out, "Fine fritters!" Damita stopped and bought two of the rice fritters. "Very hot," the black woman said, grinning as she took the coin from Damita.

Damita turned and handed one of the *calahs* to Charissa. "Eat it while it's hot," she said, smiling.

"Thank you," replied Charissa, without expression. She took the *calah* and bit into it, but she felt little friendliness. It had been four months since the beating had taken place, and during that time the two young women had been wary of each other. Damita had made some effort to reconcile with the slave girl but was ready to give it up as hopeless. Charissa never spoke of it, but her eyes showed a cold bitterness whenever she looked at her mistress.

The two women passed by a woman who cried out, "Blackberries—berries very fine!" Another, called a praline mammy, vended pecan and pink or white coconut pralines from a basket.

Damita paused in front of an Indian woman who sold herb roots. She bought some of the filé, or pounded, dried sassafras leaves, for making gumbo. As she was doing this, Charissa bent over and touched the fat cheek of the woman's baby, who grinned at her and made her smile.

Damita saw this and said, "That's a beautiful baby, isn't it, Rissa?"

She insisted on using the nickname, which rankled the young slave. "Yes, ma'am, very nice."

As the two made their way through the market, Lewis Depard hailed from across the street. He took off his hat and greeted Damita with a warm smile. "How fortunate to meet you, Damita. You are shopping, I see."

"Yes. Our cook asked me to pick up some things. How are you, Lewis?"

"Could not be better." Lewis did indeed look handsome, and he sounded eager as he said, "I was going to call on you later in the day, but we are well met."

Charissa stood by, listening to the two. It was as if she did not exist. She had noticed that slave owners were able to blot out their human possessions, treating them like furniture. At times she wanted to scream, *Look at me! I'm a human being. Don't ignore me.* But this, of course, would not have been wise.

She shrugged her shoulders in the morning heat, and the memory of the brutal beating rose in her mind. The pain was gone, but she still had fine scars left from the wounds of the rod. Alfredo had replaced Garr Odom with an older man named Batist Laurent, and she was grateful to her master for getting rid of him. Alfredo had been kinder than she expected, calling a doctor in to treat her and keeping her from work for two weeks after the beating.

But Charissa could never bring herself to forgive her mistress. She knew Damita only as a thoughtless young girl, who perhaps cared for her own people but had no compassion at all for the poor or especially for slaves. She looked at Damita, whose eyes were bright as she spoke to Lewis Depard. *She'll probably marry someone like him. She can marry anyone she wants to.*

The couple began to walk, and Charissa followed. Lewis said, "I was coming over to ask if you would go to the Quadroon Ball with me tomorrow night."

"I'm not sure Mama would let me go."

"Oh, I think she would, if you asked right." Lewis smiled, his white teeth flashing against his olive skin. "I notice you get pretty much you want. It might be wiser to get permission from your father. You wind him around your little finger—as you do every man you meet."

"What a frightful thing to say!"

"No offense. I think it's charming. Will you go?"

"I will if Papa says so. I'll send you word."

"Good. You'll enjoy it, I'm sure."

Damita found her father standing at the iron railing of the balcony, looking at the sidewalk. He seemed preoccupied, and she hesitated for a moment, making her plan. She knew that she could get almost anything out of him she wished, but going to the Quadroon Ball was not something most young ladies did. She had confidence in her wiles, however, and moving forward, she tucked her arms under his and hugged him from behind. "Papa, what are you doing?"

"Nothing. Just watching the people go by."

Damita saw that a heaviness hung about her father. It troubled her. "What's wrong? Don't you feel well?"

Alfredo turned and looked at her. He tried to smile, but it was a weak effort. "I get a little weary of struggling, daughter."

"Come. Sit down and tell me about it." Damita pulled him to a wrought-iron bench, and when he sat, she held his hand in both of hers. "What's wrong? Is it business?"

"I'm afraid so. The cotton crop was disastrous this year."

"What happened?"

"It was the drought. Ordinarily, we have too much water in this area, but this growing season, the rains didn't come. The crops were very poor." He shook his head and added, "I don't know how in the world I'm going to arrange to pay off the loans."

Damita did not know much about business, but she had heard

enough from her parents to understand that the plantation was heavily mortgaged. She squeezed his hand, saying, "Why, Papa, they'll be glad to renew your note."

"I hope so, but I never get ahead, daughter. Most years we just make enough to pay the interest and a little on the principal. This year, it's going to be even harder. I'm afraid I'm going to have to sell off some of the slaves."

Damita knew that many slaves worked out on their plantation. She did not know any of them personally. In fact, those who actually grew the cotton and lived in their own little houses by the fields were completely foreign to her.

"Damita, I may have to sell Charissa."

"Sell Rissa? Oh, Papa, I hope you don't do that."

"I don't see why. She hasn't been satisfactory, has she, since—"

He broke off, but Damita knew exactly what he meant. "I think I can do something with her. She's still resentful over the beating she got, but that will pass in time." Damita did not believe this, but for some reason, she wanted to hang onto the slave girl. It had become a challenge to her. "I'll tell you what, Papa. I won't buy any new clothes, and Mama and I will get together and cut other expenses. Perhaps we could even go live on the plantation and rent this place out."

"I'd hate to do that. Your mother loves the town house so much. And you'd be bored on the plantation."

"We'll do whatever we have to do, but promise me you won't sell Charissa."

"I can't promise that, Damita, but I will say this: It will be a last resort."

Damita accepted his statement as a guarantee and began to talk about other things. She was always able to cheer her father up, and finally, when she saw he was in a more agreeable mood, she mentioned casually, "Oh, yes, I almost forgot. Lewis Depard wants me to go to a ball with him tonight."

"Another ball? Don't you ever get tired of them?"

"Oh, they are a bit boring, but Lewis is entertaining." She was hoping that her father would not ask which ball, and he did not. He merely said, "All right, daughter. Do you care for Lewis at all?"

"Oh, as I said, he's entertaining." Damita shrugged. "But he doesn't have much depth. I don't think he ever has a serious thought."

"I hear he shows a passion for dueling. He's getting quite a reputation for that. He's already had several duels, hasn't he?"

"Yes, he has, but he hasn't killed anybody. He's such a good swordsman, he just pinks them in the shoulder and then it's over."

"I don't like this dueling thing. I never have. The best man isn't always the one who can use a sword—or the pistol—the best."

Damita agreed with him at once, then kissed him. "Don't worry, Papa. Everything will be all right."

The Quadroon Ball was held next to the Theatre d'Orleans. Gambling took place on the first story, and the ballroom was above it. As Damita stepped inside for the first time, what she saw stunned her. The dancing area was without equal in New Orleans. The floor and walls were made of beautifully finished hardwood. Expensive chandeliers decorated the high ceiling. She glanced at the balcony that overhung Orleans Street, and as Lewis took her to the back, she saw a curving stairway leading to a cool, expansive courtyard filled with flowers.

The dance had already started, and although Damita had seen quadroons and mulattoes before, the variety of their skin colors caught her eye. Some of the women had skin the color of a ripe peach, others of soft, brown velvet. Some were ivory, and others were creamy white. She studied them, noting that the eyes of most of the women were brown or ebony, but that some had blue or green eyes. Almost all of them had very wavy hair, most of it reddish or light brown. They also had finely rounded figures and had learned how to carry themselves well. They held their heads high, but their lashes veiled their eyes.

"I never saw so many beautiful young women."

"It is a sight to behold," Lewis said with a grin. "But you're the most beautiful of all."

"You flatterer! You men can never tell the truth."

"But I mean it, *chérie,* you know I do." He took her arm and said, "Come, you're the best dancer I know. Let's give them something to watch."

Damita was, in fact, an excellent dancer. She loved to dance and showed natural grace. Lewis swung her around the floor, and the elaborate dresses of the women—green, crimson, yellow—made a kaleidoscope of color. The music filled the hall, and the hubbub of voices made a pleasant sound.

After several dances, Lewis said, "It's time for refreshments." He led her to where several long tables stood. Behind them, black men wearing white jackets and flashing smiles served liquors of all sorts—champagne, sherry, bourbon—as well as platters full of delicious bits of food. Damita refused the alcoholic drinks, taking instead a glass of punch. Lewis ordered a bourbon.

Lewis's many friends bombarded him, asking for dances with Damita. He reluctantly surrendered her, warning one young man, "Just one dance, Daniel. Then I must have her back."

"We shall see about that," the young man said, grinning. He swung Damita off to the dance floor, and Damita found that, like Lewis, he was charming and talkative, but he held her much too tightly.

Suddenly a voice said, "I believe that I must have this dance with the lady."

Damita turned quickly and saw a man, at least six feet tall and dressed in the latest fashion, smiling at her. The bluest eyes she had ever seen sparkled from a handsome face framed by auburn hair. She had no time to protest, nor did Daniel, for the man simply took her in his arms and swept her into the dance. "My name is Yancy Devereaux. I would be pleased to know your name."

"I do not give my name to strangers."

"What an unfriendly thing to say!" Devereaux had a wide mouth, and his eyes were deep set. He was roughly handsome. His skin was tanned, and Damita was aware of the power in his hands, which were broad and thick.

"If you won't give me your name, I'll think New Orleans ladies are proud."

Damita hardly knew how to respond. The man impressed her; he had a strength that seemed to flow out from him, and she felt like a child in his arms. "You are a Kaintock, aren't you?"

"Not me. I come from Virginia."

"We call all Americans 'Kaintocks.'"

"Well, that's hardly true, is it?"

Damita felt herself drawn to the man and rebuked herself for it. *He's nothing but a rude American! Probably comes down on the flatboats.* But the thought was wrong, and she knew it. She had seen the flatboat men—dirty and muscular, wearing rags, foulmouthed—and this man was none of that. He spoke easily of the ball, and finally the dance ended. "Thank you very much, mademoiselle. I wish—"

A voice cut in, saying, "You are insolent, sir!"

Both Devereaux and Damita turned to see Lewis standing next to them. He had been drinking, and his face was flushed. His eyes shone with a belligerent light. "I must ask you not to dance with Señorita Madariaga again."

"I assume you are her husband," Devereaux said with a smile.

"That is none of your business." Lewis's eyes were flashing, and he stepped closer. "You will now leave this hall. I will not permit you to stay."

"Does the hall belong to you?"

"I will not argue. You have insulted Señorita Madariaga, and you will either leave or you must answer for it. But before you leave, you will apologize for intruding upon her."

Devereaux seemed amused, Damita noticed. He was a much larger man than Lewis Depard. Quickly, she said, "Please, sir, do as he says. It may be dangerous if you stay."

Devereaux turned to face her. "Dangerous? In what way?"

"Mr. Depard is an excellent swordsman. He has proven himself several times. He is also a skilled pistol shot."

"Really! I'm fascinated to hear it, but I refuse to leave." He turned to face Lewis. "Now what?"

"In that case, sir, I must ask you to come with me, and we'll settle this as gentlemen—although you are not a gentleman, I see."

"I expect I'm not, according to your definition. So, you're challenging me."

"Yes. Do you accept?"

"Certainly. And as the challenged party, I choose the weapon."

"Exactly. You can have sword or pistol."

Devereaux looked up for a moment at the ceiling, then looked back down and met Depard's eyes, saying, "Neither. I choose broadaxes."

Everyone had stopped to watch the scene. New Orleans loved its drama, and a murmur went up at the American's words. "Broadaxes!" Depard exclaimed in a high voice. "What are you talking about?"

"I expect you're better with a sword or a pistol than I am, but I'm probably better with an ax than you are. So, we'll get two axes and flail away at each other until one of us is dead. Will that satisfy?"

Lewis Depard turned pale. "You mock me, sir."

"I certainly do, and I mock this whole stupid idea of duels." He turned to Damita and said, "Thank you, Miss Madariaga, for the dance." Turning to Lewis, he said, "I'm staying at the Majestic Hotel. If you care to accept my terms, we will get axes and attack each other until the blood flows freely. Good evening, sir."

Daniel said to Lewis, "Never mind it. He's nothing but a boor."

"Certainly," Damita agreed. "You can't expect honor from a Kaintock!"

Chapter four

"I wish the weather hadn't turned so cold," Damita groaned. "I'm sure we'll freeze to death on that old boat. I know it doesn't have any heat."

Juanita Mendez looked up from putting Damita's undergarments in a small gray valise. She shook her head with displeasure, saying, "You complain about everything, Damita. Why don't you concentrate on the bright side of things?"

Damita was standing at the window. She looked out at the gray skies, and then at the ground below. "We should have gone to Savannah before winter got here."

Indeed, winter had proven to be harsh along the river. It was the middle of November, and people walked the streets bundled up beyond recognition. New Orleans seemed to be a different place when this happened: most of the frivolity, singing, and joy was frozen along with the ground and the trees. Damita turned and put her arm around her aunt. "I'm sorry, *ma tante*. I won't complain anymore. Here, I'll finish my packing, and you go see to yours."

"I packed last night. I'm all ready." Straightening up, Juanita gave Damita a questioning glance. "I wish that Rissa hadn't gotten ill. We could have used her on this trip."

"Yes, it is inconvenient, but I'm sure she didn't do it on purpose. I'm just relieved it isn't something serious." Rissa had been perfectly well until two days earlier, when she developed a sore throat and a high fever. As always in New Orleans, everyone was watching her carefully to be sure that she did not have cholera or yellow fever. The doctor had pronounced it some sort of throat infection.

"Actually, I don't think she's too sad at not going, *ma tante,*" Damita admitted. "I've tried my best to be nice to her, but she just won't receive any kindness. Still, I'm going up to tell her good-bye."

"All right. Then send Batist up to get our suitcases. It's almost time to leave."

Leaving her room, Damita climbed the stairs up to the third floor. Stopping before the door of Charissa's room, she knocked once and then pushed it open. She was sitting in a chair beside the single window. The light came in, breaking over the slave girl's face, revealing a wan countenance. She was wearing a robe that had once belonged to Damita, and she did not speak.

"Are you feeling any better, Rissa?"

"I'm all right."

"I'm sorry you became ill."

"Thank you, ma'am."

The wall that Rissa had built up between the two of them frustrated Damita. She still felt bad about the whipping that had scarred Rissa's back. Though she had been kinder, she had no success in befriending her servant. She concluded that she was wasting her time.

"You should have an easy time while you get well. We won't be back for a month. So, I will see you then. Good-bye."

She waited for Rissa to speak, and finally, the girl nodded almost imperceptibly and said, "Good-bye, Miss Damita." Then the words came grudgingly: "Have a safe trip."

"Thank you. I will." Turning, Damita walked outside and closed the door behind her. As soon as she stepped into the hall, she shook her head angrily. *I don't know what else to do. She'll never forgive me for what happened.* She descended the stairs and found her parents waiting in the foyer. "I've come to ask Batist to get our suitcases."

"He's already gone upstairs," Alfredo said.

"Are you all packed?" asked Elena.

"Oh, yes. We're all ready. It's a beastly morning to start a trip, isn't it?"

"Yes, it is," Alfredo agreed. "I wish you'd gone earlier. The weather's not good at all. This is no time for a sea voyage."

"Now, Papa, we'll be fine. Don't worry about us."

Fifteen minutes later, the bags were on the carriage, and the four of them were inside. Batist climbed up to the driver's seat and spoke to the horses. They pulled the vehicle forward, and Damita looked out to see Monica, her mother's maid, shut the iron gates. The woman waved. Damita returned the wave and settled back in the carriage.

"I wish we were already there," Juanita said. "Long journeys can be so tiresome."

"I hope you brought plenty of warm clothes along," Elena fretted. "I know that those ships are as cold as can be. What's the name of the ship again, dear?"

"The *Orestes*. A good ship," answered Alfredo.

"I thought we might get to go on one of those steamships, Papa."

"No, I know the captain of this one. We've done a lot of business together. Captain Williams is a fine fellow and a good seaman. I don't trust those newfangled steamships. They're always blowing up."

They chatted all the way to the dock. Then Alfredo said, "I'll see that your luggage is taken on board. We have a little time before the ship sails." The group stepped down from the carriage.

Despite the frigid air and her numb fingers, Damita was excited. She had never been on an oceangoing ship before and was eager to start her trip to Savannah. She had slept little the previous night, and now she followed the men her father engaged to transport their luggage. They had brought one large trunk and two smaller ones, in addition to the small night cases that both women carried. As they crossed the gangplank, Damita looked up at the tall masts that seemed to touch the sky. The sails were all furled, but she saw ropes everywhere. She could not imagine having to keep track of which was which.

When the group reached the deck, Alfredo inquired about the women's stateroom. A short but strong-looking Asian man smiled and nodded. "This way, please. I will show you." He led the party downstairs and then through a corridor. The hall was dim, lit by only two flickering lanterns, and when he opened the door, he stepped inside, carrying one of them. There was no window, and he lit a lamp that was mounted on the wall. "Very nice cabin," he said.

"It's so small!" Damita exclaimed.

The four of them had trouble crowding in, and Juanita looked at the bunk beds, the small table, and shook her head. "We won't have room to turn around when our luggage gets in here."

"Best you leave your big luggage in the hold," the steward said. "I will bring your small luggage here. Better hurry. The ship is due to leave in fifteen minutes."

"This is a miserable room, but you won't be in it long," Alfredo said reassuringly. "Come along. Let's go see if we can find Captain Williams."

They left Batist to put the smaller luggage inside and see to the storing of the trunks and went topside. They found Captain Williams, a robust, red-faced individual with direct gray eyes and windblown white hair. He greeted them all fulsomely and said, "So, Señor, you're sending these ladies to Savannah?"

"Yes, Captain. I want you to take particularly good care of them."

"I'll be sure to do that." He started to speak, then ran to the side of the ship and said, "No more! Don't bring any more cargo on this ship! You hear me?" He came back, shaking his head, and said, "The *Orestes* is a good ship until she gets heavy laden—then she wallows like an old lady. I've already got too much on now. It works the men hard to keep the sails trimmed when she's loaded like this."

"Captain, the weather looks bad," Elena said. "Do you think it will get better as you travel?"

"I wish I could say so, Señora Madariaga, but I fear it's not going to improve much."

"Do you think we'll meet a storm?" Damita asked with alarm.

The captain grinned, and his eyes were twinkling. "Ma'am, there's always danger of a storm at sea, but I trust we will be in Savannah before we have any really bad weather. We should make it without trouble. I wouldn't try it if I thought it was dangerous." A sailor called for his attention. "Excuse me," the captain said. "I hope you two ladies will have dinner at my table tonight. I will see you then." He rushed off, shouting directions to the crew. The sailors, agile as monkeys, began climbing up the masts.

"They'll be setting sail soon," Alfredo said. "We'd best say good-bye."

Damita embraced both her parents and kissed them. Her aunt did the same.

"You take good care of Damita, won't you, my dear sister?"

"Yes, I will, Alfredo. And I will give all the family your best wishes when we get to Savannah."

The Madariaga family crossed the gangplank, and almost instantly, the captain began issuing orders through a large trumpet-shaped object that amplified his voice. The lower sails fell into place, the wind caught them, and the ship began to move. Damita felt slightly afraid as she stood at the rail. She waved at her parents, and they waved back.

"I wish we were setting out in better weather," Juanita said.

"So do I, but we'll soon be there. You say they have a fine house?"

"Oh, yes. You'll have a good time—you'll meet lots of young people. I'm sure they'll be having balls." She looked up at the sky and shook her head and said, "I hope I won't be sick, but I fear that I will."

As soon as the ship left the harbor, Juanita began to feel nauseous, and she ate almost nothing at the captain's table. Halfway through the meal, she turned pale and whispered, "I feel so ill. I must go to our cabin, Damita."

Damita had barely managed to get Juanita undressed and into the lower bunk before the older woman began retching. The ship was rolling as ships do, creaking and swaying, and the cabin seemed to close in upon them.

The night passed, but no one slept well. Juanita suffered frequent bouts of seasickness, and Damita could only nap fitfully. Though she brought her aunt water, Juanita was too sick to swallow it. It was a miserable night.

The next morning, her aunt dropped off into a comalike sleep, and Damita dressed and left the cabin. She felt dirty and droopy from lack of sleep. Since they had dined in the captain's quarters the night before, Damita had no idea where the dining area was. She asked a sailor, who led her to it. "Right in there, ma'am," he said.

Damita entered and found the same white-clad Asian who had welcomed them on board. "My name is Wong, Miss." He shook his head apologetically and said, "I am afraid you will either have to wait or share a table."

Damita was very hungry. "I don't mind eating with other passengers."

"Very good. This way, please."

As Wong led her through the dining room, she saw that there was indeed little room. The tables were full. Damita smelled coffee and frying meat. Wong paused beside a table where two men and one woman were sitting and said, "Excuse me, please. This is Miss Madariaga. Miss, will you take this chair?"

As Damita sat down, a young man no more than twenty, she thought, with glowing cheeks freshly shaved and warm brown eyes, bowed slightly. "I am Robert McCain, and this is my wife, Esther."

Damita smiled and said, "I am happy to know you."

"And this is Mr. Yancy Devereaux."

Damita had been aware only of a large man wearing a gray suit. She turned quickly, and her eyes widened when she recognized Devereaux. He said smoothly, "Miss Madariaga and I have met before. It's good to see you, ma'am."

Damita felt blood rush to her cheeks and knew it showed. She could only say, "How do you do, sir?"

Wong asked, "Would you have coffee or tea?"

"Coffee, please."

Wong left. Damita sat, keeping her eyes on her lap. Devereaux spoke and made her look up. "I didn't expect to see you again."

"Nor I you, sir."

Devereaux nodded at the couple across from him. "Miss Madariaga and I met at one of the balls in New Orleans."

"Is that right?" Robert said. "Do you live in New Orleans, then, Miss Madariaga?"

"Yes, my family is there. I've always lived in New Orleans." Damita turned toward the petite young woman at Robert's side.

She had large, expressive brown eyes and a happy glow about her. "You're going to Savannah, Mrs. McCain?"

"Oh, yes. I'm so excited. I've never been on a ship before."

"Neither have I. We don't have the best weather for traveling, though."

"That won't bother these two," Devereaux said. "They're on their honeymoon."

A rich color rose in Esther McCain's face, and she laughed. "Yes, we are. We were married just two days ago."

"And I'm out to make the best husband the world ever saw," McCain said, beaming. He reached over and laid his hand on his wife's. "I must say, married life is the thing. You ought to try it, Yancy."

"Not everyone has your good fortune, Robert."

The three chatted with such familiarity that Damita could not help but ask, "Have you known each other for a long time?"

"Oh, no," Esther said. "We just met Yancy yesterday. We boarded the boat at the same time."

"You make friends quickly on ships," Yancy explained. "I trust that by the time we get to Savannah, we'll all be warm friends, Miss Madariaga."

Damita knew he was teasing her. She glared at him and said coldly, "I think that is unlikely, sir. In my opinion, friendship needs a good foundation. It takes a long time to make friendships really work."

"Do you think so? I'm of a different opinion. Some people I've known for twenty years and can't bear, and others, the first time I lay eyes on them, I say, 'Now, there's a chap who is going to be a good friend to me.'"

"You're that kind of fellow, Yancy," Robert McCain said with a laugh. "What do you do for a living? Are you some kind of a confidence man or card shark?"

"Robert, don't say such things!" Esther protested.

Yancy chuckled, saying, "No, nothing quite that romantic, I'm afraid. I've been a farmer most of my life."

"A farmer! You don't look like one. Farmers don't usually dress so well."

"I don't either, when I'm grubbing in the earth. You'd hardly know me then, with dirt up to my eyebrows! But I sold my plantation in

Shreveport six months ago. Since then, I've been learning how to become a gentleman. It's difficult. Old habits die hard."

Damita met his gaze. His vivid blue eyes seemed to dance with some sort of humor. She understood that he was daring her to speak of their first meeting, and she took up the challenge. "At least you have learned to dance. That's one step forward. Fine manners usually take a little longer than learning to dance does."

"Perhaps you'll be able to help me on this voyage—you and Mrs. McCain. I'd like to achieve some of the polished manners I observed in some of those young men in New Orleans, at the ball we attended."

Damita knew that her face was reddening. He was mocking her about Lewis Depard! She answered sharply, "I don't think I'm qualified to give lessons in manners."

"If I didn't believe you to be an honest man, I'd think you were mocking us all," McCain commented. "Your manners are finer than most—than mine, certainly."

"I doubt that."

"Why are you going to Savannah, if I may ask?" Esther queried. "Do you have family there?"

"No, I'm thinking of buying half-interest in a ship."

"You're also a sailor?" McCain asked, his eyebrows lifting.

"No, not really, and I'm too old to start. You really need to go to sea when you're twelve years old, I understand. But a good friend, who *is* a sailor, offered to split ownership of his schooner. He tells me we can get rich, making the run from the Bahamas to the coast."

"What sort of cargo?" McCain asked.

"Slaves are the most profitable ones, and my partner is inclined to that—but I'm not in favor of selling human beings. I've got him convinced that we can do well shipping cotton to England."

Esther McCain looked distressed, and Damita saw that she found the subject unpleasant. She turned to Yancy, saying, "You're opposed to slavery?"

"Yes, I am. I used them on my plantation, and it disgusted me. I was glad to get out of it."

"I think there's going to be trouble over slavery, sooner or later. The feeling in the North is strong against it," McCain said.

"You're probably right. So I'll have to make my money quickly and get out."

When Wong brought Damita's meal, she ate hungrily. The food was delicious, and she felt refreshed. McCain and his wife excused themselves, and as soon as they left, Yancy said, "This is awkward for you, I'm afraid."

"Yes, it is."

For a moment he did not speak. Then he said, "Miss Madariaga, I would like very much to apologize to you."

Of all the things that Damita had assumed about Yancy Devereaux, one was that he was not a man to apologize. She saw a hardness about him; he seemed a man unlikely to admit wrong or make himself vulnerable. She looked up with surprise and met his eyes. "Apologize, sir?"

"Yes, I was quite a boor at that ball. I suppose I did offend in some way. I wasn't joking about learning some manners. You don't learn manners planting seeds and harvesting crops, and that's what I've done for most of my life—first in Virginia and later in Shreveport. So, without meaning to, I know I broke some sort of rule that your friend called me to account for. I behaved badly to him and to you. I hope you'll forgive me."

Damita searched his face for some sort of mockery in his expression, but she found instead a guilelessness. She answered, "Of course. I'm sorry it happened."

"And if you notice that I make any more impolite moves, I hope you'll feel free to correct me."

"I wouldn't feel qualified to do that, Mr. Devereaux."

"Are you traveling alone?"

"No, my aunt is with me. We're going to Savannah to see her family. She's a widow, but she has a son and two grandchildren there."

Devereaux nodded, then changed the subject. "I'm afraid we're going to have some bad weather—at least so the captain says."

"I hope not. My aunt's already terribly seasick."

"Maybe it will clear off," he said lightly. "I hope so."

Damita rose, and he stood with her. "We Americans sometimes have fallings-out, and when we make it up, we shake hands. Is that impolite?"

"Why, no, I think not." Damita put out her hand, and his large one swallowed it.

"All is forgiven, then?" he asked.

"Yes. Now, I must go to my aunt. Good day, sir."

"Good day to you, Miss Madariaga."

On the third day of sailing, a calm came over the sea. The wind died down, and the *Orestes*, although its every sail was unfurled, barely moved through the water. The captain was anxious, and the sudden weather change bewildered Damita and Juanita. Damita asked one of the sailors if such things happened often, and he replied, "Pretty often, ma'am. Don't worry. The wind will pick up soon."

Juanita felt increasingly better, and that same evening, she went to the dining room. Robert McCain spotted them and strode to their table. "Please, Miss Madariaga, would you and your companion join my wife and myself?"

"That would be fine! This is my aunt, Juanita Mendez."

"Señora Mendez, I'm so happy to meet you."

"Good to meet you, sir."

Somehow Damita was not too surprised to see Devereaux seated with the McCains. She watched as Robert introduced Juanita to Yancy and to Esther. When they were all seated, she turned to her aunt and said, "Mr. and Mrs. McCain are newlyweds."

Juanita smiled broader. "Is that so? My congratulations to you. May you have a long and happy married life." She looked at Yancy and asked, "Are you married, sir?"

"No, ma'am, I'm not," he replied. "I haven't had that good fortune yet."

"Mr. Devereaux was a planter, *ma tante,* but he's going to buy part-ownership in a schooner."

Devereaux nodded, then turned to Robert. "What do you do? You never said."

"I'm a lawyer."

"Yes, and a good one, too," Esther said, smiling. She squeezed his hand. "The best lawyer in Alabama."

"You'll have to forgive my wife. She overestimates my talent."

After the meal, Juanita and Damita strolled back to their cabin. Juanita sat down on the lower bunk. "That man, Devereaux—he's quite attractive. You met him at the ball, I understand?"

"Oh, just briefly."

"I don't want to preach, but that's exactly the sort of man you don't need to be connected with, Damita."

Damita laughed and sat down beside her aunt. She put her arm around her and said, "Connected with him? Don't be foolish. He's simply a passenger."

"He's handsome, though, don't you think?"

"Oh, I suppose he's good-looking enough, but he's a Kaintock. I'd never marry an American. You know that."

Her assurances seemed to make Juanita feel better. "That's good to hear. He's not our kind. But young girls are impressionable. You be careful."

"Oh, I will, *ma tante*. Don't worry."

The *Orestes* traveled few sea miles for the next two days, but on Thursday, when Damita woke, she felt the ship moving and exclaimed, "I think the winds have come!"

"I know they have," Juanita said with a moan. "I grew sick as soon as the ship started rocking. I'm not going to breakfast this morning."

"I'll bring you some hot tea, and perhaps a soft-boiled egg."

"I don't think I could keep it down."

"You must try, *ma tante*."

Damita walked alone to the dining room. She noticed Esther McCain by herself at a table, and the young wife waved her over. Esther said, "The men are meeting with the captain in the front of the ship. I think they're worried about the weather. Will you join me?"

"Yes. Afterward, I'll have to take my aunt something. She's not a good sailor, I'm afraid."

In their lively conversation, Damita learned a great deal about Esther McCain—mainly that she was completely in love with her husband.

Esther admitted as much when she said, "I feel sinful, loving Robert as much as I do."

"Sinful! There's nothing sinful about loving your husband."

Esther smiled and shook her head. "I'm ashamed to tell you this, Damita, but I almost worship him."

Her words amused Damita. "Well, you *have* become an idolater, then."

"I almost have, but I know that I must love God first and Robert second. But I do love him as much as a woman ever loved a man."

Damita had never talked with a young bride like Esther, and she was interested. She inquired, "Do you mind if I ask you a very personal question?"

"Why, of course not. Anything."

Damita colored slightly. "I don't know anything at all about being a wife, I mean about—" She broke off and sought the proper words. "I mean, about, well, the intimacies of married life."

Esther McCain put her hand over Damita's. "I didn't know a thing about it, either," she admitted. "I was scared to death on our wedding night, but it was all right. It will be all right for you, too, if you marry a good man. Robert was so gentle. He knew I was afraid, and he spent, I think, more time talking to me and telling me he loved me than any man ever did."

Damita felt the young bride's contentment. She sighed and said, "I'm so glad you're happy, Esther."

"We're going to have a wonderful life, Damita. We're not going to get old the way other people do. We're going to stay fresh and young. Robert has promised me that. Even when we're gray-haired, he's going to write me love letters, and I'm going to write them to him, too. We're going to have children, and I'm so excited about the days and years to come." She asked Damita, "Have you ever been in love?"

"No, I never have."

"Then you must pray that God will give you a man as good as Robert."

Damita felt a warm glow in her face. "I never met a woman who loved her husband the way you love yours. I hope the same thing happens to me."

∽

The sea grew rougher all day, and word came that the ship's staff would serve no evening meal in the dining room because of the vessel's pitching. Instead, stewards would bring sandwiches to the passengers' cabins.

Juanita could only cling to the bunk silently; she could not eat at all. Damita ate just half a sandwich. She was frightened. The ship not only nose-dived and then rose up slowly, it also wallowed from side to side. She had no more appetite than her aunt did. She finally jumped down from the top bunk and told Juanita, "I'm going to see what it's like up on deck."

"Be careful, Damita. Don't get near the rail."

"I'll be all right. You lie still, *ma tante*."

As she climbed the stairs to the deck, Damita felt as if a hand were closing around her heart. The sky was black, and although most of the sails had been furled, the wind was whipping through those that still gave the ship forward motion. The sailors had rigged ropes to hold on to while moving from place to place, and Damita clung to one just a few feet from the staircase. She stood watching as the prow went down and slowly rose again.

"Pretty rough weather, Miss Damita."

Startled, Damita turned to see Yancy Devereaux, who had come up from another set of stairs. She nodded and said, "This is terrible."

"I'm hoping it'll get better."

"Have you talked to the captain?"

"Yes, but he says the glass is still falling."

"The glass? What does that mean?"

"It's an instrument that tells what the weather is, more or less. He's afraid it could get even worse."

Damita's hopes sank. She had never had occasion to fear much in her life, but now she felt helpless. She said as much to Yancy. "I wish I hadn't come on this voyage."

"I've had the same thought." He was not wearing a hat, and the wind blew his auburn hair over his forehead. He ran his hand through it and shook his head. "We may have to turn back and get to a port to wait this storm out."

The two studied the waves that seemed to rise higher than the ship. They lifted the *Orestes,* then the bottom seemed to drop out. "My poor aunt," Damita moaned. "She can't stand much of this."

"I think we'll just have to stand it."

A thought came to Damita. "Not a very good honeymoon trip for the McCains."

"No, it's not."

Her eyes still on the white waves that seemed to reach out for the ship and slap it with a huge hand, Damita asked, "Do you suppose that they'll love each other as much in a year as they do now?"

"I hope so. They're good people."

"She told me a lot. It's almost frightening, how much she loves her husband."

"Frightening? I think it's a good thing. You know, I heard about some geese that fly in from Canada. They mate for life, and if one of them dies, the mate stays with its partner and mourns." Yancy shook his head faintly. Light spray showed on his face. He wiped it and said, "I wish human beings were that faithful."

"They can be. My mother and my father are."

"Are they? That's good news."

"What about your parents?"

"My father died when I was two. My mother died when I was fourteen."

"She never married again?"

"No. She loved my dad until the day she died. I always liked that about my mother."

The ship suddenly rose up, throwing Damita off balance. She cried out and fell against Devereaux. He held her and kept her from falling.

Damita heard the screaming of the wind through the sails, but she was more aware of the fact that Devereaux was pressing her tightly against him, and that his arms had closed about her. She had known for a long time that a lone man's attention always moved like a compass to a single woman. She knew that she was attractive, and at that instant, as their eyes met, she knew that even with her storm-swept appearance, he studied her with a hungry glance.

Then he lowered his head, and she felt his lips on hers. She could have turned aside—she knew that—but she did not. Whether it was curiosity or passion, she didn't know, but she made no attempt to avoid him. His arms tightened around her. There was something demanding about his kiss, and though he was rough, he was also tender. He held her, she thought, as a man held something he was afraid he might lose.

For a moment they stood in an embrace, something besides the storm whirling rashly between them. And then she put her hand against his chest and pushed away. She was angry, not at him as much as at herself. She had responded to his advance, and she was embarrassed. "You keep your hands off me!" she shouted through the wind.

Yancy studied her face and shook his head. "Damita, you're living in a little box. You're afraid to reach out and touch life."

"You—you leave me alone! You're nothing but a rude Kaintock!" She whirled away, and clinging to the sides of the cabin, she stumbled toward the stairs. She felt her way through the dim corridor to her door, went inside, and checked her aunt's bunk. Damita was relieved that Juanita seemed to be asleep.

She quickly traded her damp clothes for the warmest nightgown and heaviest socks she could find, climbed silently to the top bunk, and slipped under the covers. She felt the ship continue to thrash, but again and again, her mind turned to Yancy's caresses. She knew she would not forget that scene, not for a long time. She thought furiously. *He dragged me down with him. It wasn't my fault!* She settled on that. *I'll be glad when we get to Savannah so I won't have to look at him ever again.*

Chapter five

A sudden lurch of the ship awoke Damita and almost rolled her off of the bunk. She managed to catch hold of a bedpost to save herself from falling to the cabin floor.

"Damita! Damita!"

"I'm coming, *ma tante*. It's all right." Damita lowered herself from the top bunk and knelt beside the lower bunk. The lamp had been trimmed until it cast only a faint yellow corona over the cabin, and her aunt's eyes were wide with fear, her lips trembling. Damita said softly, "Don't be frightened, Aunt. It's all right."

"No, we're going to die!" Juanita cried out. She struggled to get up, but her illness had made her so weak that she fell back helplessly. "We're going to die," she whispered and closed her eyes.

"No, don't say that. We'll be all right." Damita held her aunt's hand while trying to maintain her balance, kneeling on the floor. The ship, which had been tilted in one direction, slowly rose, but it did not stop when the floor was level but continued to roll. Damita was pressed against the side of her aunt's bunk. Farther over it went, and she thought frantically, *It's going to roll over! We'll all drown!*

The ship recovered and shifted back to a more even keel, but at the same time the nose of the ship went down, and Damita felt it would never rise again. Desperation rose in her, and she said, "I'm going to find out what's wrong."

"No, don't leave me, Damita!"

"I have to go, *ma tante*," she said as she thought, *If the ship goes down, we'll need to get to the lifeboats. We'll need life preservers.* She spoke gently to her aunt. "I'll go be sure that things are all right. You lie still."

Her aunt lay silently, her face pale as paper, and Damita put on a dress, a heavy coat, then stockings and shoes. The room tilted again, and she had to hold on to the top bunk to keep her balance. She assured her aunt, "I'll be back. Don't worry."

Juanita did not answer but shook her head in a gesture of hopelessness. Damita wanted to go to her, but the ship was pitching now like a wild thing. She stumbled outside the cabin and into the hallway, in which just one lamp was burning. Damita heard cries from inside some of the rooms. The passageway tilted and threw her against the wall, and she struggled to stay upright as she made her way through the corridor. She finally reached the end of the passageway, and holding on to the railing, she climbed the stairs. As soon as she reached the deck, she heard the wind wailing. The early morning hour should have brought plenty of daylight, but dark clouds covered the sky, causing a dusky twilight. She could see that the force of the violent wind had torn some of the sails. They fluttered, pale banners caught in the storm.

Damita saw sailors moving around the deck, holding on to the ropes they'd tied for safety. She walked out to talk to one of them, but when she looked up, her heart seemed to stop. Coming toward the ship was a monstrous wave. It seemed to be taller than the top of the mast, and Damita could not move.

A voice called her name. As she turned, a hand gripped her arm. "Damita, what are you doing up here?"

Recognizing Yancy Devereaux, she cried, "What's going to happen?"

Devereaux did not answer but shook his head. He was also watching the wave, but just before it struck he grabbed her and held her tight, pulling her down to the deck.

The sea picked up the ship and tossed it into the air, and Damita was on her back. Over Yancy's shoulder she could see the mountainous wave break. It snapped off two of the masts and continued to roll the ship.

"We're going over!" Yancy shouted in her ear. "Hang on to me. Don't turn loose. Can you swim?"

"No!"

Afterward, Damita was never able to remember the sequence of events that took place. She knew only that another massive wave broke over the ship, and then there was a whirling in her head. She realized that the ship had turned upside down, and then she felt water envelope her. She fought Yancy's hold but had the presence of mind to hold her breath. Under the water, she could not hear the shrieking of the wind, but she heard the breaking noises of the ship as it disintegrated. Her lungs began to burn, and fear was a physical thing that filled her completely. She was vaguely aware of Yancy's grip.

When Damita could stand the burning in her lungs no longer, she expelled the air and then automatically breathed in cold water. It brought a pain she had not imagined possible. Noise and cold and water—and then her head was out. She began coughing violently, and a voice cried, "Hold on!"

While only half-conscious, Damita grabbed Yancy. The waves lifted them high and then slapped her in the face so that more water went into her nose, and she coughed and gagged. Yancy turned her so that her back was to him, and his arm was around her chest. She clung to it and tried to cry out, but the water and wind covered every other sound.

Damita grew feeble and conscious only of the roar of the wind and the force of the water that seemed to beat at her like a club. She cried out, *"ma tante!"* but then could just struggle weakly to keep her head above the water.

Something hard struck her leg, and she felt Yancy's arm tighten. Her eyes were full of saltwater, and she could see nothing. She felt herself being pulled, and the back of her legs dragged across something rough, and then she was thrown down so that the back of her head struck a hard, wooden surface. The blow ignited a thousand pinpoints of light in her mind. She rolled over.

"All right, don't fight it anymore."

Hearing Yancy's voice, Damita opened her eyes. At first, all she could see was the leaden gray and black of the sky and the waves that surrounded her, still frothy white and lashing the air. She felt a wooden plank beneath her.

Damita lifted her head. She looked around wearily. Yancy was lying beside her, one arm over her back. The murky light limited her vision, but she could see that whatever they were floating on was some sort of wooden surface some ten feet or more square. It rose and fell violently with the waves, and once she started to slide off, but Yancy's hands caught her and pulled her back. "We're not far from shore," he yelled. "If we can fight out this storm, it'll carry us in."

Damita's mind cleared then, and she saw that Yancy's hair was plastered to his skull, his eyes were half shut, and his lips were a white line. "Where's the ship, Yancy?"

"She went down at once."

Damita could not speak. The passage of time meant nothing, and she had no way of telling how long they clung to their precarious island, bobbing up and down and spinning at the mercy of the waves. Once Yancy yelled, "If this thing doesn't turn over, we're all right. I can hear the breakers."

Damita's hands ached from the pressure of holding on to the board. She could see something far off that looked dimly like a dark line of coast. "Is that the shore?"

"Yes. When we hit, this thing will probably turn over. If it does, don't fight me. I'll pull you in."

"All right." Damita was too exhausted to suggest any other plan. The only firm object in the universe to the young woman at that moment was Yancy's arm around her, like iron pressing her down, holding her steady. She laid her cheek against the rough surface of the board and waited. The roar became louder, and they seemed to move faster.

"Here it comes."

Damita grew tense, and then she felt the plank begin to turn. "Let go!" Yancy yelled. She released her grasp, and he plucked her up and pulled her off to one side. As the board turned over, it struck her left foot, but she had no time to think of that pain, for her head had gone underwater again. She held her breath as best she could. She remembered that Yancy had said not to fight, and it took all of her strength to keep from grabbing at him. He turned her around as if she were a child, his arm went around her chest, and just as she could hold her breath no longer, they both rose above the surface. He did not speak, but she could feel his powerful strokes.

Finally, he yelled, "My feet hit bottom. We're all right." He stood up, his chest above the waves.

Damita's feet touched sand, and she cried out, "I feel it!" She waded out as he half-carried her. The wind tore at them as it raced across the beach. Damita trembled from the cold.

Yancy leaned forward and said in her ear, "We've got to get out of this wind. Let's make for those trees."

The two pressed against the wind and hurried across the beach to a line of trees. As soon as they stepped inside their comforting cover, the wind seemed to mitigate, but Damita was shaking so violently she could hardly stand. Yancy held her and said, "Come on. We'll try to find some shelter. There must be something."

The two stumbled along through the trees, Yancy's left arm supporting Damita. She would have fallen more than once, but he pulled her up, saying, "Come on. We can make it. You're doing fine."

Fatigue came then like a blow, and Damita did not think she could lift her feet another step, but Yancy kept pulling her forward. He finally stopped. "Look, here's a road. There's got to be something down it. Come on." The sound of the crashing breakers grew fainter. A hundred yards later, Yancy said, "Look, there's something there."

Damita could see only the vague shadow of a tall vertical object. "What is that?"

"It's an old chimney. There was a house here, but it's burned." Then he cried out, "A barn! We can at least get out of the wind."

Damita felt new strength. The barn was small, but at least it had a roof. When they had reached it, Yancy opened the door and looked inside. It was practically pitch black. A couple of small holes in the walls of the old structure admitted only faint, grayish light. Yancy said, "Stand here a minute. Let me feel my way around."

Shaking as she never had in her life, Damita waited. She rubbed her arms together, but her fingers were numb with the cold. The coat she wore was, of course, soaked, and she felt encased in an icy embrace.

"Here, we're in luck."

"What is it?"

"There's a lot of old hay here, and we can get under it. It'll help some. First, take off your clothes and wring them out. They'll never dry out like that."

"Take off my clothes?"

"Yes. I'm going to do the same." Yancy walked a few steps away, faced the opposite wall, and began removing his shirt.

Damita hesitated only an instant, then she pulled off the coat and quickly stripped down to her undergarments. She wrung out her dress, but the coat was too heavy. She put on her clothes, so cold and clammy that she shuddered beneath them.

"Are you dressed?"

"Yes."

"Here, come over here."

"I couldn't wring the water out of this coat."

"Let me try." Yancy did his best with the sopping garment. "Here, lie down." Damita felt her way past him, and when her feet crunched on the old hay underfoot, she lay down, and he joined her. "Pull all the straw you can over yourself." Damita grabbed handfuls and threw them over her legs and torso. The smell was rank and chaff got into Damita's nose and made her sneeze. "We'll put your coat over the top of the straw," Yancy said.

"I've got to get warm," she whispered. "I'm so cold."

Yancy put his arms around her and drew her to him. They were face-to-face, and Damita felt a faint heat in his body. Terror was still in her, and as his arms went around her, she put her arms around his neck greedily to absorb some of his warmth. She felt him reaching back, pulling more straw over them, and finally she felt the first small indications of her body temperature rising.

"I didn't think we were going to make it," she whispered.

"Neither did I." The two of them listened to the wind as it whistled through the cracks of the barn. Both of them were thinking of the ship.

As Damita's shaking began to subside, Yancy said, "You're getting better. We're going to live."

"Do you think anyone else is alive?" she whispered.

Yancy answered, "I doubt it, Damita. She went down too quick. It's a miracle that we lived."

Tears filled Damita's eyes, and she put her forehead against his chest and began to weep. Memories of Juanita's thousand kindnesses flew through her mind. She could not bear to think of the body down in the cold darkness of the sea. Her own body shook—not from cold, but from her sobs. Yancy held her without speaking. Once he whispered, "I'm sorry about your aunt, but it was quick."

She stopped crying, and she lay in his arms, trying to regain something that she had lost. He held her without speaking. She felt the warmth of his breath on her face, and she savored the closeness of his body. But then she began to realize that this was a man she was holding, and who was holding her. She felt his hand on her back begin to stroke her, and she lifted her head. He leaned forward and pressed his lips to hers. As he kissed her, she felt a soft, wild, half-giving and half-refusing in her own body. Everything for that moment was unreal: the sinking of the ship, the desperate fight to stay alive, the wind howling outside their cocoon. But his warmth was real, and the touch of his lips on hers was real. She felt that his caress kept loneliness and fear away.

Her mind would not function. It seemed to have become incapable of thought. Yancy's growing passion made a turbulent eddy around them both, and then she knew that he was not alone in his desires. She returned his kiss with a fierceness that shocked her.

At that moment she was helpless and open to his strength. She longed for love and assurance and security and hope, and they all seemed to lie within his arms.

Suddenly, Yancy jerked away and took a deep breath. He slid himself away from her. His withdrawal stunned Damita. "What's the matter?" She tried to pull him back.

He caught her hands in his and did not answer for a moment. When he did, his voice was hoarse. "This is a bad time for you, Damita. You're not yourself."

Damita could not believe what was happening. She had offered herself to him, and now he was refusing her. She whispered, "Don't you want me?"

"Not like this." He moved away from her slightly. "You'd hate me, and you'd hate yourself, too, when this was over." He turned away and said roughly, "Try to sleep. It'll be light soon, and we can walk out of this place."

Damita felt devastated. He had rejected her, and the thought ran bitterly through her mind.

And then, shame came, burning like a fire in her conscience. She turned over quickly, curling up, her eyes tightly shut. As she lay in the darkness, she could hear his breathing and knew that he was not asleep. She knew she would remember this moment all of her life. She would remember that she had cheapened herself to a man who had pulled away from her. A flash of violent emotion coursed through her—the closest thing to hatred that she had ever felt. Something inside murmured that what he had done was right and she was wrong, but it was only a faint voice. And she writhed silently in shame.

Chapter six

"Do you feel up to walking?"

Damita rose and brushed the straw from her dress and hair. She had slept fitfully and found upon waking that she was still angry at Yancy Devereaux. The memory came flashing back, of how she had clung to him and how he had turned away from her, and it left a bitter taste in her mouth and in her spirit. "Yes," she said in a steady voice. "I'm all right."

As Damita stood, Yancy handed her her coat and said, "You'd better wear this. It's still damp, but it'll cut the wind." She took the coat and slipped into it. When they stepped outside, he glanced at the sky. "We'll try this road. Surely we'll find something."

"All right."

Yancy started to speak, then, seeing the adamant look in her eyes, he said merely, "Let's go. There are fresh wagon tracks along here. We ought to find a house somewhere."

Ten minutes later, they rounded a bend in the road, and Yancy said, "Look, there's a place."

Damita followed his pointing finger and saw a house built up on a slight hill. Smoke was rising from the chimney, and she felt a wave of relief. "Someone is there," she said.

"Yes. Come on."

The house they approached was two-storied, unpainted, and

weathered to a silver gray. A pasture lay beyond it, with several cows and two horses. A large, whitish dog arose from the porch and slowly approached with his head down, baring his teeth. "It's all right, boy," Yancy said.

Even as he spoke, the door opened and a man stepped out. "Be quiet, Rex," he said and looked the couple. He was a tall, lanky individual wearing overalls and a gray sweater. His hair was tousled, black and gray, and his skin was tan and leathery-looking. "Hello," he said. "You folks lost?"

Yancy answered, "We were on the ship *Orestes.* She went down last night."

"Went down? You mean sank?"

"Yes. Could you get us in out of the weather? The lady is exhausted."

"My name's Moore—Caleb Moore. Come on inside." The man turned and opened the door, calling, "Esther!" A woman appeared in the doorway, and her eyes widened. She was wearing a white apron over a blue dress and seemed to be about the same age as her husband, somewhere in her fifties. "My stars! What in the world?"

"These folks were in a shipwreck."

"Come on in. It's a wonder you're not frozen."

Damita walked inside the large kitchen, and a stove that threw off waves of heat drew her immediately. She walked over to it, held her hands out, and then, inexplicably, began to tremble again.

"Here, you can't wear those wet clothes. Come along with me. What's your name?"

"Damita Madariaga."

"Miss Madariaga, you come along to my bedroom. My clothes won't fit you very well, but you can get dried out. Caleb, you get this man some of your dry clothes."

"Sure." Caleb Moore stepped into a bedroom and came out with an armload of underwear, socks, shirts, and a pair of pants. "You can wear these. What'd you say your name was?"

"Yancy Devereaux." The men shook hands, then Yancy slipped off his damp, dirty clothes and into the clean ones his host offered. The older man pulled a sweater from the back of a chair and held it out. "You might want this for a time."

"Thanks, Mr. Moore."

"Caleb's all right. I'd better get out there and see if anybody else made it."

"I'll go with you pretty soon. I doubt if we'll find anybody alive. There'll be bodies coming in."

Shock appeared on Moore's face. "How many were on the ship?"

"A little more than two hundred."

"Got to be some of them left alive. You two made it."

"I doubt it. It was a miracle that we got here. A large board broke off the ship, and we managed to get on top of it, and it brought us in to shore. If we had been farther out, we wouldn't have made it. What's the closest town?"

"St. Augustine. It's about fifteen miles from here."

At that point, Esther Moore appeared and went to the stove. "You folks need something to eat."

"Coffee would be good."

"It's on the stove. Caleb, you pour. I'll just whip up some ham and bacon and eggs, and we've got biscuits left over. It's not fancy."

"It's just what I need, Mrs. Moore."

As Esther rattled dishes and broke eggs, Caleb fired questions at Yancy. The weary young man felt drained but obligated to answer. Damita emerged from another bedroom, wearing a faded, ill-fitting dress. Her hair was still wet, and she was drying it with a towel.

"You come and sit right over here, Miss," Caleb said. "My wife's the best cook in Florida."

Indeed, Esther was an excellent cook, at least as far as breakfast was concerned. Both Yancy and Damita ate quickly and then took seconds. Afterward, Damita was stirring her coffee when Yancy said, "Caleb and I are going to the beach to see if there are any more survivors. Why don't you lie down awhile?"

"I'm all right," Damita said shortly. She looked up and started to say something about her aunt but knew such talk was useless. She sipped the coffee, and the two men left. Esther Moore filled her own coffee cup and sat beside her.

"A terrible thing. Did you have friends on the ship?"

"My aunt."

"Oh, my dear—I'm so sorry." She reached over and put her work-worn hand on Damita's and said, "Maybe she made it ashore."

"I don't think anyone did. I believe Yancy and I were the only ones."

"Was it a big ship?"

"There were more than two hundred people on board."

"Lord help us!" Esther Moore cried, her eyes widening. "Listen, as soon as Caleb comes back, we'll get you in to St. Augustine. You can catch a ship back from there, or perhaps go overland. The ship would be the quickest."

"I hate to be a bother."

"Don't be foolish. What are people for, except to help in time of trouble?"

The two women sat quietly then, and Esther tactfully did not mention the wreck anymore. She put Damita's and Yancy's clothes by the stove, and they soon dried out. Esther ironed Damita's dress, and the young woman put it back on. The coat was still hanging in front of the stove when the two men came back.

"Did you find anyone, Caleb?" His face was dark. "Not alive," he said. "We'll have to go into St. Augustine and report this."

"I know. You go hitch up the wagon. I'll go with you. Where do your people live, Miss Damita?"

"In New Orleans."

Esther said, "You are welcome to stay with us, but I know you are anxious to get home. There's nearly always a ship leaving St. Augustine for New Orleans. You can get a hotel there until one leaves."

Caleb studied her face, started to say something but then changed his mind. "I'll go get the team hitched up. The weather's clearing off."

Damita and Yancy stood in front of the Royal Hotel and said their good-byes to the Moores. She and Yancy had gone to the court-house to give notice of what had happened, and then the Moores had driven them to the hotel. The two couples shook hands, then Damita suddenly moved forward a step and hugged Esther. She had never embraced a woman in Esther Moore's class before, but gratitude was rich in her. "I can't thank you enough for helping us."

"You get on home now, and let your people baby you and take care of you. We'll be praying for you, me and Caleb. And I'm sorry about your aunt." The Moores climbed up on their wagon, Caleb snapped the reins, and they ambled out of town.

Now Yancy and Damita stood in front of the hotel, and Damita said, "I don't have any money. It was all in my stateroom."

Yancy smiled briefly. "I carry my cash in my money belt, so we still have some." He patted his side and said, "It got a little damp, but it's all right."

"My father will recompense you for anything you spend."

Yancy looked at her. "Come along. We'll go register."

The two walked into the lobby of the hotel, and the clerk smiled at them. "Yes, sir. May I help you?"

"We need two rooms, one for this lady and one for myself."

"Yes, sir, we have two. Please register right here." The clerk was a short man with fair skin and sky-blue eyes. When they finished signing in, he smiled and asked, "Will you be staying long?"

"I hope not," Yancy said. "We need to get a ship out of here. This lady needs to catch one bound for New Orleans. Do you know of any?"

"No, sir, I don't, but you can go down to the docks and find out very easily."

"I'll do that." Yancy took the keys and nodded, then the two turned and walked up the stairs.

Yancy opened the door to room 206 and handed Damita the key. "You lie down and get some rest. I'll go find out about a ship. When I get back, we'll have something to eat."

"Thank you."

"You're welcome, Damita." He hesitated and said, "I know it's been rough, but it's not over yet."

"What do you mean?"

"Sometimes the past haunts a person. Didn't you know that?"

"I don't know what you're talking about."

"I mean, you don't always have time to think about how difficult things are, but later, you look back and wonder how you lived through them."

Damita's life had been so carefree up to that point, the idea of the past's haunting her was foreign. But as Yancy spoke, she recognized that she would always remember the horror of the wreck, and other things as well.

"Try to get some sleep," he said and walked back down the stairs.

Damita awoke with a start at the gentle knock on her door. She sat up and looked around, remembering where she was. "Who is it?" she called.

"It's me, Yancy. Do you want to go eat?"

Realizing she was hungry, she got up and said, "Yes. I'll meet you in the lobby in fifteen minutes." Quickly she dressed and did the best she could with her hair. She had no brush, no comb, no cosmetics, nothing but the water-damaged clothes she was wearing. Leaving her room and descending the stairs, she walked into the hotel restaurant she had seen when they registered. As she approached Yancy at a table, he arose and drew back a chair for her. "I thought we'd have something to eat, and then maybe go buy you something to wear and other things you'll need."

"That's thoughtful of you," she said, thawing a little. "Did you find out about a ship?"

"There's one leaving tomorrow. Not much of a ship, but at least it's going to New Orleans."

"Could you get tickets on it?"

"They don't ordinarily take passengers, but the captain said that he'd make an exception after I explained what had happened. They're on the last leg of a journey—they've been down in Venezuela."

The waiter came, and the two ordered steaks. When the food arrived, the meat was tender and tasted wonderful to Damita. She ate the entire steak, and Yancy grinned, saying, "You're starved to death. You're going to get fat if you eat like that."

"No, I don't think so." She said, "I'm sorry I have to depend on you, but my father will pay you when we get back."

"I'm not going back."

Damita stared at him. "You're not going back? Why?"

"Nothing to go back to New Orleans for. I'm headed to Savannah."

"Oh, I see." Damita felt lost for a moment, then she made the best of it. "You can give me your address, and I can have him send you the money."

"To perdition with the money! Who cares about it?" Yancy said roughly. He picked up his coffee, sipped it, and said, "I thought hard times drew people together, Damita. That was a horrible experience. We were hanging on to each other, and we were all we had. I'll never forget it, but evidently, you don't want to think about it."

Damita studied his face. He had not shaved, and his whiskers had a reddish glint. His face looked thinner even in the short time since the shipwreck, but his eyes were blue as cornflowers and intense as anything she had ever seen. She remembered how she had clung to him and returned his caresses. Her face flushed, and she knew she could not hide her thoughts from him.

"Look, Damita, we barely survived a disaster. You had lost a beloved relative. We were cold and alone, and the only thing we had on earth was each other. When something like that happens, your defenses are down. It can happen to anyone." He reached over and put his hand on her wrist. "Don't be ashamed of being human, Damita."

Her first impulse was to give him the same kind of warmth and confidence that he was showing toward her. But she could not forget that he was the one who had broken away from their embrace. Damita, who had always prided herself upon her ability to stand, had nearly fallen. It was Yancy, the rough Kaintock with no manners, who had shown strength. This galled her anew. If she had been the one who had drawn back, she could have borne it. But she had not, and both of them knew it. She tightened her lips and gave him a level look. "You saved my life, Yancy, and for that, I'll always be thankful."

Yancy saw that she was hardened against him and removed his hand. He studied her for a moment and then shook his head. "You've got too much pride. One day, if you're lucky, you'll lose it. And then, you'll have to admit that you're human just like the rest of us. If that ever happens, you'll be a real woman with real pride.

The ship leaves in the morning at nine o'clock. I'll be in the lobby, waiting to take you there. Good night."

Damita watched, shocked, as Yancy stood and walked out of the restaurant. He disappeared around the corner, and she felt deflated, and that she had somehow demeaned herself. Her mind returned to the time that she had lain in his arms and shame came. *I'm no better than the women at those balls who give themselves to men for money,* she thought. *I'm the same as they are.* Her hands clenched. She rose and went to her room, and when she had shut the door, she lay down on the bed and tried to blot everything out of her mind.

The ship was terrible. It was filthy and smelly, and the sailors leered at her. Even the captain was drunk.

Yancy had brought Damita on board and introduced her to Captain Passen, who had not shaved recently and had a rank odor about him. He had grinned and said, "You're all right, lady. My first mate will give you his cabin for the trip."

"Thank you, Captain, and thank the mate for me."

"We'll be settin' sail in half an hour. You better get your good-byes said. Don't worry, little lady. We don't get many passengers, but we'll have time to get acquainted."

Damita turned toward Yancy, and they moved a few steps away from the captain, aware of the eyes of the crew. The two of them had hardly spoken all morning. She looked down at her hands, unable to meet his eyes.

"What's the matter?" he asked.

"Nothing. Nothing's wrong."

"Are you afraid?"

Damita lifted her head and nodded. "Yes, I'm afraid of these men."

Yancy studied her for a moment, then shrugged. "I'm in no big hurry. I'll pay my passage and take you back to your parents."

"I . . . I thank you for that, Yancy," she said a bit stiffly.

"No bother," he said without expression and left her to go make arrangements with the captain.

The first mate's cabin stank of stale flesh, alcohol, and tobacco smoke. As soon as Damita saw it, she knew she would not be able to sleep on the bed because the covers were so soiled. Yancy arranged to get fresh bedding for her.

The first day she spent almost entirely in her cabin. On deck, the men had whispered loudly enough for her to hear crude remarks that brought color to her face.

Yancy left her alone. On the second day of the voyage, Damita left her cabin and saw him standing in the prow of the ship. She took a deep breath and walked over. He nodded, saying, "We'll be in New Orleans by late afternoon."

"That will be good."

"It's been an unpleasant voyage."

"It hasn't been all bad, and I thank you for coming with me." He did not answer, and she leaned against the rail. "I can't stop thinking about my aunt. She was so good to me," she said, describing some of her aunt's qualities.

Yancy said quietly, "It's hard to lose someone like that. I'm sorry."

The silence continued, and Damita said, "I can't put the McCains out of my mind."

"I've thought about them a lot too."

"Esther was so happy. She had her future completely planned out. Now it's all over."

Yancy studied Damita's face. He knew she was a girl with great vitality and imagination, and he saw now her will and the pride in the corners of her eyes. He was also aware of the clean-running, physical lines of her body. He well understood the reserve that had come between them since that day in the barn, and he realized it would always be there. "They were happy for a while," he answered.

"But such a short while. What was it? Only five or six days."

"I think it was longer than that. He courted her for more than a year. That was a happy time for them."

"But still, Yancy, it's so short."

Something was in his eyes that she could not read. He shrugged. "We don't have any guarantees."

His answer was enigmatic. He himself was a man she could not understand, and abruptly she asked him, "When we thought we were going to die, were you afraid?"

"Of course I was."

"I'm surprised. You don't seem to be afraid of anything."

"You're wrong about that, Damita."

Damita studied him even more carefully. "What are you afraid of, Yancy?"

"Growing old. Getting helpless. Being alone with no one to care." He hesitated, then added, "What comes after death."

Damita suddenly realized that she was afraid of those things, too. She said as much, and he nodded.

"I think most people are, but my mother wasn't."

"Your mother?"

"After my father died, life was hard. We had no money, but she was a happy woman. She had a joy inside her I've never seen in anyone else. She went about the house singing songs about Jesus. I'll never forget that. And when she came to death," he added, "it was as if she were going on a vacation. She couldn't wait to get on 'the other side,' as she called it."

"That's wonderful."

"You know, Damita, I've met a few atheists. Some of them were pretty smart men, but my mother's the answer I have for them. I saw God in my mother."

Somehow Yancy's simple words touched Damita. "What was her name?" she asked.

"Her name was Kate. I wrote a poem about her once—the only poem I ever wrote."

"You wrote a poem?"

Yancy looked embarrassed. "Yep, I did."

"I'd like to read it."

"I don't have it written down."

"But you know it."

"Oh, yes, I know it."

"Would you say it for me, please?"

Yancy was taken aback. "I've never said it for anybody."

"I'd like to hear it."

The wind was not strong, but it blew Yancy's auburn hair over his face. He looked embarrassed but said, "All right." He stared at the sea and said:

> When she was thirty-three Kate Devereaux slipped
> Away from earth, and I was there to see
> Her debut into immortality.
> Death for her—a fine wine to be sipped
> Before her voyage on a darkling sea.
>
> So deep she lay in downy feather bed,
> Beneath the handmade quilt I saw no form,
> But lightly swelled the patterns cuneiform
> Of orange circles squared in turkey-red—
> Primly gay, her deathbed uniform!
>
> First light, Kate willed away her best:
> Husband, children, home, to God's defense.
> And then her heart, in spritely cadence,
> Drummed, then slowed—then settled down to rest.
> So well she endured her going hence.

"That's . . . that's beautiful."

Yancy saw that Damita had tears in her eyes. "Why, it's nothing to cry about," he said gently.

She could not answer but dashed the tears away. "I think your mother must have been a wonderful woman." The poem had moved her, and Yancy Devereaux had become even more of an enigma. *How could a man like this write words like that?*

One thing turned out well: Word of the ship's going down had not yet reached Damita's parents. When she had appeared at the door with Yancy at her side, Alfredo and Elena had stared at them in shock. She explained quickly what had happened, and they expressed grief and sadness over the loss of Juanita, mingled with rejoicing that Damita had survived.

Alfredo had almost swamped Yancy with his thankfulness. When Damita had told him how he saved her, Alfredo hugged the young man, something neither his wife nor his daughter had ever seen him do. Elena also had taken Yancy's hand and kissed it in the Latin manner. This had embarrassed Yancy.

"You must stay with us for a time. You must give me a chance to show my gratitude," Alfredo had said. And at his and his wife's insistence, Yancy had agreed to stay for a few days, at least until he could find a ship to Savannah.

In the days that followed, Damita felt an almost crippling discomfort when she was near Yancy. She had insisted that her father give him a reward, which Alfredo tried to do, but Yancy firmly refused it.

No ship was headed for Savannah for five days, and during those days, Damita saw a great deal of the tall visitor she had brought into their lives. She saw how quickly her mother and father accepted him. They told her separately they were shocked that an American could be so nice. Elena said, "Why, with a little training in manners, he could pass for one of us."

Damita smiled. "I doubt he would like to do that, Mother."

Damita also noticed how well Yancy got along with the servants. Within a day's time, he knew each one of them by name and most of their histories. He had become a favorite of Ernestine, the cook, and also of Dolores Aznar, the housekeeper.

Damita noticed more than once that Charissa seemed to be taken with Yancy. She once saw them sitting together in the kitchen, cracking pecans, and when she entered, Yancy said, "We're going to make some pralines. Charissa's going to show me how."

"I'm sure she makes very good ones."

"We have a lot in common, Charissa and I. We've both picked lots of cotton, haven't we, Charissa?"

"Yes, we have," Charissa said, smiling at him. "I've picked enough to last me a lifetime."

"So have I. I'd rather make pralines with a pretty girl anytime."

Something about the scene had disturbed Damita. She could not put her finger on it, but she filed it away in her mind.

On the day before he was to leave, Yancy visited the garden market with Charissa. He helped her carry the packages back, and the two deposited the groceries in the kitchen with Ernestine. Then they went outside to the courtyard, where Charissa asked him to tell her what life was like where he grew up in Virginia.

The two of them stood beside a wall, and Yancy began to describe bear hunting to her. Charissa's eyes glowed as he talked.

"One time, my friend Ed and I were hunting bear, and we hadn't had any luck tracking one at all. Then suddenly, one came roaring out of nowhere. He reached out just like this, and he grabbed me, and I knew I was a goner."

To illustrate his point, Yancy put his arms around Charissa. "He had big, long, white teeth, and I just knew he was going to bite my head off."

"What are you doing?"

Yancy turned and saw that Damita had come out into the courtyard. He stepped back and smiled. "Why, I was just telling Charissa—"

"I could see what you were doing. Mr. Devereaux, I would appreciate it if you would not trouble the female servants."

"He was just telling me a story," Charissa said.

"You keep out of this, Rissa."

"My name is Charissa."

"You be quiet, or I'll have you whipped!"

"You've done it before, haven't you?" Charissa stared at her mistress for a moment, then turned and walked away, her back stiff.

Yancy glared at Damita. "You had that girl beaten?"

"That's none of your business."

Yancy's smile had disappeared. "That's your way, isn't it? Somebody doesn't do what you like, you have them punished! If you don't own them, then you take it out in other ways. You're nothing but a spoiled brat, Damita! Other people who went down on that ship were more fit to live than you are." He walked briskly out of the courtyard and back into the house.

Damita stood silently. She began to tremble and turned to go talk to Charissa, but she knew that would be useless. She looked at the door into which Yancy had disappeared. *It's all his fault,* she thought angrily. *Everything he does hurts me somehow. I'll never have anything to do with another Kaintock as long as I live!*

PART TWO

· Spring 1832 ·

Charissa

Chapter seven

From the surgical viewing area, Dr. Aaron Goldman watched the operation that took place below him with avid interest. He was a small man with coal-black hair despite his sixty years, and he exuded a certain elegance. All of the other doctors who had gathered to watch the operation wore black, but Goldman gave the Prince Albert coat he wore a special sort of dignity. He ran his hand over his hair, then shook his head in wonder. Turning to the man who sat beside him, he said, "Dr. Pryor, *that* is what I call a fine piece of work."

John Pryor was much younger. He was also much larger. As the two stood up to leave, he towered over Goldman. He took one more look at the patient being wheeled out and at the surgeon walking toward the door of the operating room. "I've never seen a better man with a knife," he admitted. Pryor was a broad, tall man with blunt features, red hair, and direct brown eyes. He wore a beard and now he stroked it thoughtfully. "He's very young to be so good."

"Yes, he's only twenty-six. Come along. Let's be on our way," Goldman said. "I want to find out how his father's doing."

"You know the family, then?"

"Yes, his father is Irving Whitman. I've known him since we were young men in medical school together." He turned, and the two men joined the others filing out of the balcony that circled the operating room. They made their way into the hall, and as they turned toward the stairs, Pryor asked, "What sort of training did he have, Dr. Goldman?"

"His father is one of the finest physicians I've ever known—a skillful surgeon and all-around physician. His wife died years ago, and they never had any children. Irving missed her terribly. We were afraid, for a while, that he might take his own life, his loss so devastated him. I don't know how he ran across him, but he adopted this boy and named him Jefferson. The two were inseparable, and I suppose Jeff just soaked up everything his father taught him. He's a bright young man with a brilliant future."

"Will he stay here in the hospital?"

"I suppose he will. His father is very closely tied to this place. Oh, there he is. Come on, I want you to meet him."

Pryor hurried along with Aaron Goldman, who walked fast for a man his age. As they approached the young physician, Pryor studied him and thought, *Well, he'll never take any prizes for beauty.* He waited as Goldman approached first, and the young surgeon turned to greet him. Jefferson's eyes lit up with pleasure as he shook hands with the older man. Jefferson had coarse black hair and expressive brown eyes and was quite tall: six feet, three inches, Pryor guessed. There was nothing fine about the tall, lanky body, or the face itself. Whitman's face was craggy, with deep-set eyes, high cheekbones, and hollow cheeks. He was very lean, but when he was introduced and Pryor took his hand, he felt the strength of the young man's grasp.

"How's your father, Jefferson?"

"Not much improved, I'm afraid, Dr. Goldman. He has his good days and his bad ones."

"I was hoping he'd gotten better. Does he go out at all?" Goldman asked.

"Yes, sir. On his better days, I take him riding in the carriage. Sometimes we walk a little, if the weather's fine. Last week was good for him, but now he's very weak."

"Give him my best wishes, and tell him I'll be by to see him later this week, to beat him at chess again."

A smile spread across Whitman's face. "I don't think you've beaten him in fifty years—at least, so he tells it."

"I let him win just to make him feel better," Goldman said, his eyes sparkling. "Say, that was a fine job you did in there."

"Thank you, Dr. Goldman. I'll look forward to your visit."

Whitman departed, and John Pryor murmured, "He doesn't look like a doctor, does he?"

"No, he looks more like an outdoorsman, which he is, as a matter of fact. He loves hunting and fishing and goes every chance he gets."

"He's an amazing surgeon, if what I saw was any sample, and I suppose he has a good thing here with his father's influence."

Goldman shook his head and said firmly, "Jefferson Whitman's made his own way. His father may have had some input in getting him into this hospital, but the rest he did on his own. He's a fine young fellow."

Spring of 1832 brought St. Louis the mildest of warm, soft breezes. As Jefferson Whitman guided the mare to a stop beside the tall three-story brownstone, he waved at Marcus Stoner, the free black man who was kneeling in the garden that stretched beside the house. "Hello, Marcus," he called out. "What are you planting now?"

"Just a few pretty flowers. You gonna like 'em when they come up, Dr. Jeff."

The black man, short and stocky, stood and followed the buggy around to the large hitching area in the back. To the right was a carriage house, and behind was a half-acre field, green with grass.

"Let me unhitch for you, Dr. Jeff."

"You might as well turn Penny out into the pasture. I won't be going anywhere the rest of the day."

"Yes, sah. Did you have a good day, Doctor?"

"Very fine. Did my father sit on the porch today?"

"Not today, sah. Mrs. Shultz, she say he's not doin' well. I was hopin' this warm weather would be good for him."

"So was I."

Marcus said with a grin, "He's got a good doctor takin' care of him. You give him my best wishes and tell him I'm prayin' for him, and my prayers don't never fail."

"I'll tell him, Marcus."

Jeff picked up his medical bag and walked in the back door. He found Olga Shultz, the housekeeper, and Ellie Middleton, the maid, preparing the evening meal. "Hello, ladies," he said. "Something good for supper tonight?"

"Yah. Vat you expect? I cook something bad?"

Mrs. Shultz was forty-eight and had been in America since she was fifteen, but she still had her German accent. She was a heavy woman, blonde and blue-eyed, with a perfect complexion. A widow, she was totally devoted to Irving Whitman; he had shown kindness to her as an immigrant, unable to speak a word of English and new to the country. Olga nudged the maid at her side and said, "Why you just stand there, Ellie? Take the doctor's bag up to his room."

"Oh, yes, I'll take it, Dr. Jeff!" Ellie was twenty years old, a thin woman with brown hair and pale blue eyes. She obviously adored Jefferson Whitman, which at first had amused Olga Shultz; now she was impatient with the girl.

"Oh, don't bother. I'll take it myself, Ellie," Jeff said.

"Oh, no, sir, let me do it!" Ellie reached out, and when his hand touched hers as they passed the bag, she blushed, swallowed hard, and ran out of the room.

"That is a foolish girl. She thinks she's in loff with you."

"She just can't resist my good looks. No woman can." Jeff looked down at the housekeeper with fondness. "How's Father been today?"

"Not gute. I couldn't get him to eat his lunch, but he'll eat tonight. I made him a gute German meal." She reached out and poked the tall man's ribs. "And you, you never put on a pound. You're skinny as a rail."

"Not because I don't get good cooking. I'll go visit Father, and then I think I'll lie down before supper."

"Don't you be fooling vid dot Ellie! She's got no sense at all."

Jefferson grinned broadly. "I can't promise a thing, Olga. I'm a wicked, wicked man." He laughed and turned down a short hall that opened into a large foyer. He walked to the bedroom that they had provided on the first floor for convenience's sake. He knocked on the door, and hearing his father's voice, he stepped inside. He saw that his father was pale and wan, but he showed no reaction. Smiling, he said, "I hear you've been misbehaving. Olga says you wouldn't eat your lunch."

"That woman wants to stuff me like a pig. Sit down. Tell me about what's been going on. I'm surprised the hospital is still open without me there to see to it."

Jeff pulled a chair close to the bed, sat, and began to speak of the activities of the day. Without seeming to, he studied his father carefully. At the age of sixty-four, Irving Whitman had been a strong man up until a year ago. The illness had baffled most of the doctors. Whatever it was had drained his strength and the color from his face. He had always been a handsome man, with silver hair and unusual green eyes, but now he looked frail.

Jeff told him about his various doctoring activities, including the finite details of each one. When he finished speaking of the last surgery, he mentioned, "I saw Dr. Goldman today. He says he's coming out to see you this week."

"He's too busy for that."

"I don't think so. I never knew Dr. Goldman to promise a single thing he didn't carry out." Jeff felt a pang in his heart. Irving was all the family he knew, and his father's illness pained him. He forced a smile and said, "I'll going to go clean up a little bit. Olga tells me she's made a fine meal. Do you feel like going to the table?"

"Certainly."

Jeff was fairly sure that his father did not feel like it, but it was good that he made the effort. "All right. We'll have a contest and see who can eat the most."

"This is fine cooking, Olga," Jeff said. He had eaten a great portion of the meal, which included tender pork chops, carrots and broccoli from the garden, and new potatoes, white and steaming as they burst out of their jackets. The freshly baked éclairs that served as dessert seemed to melt in his mouth.

Mrs. Shultz beamed but saw that Irving had eaten almost nothing. She opened her mouth to protest when she caught Jeff's eye. He shook his head, and she swallowed her scoldings.

"Let's go sit on the porch and watch the fireflies," Jeff suggested.

"I think I'd rather lie down."

Jeff recognized fatigue in his father's face. "Of course," he said. "I'll tell you what—let me read to you. You always like that."

"All right, but I don't want any adventure stories tonight."

"You can choose."

Fifteen minutes later, Irving Whitman was propped up in his bed, his hands folded, and Jeff was roaming the bookcases. "Nothing here but science and medical books."

"Read from this."

Jeff turned and walked over and took the worn, black Bible that his father indicated on the table beside him. "Fine," he said. "Would you like something from the Gospels?"

"No, I want you to read the Song of Solomon."

Surprise showed in the younger man's eyes. "The Song of Solomon?"

"Yes."

Jeff shrugged, sat down, and opened the Bible. The book was ragged, its thin pages creased and yellowed with age. He remarked, "We need to get you a new Bible. This one's worn out."

"No, I like that one. It's like an old friend."

"I wish mine were as worn as yours." Jeff found the book and began to read. "The song of songs which is Solomon's. Let him kiss me with the kisses of his mouth: for thy love is better than wine." He looked up and said, "This really is an odd book! I never know what to do with it, Father. Some of the lines in it are embarrassing."

Irving smiled. "I heard a pastor say once that this is the hardest book for unspiritual people to read."

"I guess that's me."

"Go ahead and just read it."

Jeff continued through the first chapter to verse thirteen:

> A bundle of myrrh is my well-beloved unto me; he shall lie all night betwixt my breasts. My beloved is unto me as a cluster of camp-

fire in the vineyards of Engedi. Behold, thou art fair, my love; behold, thou art fair; thou hast doves' eyes. Behold, thou art fair, my beloved, yea, pleasant: also our bed is green. The beams of our house are cedar, and our rafters of fir.

Jeff looked up, a puzzled light in his brown eyes. "I must confess, Father, I don't know what this book is doing in the Bible."

"It's always been one of my favorites."

"But why?"

"It's a book about love, Jeff," the old man said. "Everybody's interested in love, I suppose."

"But this is so—*strange*. Listen to this: 'He brought me to the banqueting house, and his banner over me was love. Stay me with flagons, comfort me with apples: for I am sick of love. His left hand is under my head, and his right hand doth embrace me.'" Jeff shook his head. "This is a pretty graphic love scene."

"Yes, it is. The whole book, on the surface, is about the love of a man and a woman. It's taking a look at the physical side of the marriage relationship."

"But why is it in the Bible?"

"I think God uses this book as He uses others: to show us His love for man. After all, Jeff, the highest form of love on earth is probably between a husband and a wife. The apostle Paul said that the two become one flesh. I don't know of any other relationship that creates such a complete union. Yes, I think it's a picture of Christ and His church, expressed in terms of a human marriage. You remember that Paul said that the church is the bride of Christ. And in the Old Testament, Israel was the wife of Jehovah."

"It's so sensual."

"So is marriage, Jeff. That's part of the love between men and women. There are other parts. When the sensual passes away, there's still love there, but for a time, physical love is part of marriage. And God honors it. Only worldly people and those with impure minds find something shameful about the marriage bed."

Jeff continued reading, pausing from time to time to let his father speak of what the verses meant to him. He knew his father was a truly devout Christian, but they didn't often read the Bible together. This night, Irving seemed unusually talkative.

When Jeff finished the book, Irving looked tired, but a light still shone in his eyes as he looked at his son. "One day, you'll get married, Jeff, and I hope you find the woman that God's created just for you."

Jeff smiled. "You're very romantic. You believe that marriages are made in heaven."

"I believe that God made Isabelle for me, and me for her."

"You loved her very much."

"Perhaps too much. Jeff, find a woman and love her as this book sets it out. Let her be the fairest thing in this world to you."

Jeff saw tears in his father's eyes, and this shocked him. He sat quietly until his father said, "I think I'll sleep now, son. Thanks for reading to me."

Jeff removed some of his father's pillows, then took his hand. He held it in both of his. It felt as thin and feeble as the bones of a young bird. "I'll remember what you said about finding the right woman. Good night, sir."

"Good night, Jeff."

Jeff turned the lamp down very low and left the room. In the hall, he met Olga, who asked, "Is he all right?"

"He's not as well as I'd like. He was in an odd mood tonight. He talked about his wife."

"Vat did he say?"

"He talked about how much he loved her, and how he wants me to find a woman I can love that way."

"He is such a good man. I pray every night and every morning, too, und all day that Gott vill get him up from dot bed."

"So do I, Olga." He put his arm around the woman, hugged her, and said, "Good night."

Jeff went to his own bedroom then, undressed, and got into bed. He was tired to the bone; he had started his day at five o'clock, and now it was after midnight. Yet he lay unable to sleep, thinking about the evening with his father. Finally he realized, *Something is troubling him. But I don't know what it is.* As he pondered what it could be, sleep overtook him.

For the next two days, Jeff worked hard and rode home as quickly as he could, in case his father wanted to talk some more, but Irving kept conversations short. Jeff grew more and more convinced that something was disturbing his father, but he respected the old man's privacy and would not ask him outright.

On Thursday night, Irving ate very little and went to sleep early in the evening. Jeff was in the library next door to his father's bedroom, reading, when he heard Irving's bell ring. He jumped to his feet and met the housekeeper in the hall, coming from the kitchen. "I'll see to him, Olga."

He entered Irving's room and saw that the bed was rumpled, as if his father had been thrashing around. Irving looked up at him with desperate eyes.

"What is it, sir? Are you in pain?"

"Not physically."

Jeff hesitated, then said, "You didn't bring me up to be nosy, but I wish you'd tell me what it is." For a moment, he thought that he had stepped over the line: His father stared at him almost harshly. He began to apologize, but Irving interrupted him.

"Sit down, Jeff. I must talk to you."

Jeff pulled a chair close to his father's bed and leaned forward, his hands clasped together.

The words came from the older man slowly. "You're right. I am troubled. I have tried to keep this thing to myself, but I can't do it any longer, son."

Jeff had no idea what was coming. He said, "Tell me, Father. If it's something I can fix, I'll do it."

The gaslight burned steadily, throwing shadows on the face of Irving Whitman. His cheeks were thin, his lips pale. He closed his eyes for a time, and when he opened them to meet those of his son, they showed torment. "I have something to confess to you, Jeff. It may be that you will despise me after you've heard what I have to say."

"That won't happen!"

"Perhaps it should. I committed a terrible sin, Jeff."

"I can't believe that, sir."

Irving began to tremble, and he lowered his head. Finally he said, "It was five years after my wife died, Jeff. God knows I loved her more than life, and after I lost her, I nearly lost my mind. I was so lonely, Jeff. I really had no one until I adopted you, and you were only a child."

Jeff did not move. He had never seen his father in this mood. He waited, scarcely daring to breathe.

"There was a young woman, a slave on the plantation. She was a beautiful quadroon. Her name was Bethany. I . . . I don't know how it happened. I had never had any affairs, but without going into details I had a . . . relationship with her. She had no choice, of course. I think she really cared for me."

Irving broke off then and found it difficult to speak. "I cared for her, too. I can't explain how I could so turn aside from everything that I knew was right. I wasn't a Christian at the time, but I knew what I did was wrong. Then I found out she was pregnant, and I was scared to death."

Jeff did not move a muscle, nor did the shock that he felt show in his face. He waited and finally, when his father seemed unable to continue, he whispered, "What did you do?"

"What could I do? She was a black woman in the eyes of the society I grew up in. I went around for weeks in agony not knowing what to do. When I found out she was carrying my child, I panicked. I . . . I sold her to a neighboring planter named Franklin Demarr."

"You're not the first man to fall into temptation," Jeff said quietly.

"Don't make excuses for me! I was absolutely miserable, and I took the easy way out. I buried myself in work, but I never could forget Bethany, for I knew that I had wronged her terribly. I tried to make up for what I had done by being a good man, but I could never put it away." Suddenly, he turned and faced Jeff. "How can I face God with this on my soul, Jeff?"

Jeff swallowed hard. "You've asked God to forgive you, haven't you?"

"Yes, and God did save me. And I thank Him for it, and for the blood of Jesus. But Jeff, I owe this woman and this child something."

"You want me to help you with this, don't you, Father?"

"Yes. I want you to find Bethany and the child, and I want you to purchase them. I want you to buy them out of slavery and bring them here so we can give them a better life. Will you do this?"

Jeff took his father's hands. He saw the tears in his father's eyes and felt some in his own. "Yes. I'll leave right away, and I will do exactly as you say. I'll find the woman and the child, and I'll do whatever I can to help them."

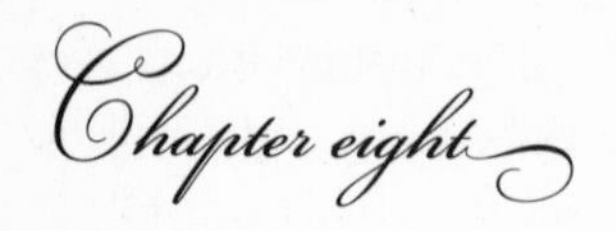

Chapter eight

Jeff stepped off the train, half-choked by the cinders that poured out of the engine. His bag in hand, he immediately looked around for a carriage. Independence, Missouri, had only a small train station, and he soon spotted two carriages along the curb. He walked toward the man standing by the first one and asked, "Can you take me into town?"

"Yes, sir." The speaker was ruddy-faced, wearing a pair of brown trousers and a flamboyant yellow shirt. He grabbed Jeff's bag, tossed it in the back carelessly, and then hopped to the seat. "Where can I take you, sir?"

"I'm looking for a man named Franklin Demarr. I understand he lives at 611 Elm Street."

"You just sit back, and I'll have you there in no time, sir."

Jeff held on as the driver wheeled the horses around abruptly, throwing him to one side. Jeff was tired after his long train ride, but he had dozed a little during the night. He pulled out his watch and saw that the time was shortly after ten o'clock; today was the twentieth of April. Jeff leaned back, wondering how he would approach Franklin Demarr. It was, after all, a delicate situation. He had thought about it since he left home and concluded, *I can't tell him the whole truth. I hope he'll be understanding.*

Ten minutes later, the carriage pulled up in front of a tall two-story frame house. "This the place?"

"I suppose so." Jeff got out and asked, "Would you mind waiting for me? I'll be glad to pay you for your time."

"Yes, sir."

Jeff ascended the steep steps and knocked on the door. He waited apprehensively, and when it opened, he found himself facing a middle-aged woman with kind gray eyes.

"Yes, what is it?"

"I'm Dr. Jefferson Whitman, ma'am. I'm looking for Mr. Franklin Demarr."

"He's my father-in-law. Is he expecting you?"

"No, ma'am, but I do need to see him."

"Come in. I'll see what he says."

Jeff stepped inside the spacious foyer, and the woman disappeared down a hall. A few moments later, she returned and said, "He said he will see you. He's in the last room down the hall."

"Thank you, ma'am."

When Jeff found the door and was admitted, he faced a silver-haired man, who rose from a desk, walked over, and said, "Yes? Your name is Whitman?"

"Yes. I'm sorry to intrude, sir, but—"

"I knew some Whitmans when I was younger."

"They were my father's parents, I suppose. My father's name is Irving Whitman."

"Why, yes, I know your family well. And I remember Irving was a doctor."

"That's right, sir. Irving is my father."

"Come in and sit down." Demarr pointed to a sofa and and offered Jeff some tea. When Jeff declined, the older man leaned back and said, "Can't imagine why in the world you'd be looking for me. I haven't thought of Whitman in oh, fifteen years. Is he still alive?"

"Yes, sir, but he is very ill."

"I'm sorry to hear this. I heard good things of him. I have a sister who lives in St. Louis. She says he's practicing there."

"Yes, sir, and so am I."

Jeff answered some questions about the Whitman plantation, and when the conversation began to falter, he said, "This is going to sound strange, but I'm looking for the records on a slave my father sold to you quite a few years ago."

"A slave?"

"Yes. Her name was Bethany. I don't know any last name. I don't think there was one."

"Why would you want to find a record on a sale that old?"

"My father asked me to do it. I can't give you his reasons."

Franklin studied Jeff, then shrugged his shoulders. "Well, I have the books right here. We sold the plantation years ago, but I kept all the records. Don't know why." He rose and walked over to a bookcase, ran his finger over some volumes, and pulled down a ledger. He brought it back to the desk, opened it up, and began to scan its contents. "Here it is. One mulatto, Bethany, purchased from Whitman."

"You sold your plantation. Then I suppose you sold off all your slaves. Would you have a record there of who bought this woman?"

"It's right here. Sold: one mulatto with her daughter to a plantation owner named Donald Barton."

"Is there an address there for Mr. Barton?"

"He has an office in Memphis. I don't know where it is, but it shouldn't be hard to find."

"Thank you very much, Mr. Demarr."

"Tell your father I remember him."

"I'll tell him. You've been a great help, sir."

Jeff's trip to Memphis was hard and dull. He had to change trains twice from Independence, and by the time he reached Memphis, he was exhausted. He had no trouble, however, finding Donald Barton, who was a prominent businessman in real estate.

Jeff arrived too late that day to call on the man in his office, but first thing the next morning, he walked in the door and met a tall, distinguished-looking man who smiled winningly. "Mr. Barton?"

"Yes, sir. I am Donald Barton."

"I'm Dr. Jefferson Whitman."

"Sit down, Doctor. Are you a resident here?"

"No, I'm from St. Louis."

"If you're thinking of settling, I can help you with a business address or with a residential property."

"I'm afraid not, Mr. Barton. I'm actually searching for two slaves you purchased four years ago."

"Oh?" Barton dropped his smile. "What is your interest, sir?"

"I'm trying to trace the two at the request of my father."

"What were their names? I sold my plantation, and I know that most of the slaves are now gone."

Jeff told him Bethany's name, and Barton said, "Oh, yes, I remember her and her daughter, Charissa, well. Fine-looking stock. But I sold them off to Leroy Hampton."

"Does he live in this area?"

"Oh, no, he has a large plantation outside of Baton Rouge."

Jeff rose. "Thank you very much."

"You sure I can't show you some property?"

Jeff smiled. "No, thank you. I'll be leaving."

He went directly to check on a packet. He was tired of trains and was glad to find that a fast packet was leaving the next day at eleven o'clock. He reserved a stateroom, then returned to his hotel for the night.

When Jeff left the packet at Baton Rouge, he had no idea where to find Hampton, so he visited the courthouse. It took a little persuasion, but he used what charm he had and discovered from the clerk, who seemed familiar with most of the population, that Leroy Hampton had died. The clerk did manage to give Jeff some useful information: "His wife's running the place now. You'd have to see her. You can find her easily enough."

"How do I get there?"

"If you hire a carriage, tell the driver to take you out the old Military Road for three miles. When you get there, ask anybody, and they'll tell you where the Hampton place is."

"Thank you very much."

"You're welcome, sir."

Jeff quickly found a carriage. The driver urged the bays to a fast pace. They passed through the center of Baton Rouge and then the outskirts. Three miles later, the driver hailed a pedestrian, asking, "Can you tell me where the Hamptons live?"

"Right over there. That big white house with the blue shutters."

The driver thanked him. When he pulled up in front of the house, Jeff got out, asking him to wait. He climbed the steps to the porch and knocked on the door. There was long pause before it opened. Then a thin, narrow-faced woman with suspicious eyes appeared and asked, "What is it?"

"My name is Dr. Jefferson Whitman. I'm looking for Mrs. Hampton."

"That's me. What do you want?"

"I'm looking for some information, Mrs. Hampton. Could you give me a few minutes?" The woman hesitated, and it seemed as though she was going to shut the door. But then she shrugged and said, "Come in."

Jeff stepped inside, and she led him into a drawing room. The room smelled musty, and the windows were all closed, even though the day was hot. Jeff stated his business. "I'm looking for a slave woman and her daughter. Her name is Bethany, and her daughter's name is Charissa. Donald Barton said that your husband purchased them a while back."

The woman stared at him. "Why do you want to find out about them?"

Jeff saw the hardness of the woman's glance and said, "I had it in my mind to purchase the pair." Since this really was his intention, he felt as if he was telling her the truth, if not the whole story.

"You're too late."

"Too late?" Jeff said. "What do you mean?"

"The woman's dead. She died some time ago."

Jeff felt the heavy weight of disappointment. "All this for nothing. The girl, is she here?"

"No. I sold her. It's hard times. I had to cut back."

"Would you mind telling me whom you sold her to?"

"Yes, I would. I know men like you. She's a good-lookin' wench, and I know your purpose. You don't intend to put her pickin' cotton."

"You're entirely mistaken, Mrs. Hampton."

"I know you want the girl for evil purposes. I won't help you. Now, please leave!"

Jeff had no choice but to do as she said. He heard the door slam behind him as he climbed into the carriage. The driver waited for directions, and Jeff finally said, "Take me to a hotel."

"Yes, sir. Any particular one?"

"No. Just a respectable place. A room for the night."

"Yes, sir."

Jeff toyed with the food on his plate. He had taken the room, cleaned up, and spent the day wondering what to do next. He was sure there were ways to find the records of sale, but he was not sure how to go about it.

A voice jarred him out of his thoughts: "Do you mind if I join you? It looks like the tables are all taken."

Jeff looked up and saw a broad-shouldered, middle-aged man. "Not at all. Have a seat."

"My name's Vince Shoulders."

"Dr. Jefferson Whitman."

"A doctor, eh? I don't believe we've met. Do you practice here?"

"No, I'm just here on business."

Shoulders sat down, and when the waiter came over, he ordered steak and potatoes. He was a talkative individual, cheerful, and apparently quite a successful man. His clothes were fancy and he wore an ornate gold ring. "You came on business, you say? Successful, I hope."

"No, as a matter of fact, it wasn't."

"Sorry to hear that. Deals do fall through. Were you here to buy land? Maybe I can help. I'm a planter myself. I know most places around here."

"Nothing like that, Mr. Shoulders. I came trying to trace two slaves, but I haven't been able to get any information."

"Who'd they belong to?"

"Leroy Hampton."

"Oh, yes, Leroy. The poor fellow had a hard time of it at the last. He had something wrong with his belly. Went down to nothing. That wife of his wasn't much help, either. She is about the gloomiest woman I ever saw."

"You know the family?"

"Oh, yes. My place is right down the road from theirs."

"Mrs. Hampton wasn't willing to give me any information."

"She's batty, a crazy old woman. Don't know what's wrong with her. I don't know any of the particular slaves, but I can tell you where they are."

Jeff straightened up, his eyes lit with eagerness. "You can?"

"Yep. She sold the whole bunch to a fellow in New Orleans who runs an auction. His name is Saul Lebeaux. I sold him two of my hands at the same time."

"Wonder where I could find him."

"Like I said, he runs an auction in New Orleans, but if you're thinkin' of goin' there, I wouldn't, if I were you."

"Why not, Mr. Shoulders?"

"Yellow fever is bad there. Besides, that's a wicked town. Some of these days, God's going to send fire and brimstone on it, just like He did on Sodom and Gomorrah."

"I'll have to take a chance."

"Watch yourself. There are all kinds of temptations in that town." He broke into a grin and said, "I go over myself to get tempted every once in a while."

Jeff finished his meal and and shook hands with Shoulders. "Thank you, sir. You've been a great help to me."

He lay awake that night for a long time, thinking of his father, and hoping that he would find some trace of the girl called Charissa from Saul Lebeaux.

Chapter nine

The waters of the Mississippi were a rich brown, almost like chocolate, Jeff thought as he stood on the deck of the steamship *Myra Belle*. The paddles drove the vessel through the water at a fast clip, churning up a frothy wake. Jeff found something hypnotic about the water's motion, and despite the noise of the turning paddles, he actually forgot his misson for a moment.

Then he turned and made his way toward the bow, where a crowd had gathered. The region they were approaching was more liquid than solid, it seemed. On both sides of the channel, bayous were filled with strange-looking trees, cypress, he supposed, that bore on their branches what looked like shredded bird's nests. He had asked one of the crew about them and learned that the gray clumps and strands were Spanish moss.

As they passed through the channel, Jeff was fascinated by the long-legged herons that walked solemnly in the shallow water, occasionally bending to spear a fish. The noise of the ship's passage stirred white birds that Jeff did not recognize. In their flight, they mingled with the seagulls that constantly rent the air with their raucous cries.

Restlessly, Jeff moved along the railing and thought of his father. Ever since he had learned the secret that had plagued the man he respected above all others, he felt more uneasy than he could ever remember feeling before. Until then, his life had been fairly easy, and never had he doubted the honor and the integrity of Irving Whitman. Now he felt torn in two by the quest he had undertaken. As the brown waters parted for the *Myra Belle,* he thought over and over about what sort of future might lie ahead, not so much for himself, but for his father. *What if I find the girl and bring her back? What place would she have? I haven't seen much of slavery, but I know it's harsh. How will Father explain her presence to others?* The thoughts troubled him, and he shook his head to clear them away.

The steamboat let out a shrill, clarion call, and the whistle startled the flight of the white birds that fluttered upward, making an irregular pattern against the sky. The sun was hot, for April along the Gulf Coast had a humidity and a power that he had not known in the milder climate of St. Louis.

He stood at the bow, and the crew began to scurry along the decks. "Is that New Orleans up ahead?" he asked one of them.

"That's it, sir. We'll dock within fifteen minutes."

More vessels appeared on the river. Many of them were outgoing, and Jeff watched steamships and those equipped only with sails pass by. Some were side-wheelers that kicked up the brown waters of the Mississippi as they pushed their way steadily toward the gulf. Once he was startled to see what he thought was a log suddenly break into life. He straightened up and narrowed his eyes, then realized that it was an alligator. He watched as the beast, which was at least ten feet long, made its way under the water, with just its snout and eyes peeking above the surface. Jeff kept his eyes on the alligator until the *Myra Belle* passed it and wondered what such a creature's attack would be like.

He turned his attention to the crowded harbor. The *Myra Belle* nosed into the dock, and the sailors let down the long loading walkway next to a stack of cotton bales. The captain and his mate bellowed orders, and Jeff returned to his cabin. He threw his belongings into the suitcase, then joined the passengers who were departing. He asked a carriage driver if he could recommend a hotel.

"I know them all, sir. How much would you like to spend?"

Jeff answered, "I want one close to wherever the slave auction is."

"Why, that would be the St. Louis Hotel," the driver replied. He was a swarthy, muscular individual with his shirt sleeves cut short, exposing massive corded arms. "A fine place but a mite expensive."

"That'll be fine. Take me there."

Jeff drew the razor down his face, wiped the foam off on a towel, and studied himself in the mirror. *I look tired and washed out,* he thought, *but that's only natural.* He splashed water on his face and then picked up a comb. He was not a man who gave a great deal of thought to personal appearance, but he liked to be clean. Finished with his grooming, he went downstairs. He'd had no trouble getting a room, and now he was struck by the lack of activity in the hotel. The lobby was almost empty. He asked the desk clerk, "Can you tell me how to get to the auction?"

"Yes, sir," answered the man, who was dressed in finery. His shirt was gleaming white and his coat a rich brown fabric. "You'll find it on Royal Street. Go down that way for three blocks," he instructed, pointing. "It's right next to the Creole Hotel. Anyone can point it out to you."

Jeff hesitated a moment. "There's not much going on in the city, is there?"

The clerk's eyes grew hooded. He lowered his voice as if whispering a secret: "It's because of the yellow fever epidemic. Ordinarily, this time of year the hotel would be full, but the sickness is everywhere. Bronze John is bad this year."

"Bronze John?"

"That's what some call yellow fever."

"I've heard your people have struggled with that here, off and on."

"It's not as severe yet as it was four years ago. I lost my parents in that one. You'd think the doctors could do something, but they really can't."

"Is the city correcting the sanitary conditions?"

The clerk shrugged. "There's not a lot they can do, I guess. You've never been here before?"

"Never have."

"The city's lower than sea level. It's built in something like a saucer, and the rainwater collects in the gutters, and it ponds around the houses. And sometimes it gets like a swamp."

"Isn't there any underground drainage, sewers, things like that?"

"No. Nothing." The clerk seemed discouraged and passed his hand across his face, as if brushing away something troublesome. "You'll see what happens if you're here long enough. The water stays where it falls, gets stagnant, and makes kind of a green scum. It looks like velvet, but it stinks. Of course, the city's slops and garbage and dead animals don't help much."

Jeff wanted to ask, *Why do you live here, if it's so bad?* but he refrained. People sometimes lived where they had to. He thanked the clerk and headed out to find Saul Lebeaux. He was intrigued by the architecture along the streets. He noted the two-story buildings, which were everywhere, supported by rows of iron posts that fit into a curb. The delicate ironwork on the galleries made a fine weaving shaped like leaves and flowers. All of the upper galleries had waist-high railings, and he saw people sitting in many of them. It made a graceful sight, with the scrolled panels of filigree that topped most of the homes. The sunlight was filtering onto the geraniums, wax flowers, ferns, and here and there a big birdcage that decorated the galleries.

As he watched for the Creole Hotel, he passed a black woman carrying a bucket, her head swathed in a white turban. Right behind her were a pair of dandies, and the two were eyeing a beautiful young woman across the street with her apparent escort. The couple was dressed at the height of fashion, and the man carried a long cane. Jeff had heard that many of these canes concealed swords, which the hot-blooded Creoles drew on the least provocation.

He passed the Creole Hotel to find a short flight of steps leading to a formal doorway. Men were coming and going, and he asked one of them, "Is this where the auction is held?"

"Yes, sir. This is the place."

Jeff stepped inside and took in the large room at a glance. There was no activity, it seemed, although a few prospective buyers were wandering around, smoking long, thin cigars. The sound of their talk filled the place. Jeff saw a man come from a door in the back and approached him, saying, "I'm looking for Mr. Lebeaux."

The man said, "You have some stock to sell?"

"No, it's another matter."

"Go in the back. He's in his office," he said, gesturing toward the door.

Jeff nodded his thanks, found the office, and entered. "I'm looking for Mr. Saul Lebeaux," he said to the man who was standing at the window. He was a swarthy man, with jet-black hair plastered against his skull and a fine black mustache, carefully trimmed. He was wearing a white suit and a black string tie, and the purple smoke from his cigar curled lazily into the air. "That's me," he said. "What can I do for you?"

Jeff expected to be asked to sit down, but Lebeaux was not hospitable. "I am Dr. Jefferson Whitman," he said. "I'm from St. Louis."

Interest quickened in the dark man's face. "You've come, perhaps, to buy?"

"No, Mr. Lebeaux, I'm not a prospective customer." He saw Lebeaux's interest dissipate and said quickly, "I'm trying to find a young woman you purchased from Mrs. Leroy Hampton in Baton Rouge."

"I did make a buy there. You interested in one of them?"

"The name I have is Charissa. It's the only name I know. She would be, I believe, about sixteen."

Lebeaux's eyes were fixed steadily on him. "What is your interest, doctor?"

"It's personal."

Lebeaux's mouth twisted into a grin. There was something evil in his expression.

Jeff ignored it. "Could you give me any information about the girl?"

"You know her, do you?"

"No, I've never seen her in my life, but another party has sent me to find out her whereabouts."

"I might remember—for a price. A memory works better when it's primed by cash."

Lebeaux repulsed Jeff, but he knew he had little choice. "Fifty dollars," he said flatly.

"Give it to me."

Jeff reached into his pocket, pulled out a leather wallet, and extracted some bills. He handed them to Lebeaux, who stuffed them into the pocket of his shirt. "The girl's the property of Alfredo Madariaga."

"Does he live here in town?"

"He has a place in town but a larger plantation just north of the city. It's a prominent family, but I'll tell you, you're probably wasting your time if you want to buy the girl."

"Why do you say that?"

Lebeaux puffed on the cigar and said, "They're proud. A little brash, I think. The girl was supposed to be a maid for the daughter in the family, so I doubt they'll sell her. That's all I know."

Jeff nodded curtly and said, "Thank you, sir," turned, and left the auction house. The encounter had left a bad taste in his mouth, and he walked slowly along the street, wondering what his next move should be. He felt ill-suited for his mission. He had spent much of his life in classrooms, then in examining and operating rooms at the hospital. Yet he knew this was an undeniable request. His father needed Jeff to find the girl and help her, to rest his conscience. A thought snapped into his mind. It came with as much finality as a key turning in a lock. *I'll find Debakky. He'll be able to advise me.*

The one person he knew in the entire city of New Orleans was Dr. Elmo Debakky. Jeff's mind had been so filled with his quest, he had completely forgotten about his old friend. Although Debakky was two years older than he, the two had been close during their medical training in St. Louis and stayed in contact afterward. Jeff remembered the address and asked a coachman to take him to it.

The driver agreed, and Jeff got in the cab. The driver picked up the lines and spoke to the horses. He drove along several streets, making turns, and once again Jeff marveled at the lack of traffic. "Business isn't good?" he asked.

"No," the driver said and cursed fluently in French and English. "The fever's got everybody scared."

"What about you? Aren't you scared?"

"Me? No! If a man's time has come, he will get the fever wherever he is. You can't run from death."

The cab drew up to the house, which was set back from the street. It was a large, two-story structure with a steep roof and gables, and the only resemblance it bore to other architecture in the city was the gallery along the upper story. A sign out front said *Dr. Elmo Debakky*. Getting out, Jeff paid the driver and walked up the steps. When he knocked on the door, an attractive mulatto woman in her late twenties stood before him. "Yes, sir?"

"I am Dr. Jefferson Whitman. I'm a friend of Dr. Debakky's. I'd like to see him, if he's in."

"Yes, he is. Come inside, please. I am Mrs. Bozonnier, the housekeeper." She shut the door behind him and said, "If you'll wait, sir, I'll tell the doctor you're here."

"Thank you." Jeff looked around at the large foyer with expensive-looking pictures on the wall. Doors on each side of the hall before him were open, revealing rich carpets and sunlit rooms. On his right was the library, on the left was apparently a parlor.

"Jeff, what in the world are you doing here?"

Jeff smiled as Elmo Debakky hurried down the hall. Debakky was a cheerful-looking man, short and somewhat heavy. It was not fat but muscle, as Jeff well knew, and when Debakky took his hand, he winced at the iron grip. "Don't break my hand, Elmo."

Debakky slapped Jeff on the back. He wore his blond hair rather long and had intense gray eyes set in a round face. He did everything quickly, speech or action, and now he said, "Come into the parlor. Rose, bring us something refreshing to drink."

"What shall it be, Doctor?"

"You always choose best," he said, smiling. "Come on, Jeff. By George, I'm glad to see you!" He led his friend into the parlor.

"Elmo, I hope I haven't caught you at a busy time."

"As a matter of fact, you have. This yellow fever keeps all the doctors busy. What are you doing in New Orleans? Sit down. How's your father?"

Jeff answered the rapid-fire questions from a horsehide-covered chair. He had little time to do more than that when the housekeeper came in, carrying a tray.

"I thought tea would be nice," she said. "Lunch will be ready soon, though." She looked a question at Jeff.

"Put enough on for two, Rose. Jeff, where are you staying?"

"I took a room in the St. Louis Hotel."

"You go get your things and come here. I just rattle around in this big old house." Elmo Debakky's face was filled with gladness. "Now, help yourself to that tea. Rose here makes the best tea in New Orleans—or anywhere else, for that matter."

"I'm sure she does." The two men sipped tea, and Elmo chattered until Jeff finally had to cut in on his friend. "I'll tell you why I've come, Elmo. I'm here to buy a slave."

"You didn't have to come all the way to New Orleans for that."

Jeff shifted uncomfortably. "I'm going to have to confide in you, but it must not go any further."

Debakky's eyes grew thoughtful. He chewed on his lower lip and then nodded. "All right. What is it?"

Knowing that he could fully trust his friend, Jeff explained his story, concluding, "So, you see, it's a touchy situation. Lebeaux tells me a family named Madariaga bought the girl."

"That would be Alfredo Madariaga," he said. "I know the family."

"Lebeaux seemed to think they are proud people."

"They were, but it's pretty common talk that the family's not as prosperous as it once was. There have been some bad cotton crops. If you're prepared to pay a stiff price, you may be able to purchase the girl."

"Could you give me a letter of introduction?"

"Glad to. You'll probably find them in town here, although they may have run away to their plantation to avoid the fever."

"I've got to find her. I'm worried about Father. This thing is preying on his mind."

"It may take a little negotiating. Look, go to your hotel and get your things." Elmo reached out and squeezed Jeff's arm. "I've missed you, old boy. What I'd like to do is persuade you to stay here and go into practice with me, but I know that's impossible."

"I appreciate the offer, but I can't leave my father, and St. Louis is all he knows now."

"We'll have a good time while you are here. I'll have my man take you to get your things after lunch, and then we'll see about buying this girl."

The Madariaga plantation was expansive, Jeff discovered. He had borrowed Elmo's buggy and driven out of New Orleans, having learned that the family had indeed left town until the yellow fever epidemic passed. The house that rose out of the flatlands was enormous, white with four columns, and on all sides the fields stretched away over the land. Pulling up in front of the house, Jeff met a young black man who inquired, "Shall I put up your horse, sir?"

"No, I don't think I'll be here long. You might water him, though." He fished in his pocket, pulled out a coin, and gave it to the man, whose eyes lit up.

"Yes, suh!" he said and went to lead the buggy away.

As Jeff walked up to the stairs leading to the porch, he rehearsed in his mind what he was going to say. He was not satisfied with it. No matter how he phrased it, his explanation for coming all the way from St. Louis to buy a single slave sounded feeble.

He pounded the big brass knocker on the front door, and almost at once, it swung wide. He found himself facing an older woman wearing a gray dress and a white cap on her head. "Yes, sir?" she said. "May I help you?"

"I would like to see Mr. Madariaga, if possible."

The woman hesitated, then said, "May I have your name, sir?"

"Dr. Jefferson Whitman."

"Will you step inside, please? I'll see if Señor Madariaga is available."

Jeff obeyed, and the woman disappeared. As he waited, he silently rehearsed his speech again. The woman returned and said, "Come this way, sir."

Jeff followed the woman down the wide hallway, and then through a door on the left. The woman stepped aside to let him pass, and he found himself inside a spacious room with a beautiful oriental carpet. The walls were a pale gold and reflected the sunlight that came through the tall window at one end. The man who rose to greet him was dressed in a rather formal way, with black trousers, white shirt, and a tie. He had a smooth, olive complexion and light brown eyes, and he nodded courteously, saying, "Dr. Whitman, welcome to my home."

"Thank you, Mr. Madariaga. I must apologize for coming without an appointment, but I do have a note from a mutual acquaintance, Dr. Debakky."

Madariaga took the note that Jeff extended, read it quickly, and smiled. "Yes, Dr. Debakky was very helpful to my family once during a sickness. Will you sit down?"

Jeff accepted his invitation and decided that the best approach was to bring his business into the open as soon as possible. "I will not take much of your time, sir. I've been commissioned to find a young woman, a slave you purchased recently. I can't reveal the details, but I would like to buy the young woman, if it's possible. Her name is Charissa."

Instantly, Madariaga drew himself up straighter. "Yes," he said evenly, "I do own such a girl. Could you tell me a little more about the details of your mission?"

Jeff had known that he would have to say something, and he had come up with a story that explained his mission in the vaguest of terms. "The gentleman who sent me felt that he had done an injustice to the mother of Charissa. I believe her name was Bethany. I was sent to purchase both the mother and the daughter, but I discovered that the mother died recently. I'm sure my principal would be willing to pay any reasonable price for the girl."

Madariaga tapped his fingertips together thoughtfully and then shook his head, a puzzled look in his eyes. "This is all rather strange, sir. I hardly know what to say."

"I wish I could reveal more, but I can't."

"Do you know the girl, may I ask?"

"No, I've never seen her."

"The girl was a gift to my daughter on her graduation. I could not think of selling her unless my daughter agreed." He hesitated, then said, "She has had trouble with the girl, I must tell you. Charissa is strong-willed. Personally, I would be willing, but you must get my daughter's consent."

"Would it be possible to speak with your daughter, sir?"

"Yes. If you will wait here, I will send her to you." He left the room and turned down the hallway. There he encountered Dolores, his housekeeper, and asked if she knew Damita's whereabouts.

"She is out in the garden, sir."

"Go get her, and tell her to come inside."

"Yes, sir."

As Dolores stepped outside, Madariaga stood thinking over this turn of events. Dolores returned with Damita at her side.

"Damita, come with me, please."

"What is it, Papa?" Damita was wearing a pale yellow dress and a bonnet to shield her face from the sun. She pulled it off now, gave it to Dolores, and followed her father down the hall.

He paused halfway to the den and lowered his voice, saying, "There is a man here, a physician from St. Louis. It's a rather unusual situation. I don't understand it."

"What is it?" Damita asked with curiosity. "What does he want?"

"He wants to buy Rissa."

"Buy Rissa? He's come all the way from St. Louis for that?" Her eyes narrowed, and she asked, "But why?"

She listened as her father repeated the explanation their visitor had given, then said, "I told him that I would not sell the girl without your permission, but I want you to think carefully, Damita. The girl will never make a proper maid for you. I think you should allow the man to buy her, and we'll find a more suitable servant."

Damita looked at her father, then said, "Let me talk to him, Papa, and we will see."

"He's in my study. After you've talked, come and tell me what you've decided."

Damita entered the study and saw the tall man sitting in a leather-bound armchair. He rose to his feet and bowed slightly, and she said, "I am Damita Madariaga, sir."

"Dr. Jefferson Whitman, ma'am."

"I understand that you want to buy my maid." As she spoke, Damita surveyed the gangly figure of the doctor. Though she had a stubborn prejudice against Americans and called them all "Kaintocks," this man was a physician. She saw that he was educated and not crude, as many Americans were. Still, her voice had a hard edge when she asked, "Why do you want this particular girl?"

"Miss Madariaga, as I told your father, I have been sent to buy the girl by an individual who feels that he did her mother an injustice. That's all I can say. I am bound to secrecy."

"That sounds odd to me," Damita said, somewhat haughtily. She had seen how men's eyes followed her maid and wondered if this man had the same intentions. She met his eyes steadily. "I would have to be assured that your interest was not more personal."

"More personal? I don't understand."

"Rissa is a very attractive girl. Men are interested in her."

"But I've never even seen the girl, Miss Madariaga."

Damita was a fair judge of character, and she saw the surprise in the deep-set eyes of the man before her. He was homely, not handsome in the least, and he seemed to project honesty. Still, he was a Kaintock. She came to a decision. "If you will stay here, I will get the girl."

"I'm afraid I won't be able to tell her any more than I've told you, Miss Madariaga, but I would like to meet her."

Damita stepped outside and found the young slave. "There's a man here to buy you, Rissa."

"Buy me!" she exclaimed. "What do you mean, Miss Damita?"

"Just what I said. He's come all the way from St. Louis." She lowered her voice, then asked, "Did you ever hear of anyone named Jefferson Whitman?"

"No, ma'am, never."

"He says another man, who owed your mother a favor, sent him. Did she ever mention anybody by that name?"

Charissa was silent. "I've never heard the name before."

"Come along. I want you to see him. He's an American. A Kaintock, but he's a doctor. I suppose that makes a difference."

The two women entered the room, and Jeff was visibly startled when he saw the girl. Her hair was as black as any he had ever seen, but what caught his attention was her eyes. They were light green, exactly the color of his father's.

Both women saw his eyes widen at the girl. Damita said, "This is Dr. Whitman, Rissa. He's the man who wants to buy you."

Charissa studied the tall man. She had learned to read men's faces, and she examined the doctor's for signs of lust. Men could not cover their desires from her. Yet she saw none of this in his eyes. "Why do you want to buy me, sir?"

"The truth is, I can't say much, but the individual who sent me said that he wanted to show a kindness to your mother. He didn't know she had died. He commissioned me to purchase you and your mother."

"Who is this man?"

"I'm afraid I can't say any more than I have."

Charissa had, long ago, built a wall of defense against men, and now she stood silently for so long that Damita finally asked, "What do you say to this, Rissa?"

"I don't trust any man," she said, her voice severe.

Damita smiled. "You may go now, Rissa."

Rissa left the room, and as soon as the door closed behind her, Damita said, "Dr. Whitman, I think I must disappoint you."

Jeff stood awkwardly before her. He tried to think of arguments, but none came. The sight of the girl had shocked him; he had not expected her beauty, and the eyes were so much like his father's that he could not think clearly. "I wish you'd reconsider, Miss Madariaga," he said.

"I'm afraid I won't do that. Good day, sir."

Jeff accepted his dismissal and left without another word.

As soon as he was gone, Damita went to find Rissa, who had gone to the kitchen. "You don't want that man to buy you?"

"I'd rather stay here," Charissa replied evenly. "At least here I don't have to bed down with any man. You have made me safe from that."

Damita responded, "All right, but I'll expect to see a little better behavior in you, since I'm doing you this favor. My father wanted to sell you, but I'll keep you, on the condition you mend your ways."

"I'll try." Charissa forced out the words and bowed her head.

Damita turned and went to find her father, who was waiting for her in her room. "What happened?" he asked.

"I don't want to sell Rissa, and she doesn't want to go."

Alfredo was not particularly interested in Rissa's desires, and he was plainly disappointed. "Come into the study. We need to talk."

Surprised, Damita followed her father into the study, and he turned to say, "We're going to have to cut back."

"Cut back! But we already have! What do you mean, Papa?"

"The market has been bad. I told you before that the crops have been terrible, and I've had some business dealings that soured at the last minute."

Damita knew that her father was a gambling man, although she never mentioned this to him. Despite their discussion on the balcony those months ago, she had always assumed that he would manage to keep things as they were. Now she saw that he was deeply troubled, and this, in turn, troubled her. "I'd like to keep the girl, Papa."

"I'll see what can be done, but I can't make any promises. The man obviously has money, and as I told you before, it may be necessary to sell Rissa. Not to mention a few of the other slaves."

"So, Madariaga refused to sell the girl," Elmo said. "I'm a little surprised, since I know he's low on cash. Most of these planters are now."

"I think it was his daughter's choice. Do you know her?"

"I've seen her. Good-looking woman, but proud as Lucifer—but all those Creoles are. What are you going to do, Jeff?"

"I don't know." Jeff stood despondently in front of his friend. "If I won't be in the way, I think I'll stay for a time. Maybe an idea will come to me. Maybe I'll offer so much money, they can't turn it down."

"That might work. And it'll be good to have you. As a matter of fact, I wish you'd make the rounds with me."

"I'll be glad to do that, Elmo. You look tired."

"I need an associate. Sure you won't change your mind, Jeff? We could find a good place for your father here and move your whole staff."

"I'm afraid that's impossible, Elmo."

Elmo sighed. "I thought it would be, but I had to ask."

For the next two weeks Jeff found himself working as hard as he ever did at the hospital in St. Louis. The yellow fever epidemic had struck a serious blow, and Elmo saw patients from early morning until late evening. Jeff accompanied him and shared the load.

He had written his father several times during his journeys. He broke the news that Bethany was dead, but the girl was alive, and he'd found her. He told his father of the difficulties of purchasing the girl and asked if he wanted him to pursue the sale. Irving's reply by return mail stated: "Yes, pay any price, and buy the girl."

Jeff shared the contents of the letter with Elmo, who nodded and said, "You'll have to do it, Jeff, no matter what it takes."

On May eighteenth, late in the afternoon, a visitor surprised Señor Madariaga. He looked up from his desk in the study when the housekeeper said, "Mr. Pennington is here to see you, sir."

"Pennington? Show him in."

A worried look crossed Alfredo's face, and he rose to meet the man who entered the door. Asa Pennington was the vice president of the bank where he did business. His appearance at the Madariaga home was unusual, because they had always conversed at the bank. He covered his nervousness well, however, and smiled, saying, "Mr. Pennington, it's a pleasure to see you."

Asa Pennington was a small man dressed in plain clothing. He had a thin, pale face and tight lips. Words were money to him, and he spent them as cautiously as he did his own cash. When Alfredo asked him to sit, he replied, "No, sir, I'm in a hurry. I have several calls to make, and I'm afraid I have unpleasant news."

Alfredo licked his lips nervously. "And that might be what, Mr. Pennington?"

"We've carried your loans as long as we can without a payment, Señor Madariaga. We must have money, or I'm afraid we'll have to take action."

Alfredo knew then that what he dreaded was occurring. "Sit down, and we will go over the figures."

Pennington replied, "We can go over them, but the bank must have at least ten thousand dollars at once, or we will have to foreclose on either your town house or this plantation."

The very idea was repugnant as well as frightening. Alfredo agreed, "Of course, Mr. Pennington, you have always been most generous. The crops have been poor."

"I know. I have had to make this sort of call to five other gentlemen. But the bank must have some assurance in monetary terms."

"I will sell off some of my slaves, Mr. Pennington." Alfredo shook his head and said, "You will have the money by the end of the week."

Chapter eleven

Elena noticed that her husband had eaten little and said almost nothing during the morning meal. Her eyes shifted to Damita, and Elena thought, *She looks so tired. She's never really gotten over that terrible shipwreck, and I know she misses Juanita.*

Alfredo interrupted her thoughts when he said abruptly, "Ladies, come into my study. I have something to say."

Elena knew then that whatever was troubling her husband would soon come out. She and her daughter rose and followed Alfredo. He turned into his study and stood by the door. When they had entered, he shut the door behind him and walked over to his desk. "I have something to tell you. I've tried to keep it from you as much as possible, but that's impossible now." Alfredo hesitated.

"What is it?" Elena asked. "What's wrong? Are you ill?"

"No, I'm not ill. But I've never talked to you much about the finances, and I have to now." Perspiration shone on Alfredo's forehead. Taking out a handkerchief, he wiped it away, then straightened up. He looked at his wife and daughter and said, "I suppose you know that the crops have been bad. Our income has been cut more than fifty percent, but our expenses haven't. I know you've made some sacrifices, but they haven't been near enough. I'm afraid we're going to have to make some—adjustments."

"Of course," Elena answered. "We understand."

"We aren't in danger of losing anything permanently, are we, Papa?" Damita asked. She had never seen her father this troubled.

"It's more serious than usual. We're going to have to sell off some property, and we're going to have to seriously reduce our living expenses. I'm hoping that we won't have to sell the house in town."

"Sell the house!" Elena exclaimed. She loved their peach-colored home and living in the city. The idea of staying twelve months a year on the plantation was repugnant to her. "It's not that serious, is it?"

"The banker thinks it is. We've got to make a payment right away, and a large one. We'll have to sell some of the slaves."

Elena went to his side. "I don't want you to worry about this, dear. We'll cut back to the bone. There are many things we can do without. We have plenty of clothes, and we can give up our travel until things get better."

"Of course we can, Papa," Damita said. She walked to her father and kissed him on the cheek. "We'll all help with this. And the crop looks wonderful this year. Claude said so." Claude Napier was the manager of the plantation, and he had commented on the crop to Damita only a week earlier.

"I hated to tell you, but I had to. We'll talk about the details of it later." As the ladies turned to leave, he said, "Damita, just a moment, please."

Damita returned to his side. He said, "One of the slaves that will have to be sold is Rissa." He saw a stubborn look come to her eyes and said firmly, "I'm sorry, but I've got to have cash right away, and this physician from St. Louis is prepared to pay any price. It has to be."

Damita started to argue, but she saw the set look of her father's face and knew that it was hopeless. Her anger fell on Jefferson Whitman, who had brought this upon her. She swallowed and said, "Very well, Papa. That's what we'll do."

When Jeff went to the Debakky house for lunch that day, he was surprised when Rose Bozonnier met him, saying, "There's a gentleman to see you, sir. I had him wait in the study."

"A gentleman? I wasn't expecting anyone. Did he give his name?"

"It's Señor Madariaga."

Jeff instantly felt a lift of spirits. He could think of only one reason why Madariaga would come to see him. "Thank you, Rose." He walked down the hall to the study. When Madariaga rose from his chair and bowed slightly, Jeff bowed also. "I'm glad to see you, sir. I hope you haven't had to wait long."

"No, of course not, Doctor," Madariaga answered. He appeared nervous and stroked his mustache with a quick motion. He was not accustomed to giving up his own way, and it had cost him a great deal of pride to come. But he had steeled himself for it and said, "I will be brief, Doctor. Are you still interested in buying the slave girl Charissa?"

"Yes, I am."

"I have thought on it a great deal and spoken with my daughter. She's very fond of the girl, and I'm afraid I must ask a high price, perhaps more than you'd wish to pay."

"Name your price, Señor Madariaga."

Alfredo cleared his throat, then said, "We'll have to have five thousand dollars for her." He knew this was much more than he could get for the girl on the market, and he was prepared to bargain—something he hated to do.

Jeff responded, "If you would care to go to the bank, I will write a draft, and they will cash it for you at once."

Madariaga was surprised at Jeff's unquestioning acceptance of the price, but he felt instantly relieved that it would help toward settling the crisis at the bank. "It's not necessary for you to go with me, Doctor. If you will just give me the draft, I will take it to the bank myself."

Jeff retrieved the draft, filled it out, signed it, and handed it to Madariaga.

"Thank you, Doctor. This is quite satisfactory." Alfredo's eyes were on the draft, but then he looked up. "You may call for the girl at any time tomorrow."

"I will be there early, Señor. Will you have something to drink?"

"No, I must be going." Madariaga hesitated, then put out his hand, something he rarely did and never had done to an American.

He felt the strength of the tall doctor's grip and said, "I can't imagine your reasons, but they are your own. Good day, sir."

"Good day, Señor Madariaga." Jeff felt a surge of happiness as he watched the man leave. He went to the window and watched the man get into his carriage, then motion the driver to leave. *I don't know what changed his mind, but I'm grateful for it.* Jeff turned away from the window, and a more somber mood fell on him. *Father may be disappointed by this young woman. We have no way of knowing how this will all work out.*

Charissa stared at Damita. She had been polishing the silver when Damita entered and said abruptly, "I've got some news for you, Rissa, news you won't like. The American doctor, the one that wanted to buy you? Father has sold you to him."

For a moment, Charissa could not speak. She had put the matter out of her mind, feeling that she was secure. She saw that Damita was disturbed, even angry. "The master has sold me?"

"I'm afraid so."

Charissa felt panicked. Although she had no love for Damita, she had found a place of safety. The male servants in the Madariaga household left her alone—with the exception of Garr Odom, whom the master had finally fired. What she feared most was a return to the life she had had before. On the plantation, she had been in constant danger of being raped. Quickly she sought some sort of assurance from her mistress. "Where will I be living?"

"I have no idea. I don't know anything about this man except that he's a doctor." Damita tried to offer some hope. "He seems to be a respectable man."

Rissa had had some experience with "respectable" men, and her feelings of apprehension showed in her face.

Damita could see the girl's discomfort. For one moment, she was on the verge of apologizing again for the whipping. She well understood that Charissa had never forgiven her for it, but her pride forbade her to speak. Damita considered what it must be like to be someone's property: no rights, no say in where she would live or what she would do. Damita had been insulated from the worst aspects of slavery. Now she saw the fear on the girl's face and awkwardly said, "I wish you well, Rissa."

"When will I be leaving?"

"Sometime tomorrow. Here, I want you to have this." Damita handed her four gold coins. "We've had our differences, but I wanted to reward you for your service."

Charissa stared at the coins and then lifted her eyes. "Thank you, Miss Damita," she whispered.

Damita turned and left the room, leaving Charissa alone with her worst thoughts.

Charissa had slept little; throughout the night, she found herself growing tense as she thought about what lay ahead of her. She said little during the breakfast she ate with the servants of the family, and when the others had left, she began to help Ernestine with the dishes. The old cook was chattering as she always did when Charissa said, "I'm leaving here, Ernestine."

"You're leaving! What do you mean, child?"

"I've been sold to another family."

Ernestine saw the dread in the young girl's eyes and put her arms around her. "I'm so sorry to hear that," she said. "I truly am. But maybe it'll be good."

"No, it won't. That man, that doctor, he's the one who bought me. He's so big and strong, and he can do anything with me he wants to."

Ernestine hugged the girl with real affection. She felt the tremors in Charissa's body and said, "God's gonna take care of you, honey. Don't you ever doubt it."

"You expect me to believe in God?"

"I know you don't, but someday you will." Ernestine stroked the girl's smooth black hair and said, "Don't you remember that story about Joseph in the Bible? Everything went wrong with that man. His own brothers threw him in a pit and sold him for a slave. Then, later on, people lied on him and he went to prison. Everything was a defeat, but when they was all over, he came out of it fine. That's what I'm askin' the Lord for you."

Charissa wiped her eyes. She rarely cried, but her world seemed to be falling apart. She clung to Ernestine and whispered, "I'm afraid!"

Ernestine knew that Charissa had good reason to fear. Masters often used attractive young slaves for immoral purposes. Ernestine prayed silently, "Oh, Lord, help this young girl. She don't believe in You yet, but You take care of her, and one day she will."

Charissa was sitting silently in her room when Elena entered. "It's time for you to go. Dr. Whitman is here for you, Rissa."

Charissa had said her good-byes to the family and the servants, and now she stood and picked up the bag that contained her few belongings. Elena put her hand on the girl's shoulder and said, "I'm sorry you won't be with us, but things will be fine. Dr. Whitman seems like a good man—for an American, of course."

Charissa could not answer, her heart was so full. She and Elena walked down the three flights of stairs to the first floor. There she saw the tall man, who said, "Good morning, Charissa."

Charissa merely nodded.

"You have all your things there?"

"Yes, sir."

"We'll be going. Good day, Mrs. Madariaga. Give my regards to your husband."

"Yes, Doctor, I'll do that. Charissa, you be a good girl now."

"Yes, ma'am." Charissa stepped to the door and saw a carriage waiting.

Before Jeff could respond, Charissa climbed up and spoke to the horses. She turned once and looked at the house. It had been a haven to her. She felt loss and loneliness.

Jeff saw that the girl was frightened. *Not much chance she would be otherwise,* he thought. *It'll take a while, but she'll come around.* "Beautiful day, isn't it, Charissa?"

"Yes, sir." The reply was brief, and Charissa did not turn her head.

Jeff tried several more times to make conversation, but the girl answered in monosyllables. He finally pulled up to the house and drove around to the backyard. Charles Menton, the gardener, ran across the yard to take the horses. "You want me to unhitch the team, Doctor?"

"Yes, I suppose so, Charles." Jeff jumped out and walked around the buggy. Charissa had stepped out and stood next to it. "Charles, this is Charissa."

"How do you do, Miss Charissa?" Charles said. "It's fine to meet you."

The black man seemed friendly, but her guard was up. "Hello."

"Come on inside. Charles, you might grain those horses."

"Yes, sir, I'll do that."

Jeff strode to the back door, and when he stepped inside, he found the housekeeper waiting. "Hello, Rose. You have another mouth to feed. This is Charissa."

"Hello, Charissa."

"She'll be staying for a few days. Which room would you suggest?"

"The second door on the right when you get upstairs."

"Come along, Charissa," Jeff said. "I'll show it to you."

Charissa followed without a word. The house was impressive. It was not as fine as the one she had been living in, but it was obviously expensive. As they walked up the stairs, Jeff explained, "This is Dr. Debakky's home, but he's working at his office now."

"You don't live here, sir?"

"No, I live in St. Louis with my father. We'll be going there day after tomorrow by ship."

He opened the door and stood back, and Charissa, unaccustomed to courtesies, did not know what to do. She was trained not to walk before white people, but he said, "Go on in. See if you like it."

She entered the room, which had a high ceiling and cream-colored wallpaper with dancing figures on it. The carpet under her feet was a deep maroon, and the furniture was gleaming mahogany. Sunlight flowed through two tall windows. Charissa stood at the doorway, holding her possessions, not knowing what to do.

Jeff saw that the girl was apprehensive and said, "You'd better open these windows. It's going to be warm tonight. It's getting hot for May." He then said, "Make yourself at home here, Charissa. Dr. Debakky will be back after a while. I want you to meet him at supper."

"Dr. Whitman," Charissa said, "I have to tell you something."

"Of course. What is it?"

Charissa had to tilt her head back to look up at him, and she studied him for a moment. He was not a handsome man, but his features showed strength. Though she had planned her speech, her voice was flat as she said, "I belong to you now, sir, and I will do any work that you ask me to do." She paused, and then her eyelids dropped until her eyes were nearly hidden. Her throat was tight, and she had difficulty adding, "I'll do any work you want, no matter how hard, and I'll never complain. But if you touch me, I'll kill you if I can, even if I die for it!"

Her words shocked Jeff. He had no idea what sort of life she had led. He did not speak for a moment, but then he shook his head and said quietly, "I don't force myself on women, Charissa."

"I've heard that before, sir."

Jefferson Whitman suddenly felt compassion for the girl. She had no defense, none whatsoever, but was at the mercy of those with greater power. "You haven't heard it from me, Charissa," he said quietly. "But I understand your fears. All I ask is that you give me and my father a chance to show you how we feel about things like this. I'll see you later tonight when Dr. Debakky gets back."

He turned and left the room, and suddenly Charissa's knees felt weak. She had planned her declaration and fully expected to be beaten for it. But she had seen nothing like anger in the tall man's eyes. She went over to one of the windows, opened it, and sat down in the chair opposite it. Leaning forward, she put her head down and placed her palms over her eyes. She was trembling, but she could not pray, because she did not believe in God. Yet just sitting silently, she began to gather her courage. *We will see what you are like, Dr. Whitman, you and your father,* she thought.

Chapter twelve

When she woke the next morning, Charissa stared around her wildly, not knowing where she was. The large room, the beautifully papered walls, and the exquisite furniture—none of it seemed familiar. Then she sat up and remembered. She recalled how she had been able to take a bath the previous night in hot water the housekeeper brought. She had luxuriated in the large tub, trying each of the fancy soaps that the woman called Rose had provided. Now, as she threw the covers back, she realized she would have to wear her only other dress—a raggedy slave garment. She slipped into it and her shoes, and then looked in the mirror mounted behind a finely finished dresser. She had a comb and brush, well worn, that she had found in a dump, and she brushed her glossy black hair. It had a slight wave to it and fell beneath her shoulders. She tied it with a piece of ribbon and went to look out the window.

Just outside, sparrows were fighting over something, tumbling, and for a moment the scene brought a smile to her lips. *If birds can't even get along, how can human beings?* A knock at the door startled her. Turning quickly, she went to the door, opened it, and saw Rose.

The woman was smiling and said, "Why don't you come down to breakfast, Charissa? It's all ready."

"Yes, ma'am." Charissa stepped outside and followed the woman down the stairs. She asked, "Do you belong to the doctor who owns this house?"

"No, the doctor freed my husband and me. My husband died only last year."

Charissa had never heard of such a thing. "You mean, he just set you free instead of selling you?"

"That's right. Dr. Debakky is a fine man. I'll never cease being grateful to him."

Charissa followed Rose down the stairs and through the hallway, turning into a room at the back of the house. When she stepped inside, she saw Dr. Whitman seated at a large dining table with another man. Two more places were set across from him, but she did not notice them.

"Come in, Charissa. I hope you slept well." Both men stood.

Charissa was stunned. "Yes, sir. I did."

"This is Dr. Debakky. Elmo, this is Charissa Desjardin."

"I'm glad to know you, Miss Charissa," Debakky said with a smile. "I hope you're hungry. Sit down. Dr. Whitman and I have been waiting for you."

Charissa could not understand what the man meant. *Sit down with two white men?* She had never done such a thing. Always she had eaten in the kitchen or wherever the slaves were assigned. She blinked and did not move. Rose pulled out her chair. "You sit right down here, Charissa, and I'll sit beside you."

Dumbly Charissa sat and stared at the fine china plate and the silver before her. She could not say a word, but Dr. Debakky said, "Why don't you ask the blessing, Jeff?"

"Sure will. Lord, we thank You for this food. We thank You for every blessing You've given us. Bless this house. Bless Miss Rose and Miss Charissa, and bless us as we serve You this day. In Jesus' name, amen."

"Here, have some of these eggs, Charissa," Rose said. "And this ham is very tasty."

Charissa kept her hands beneath the table as Rose filled her plate. A young girl came in, no older than herself, with a silver tray and coffee urn.

"Mary, give us all some of that good coffee," Rose said. "Do you like coffee, Charissa?"

"Yes, ma'am." Charissa was glad when the two men began talking about the yellow fever epidemic. She did not understand most of their terms, and she was terribly self-conscious. She watched Rose covertly and picked up her fork when she did. She found she was ravenous and ate everything on her plate. Then Rose passed her some jelly and freshly baked buns. She ate these, too, and just as she was finishing, Dr. Debakky said, "I hate to leave good company, but I've got to start my rounds. Jeff, you're going to join me later?"

"Yes, I will."

Debakky said, "Good to have you with us, Miss Charissa. I'll be seeing you later."

Rose stood and began to help the girl named Mary clear the dishes. Charissa sat with her eyes down, unsure what she should do next. Finally, she looked up and saw that Whitman was sipping his coffee. When she met his eyes, he said, "We'll be leaving for St. Louis tomorrow, Charissa. Today I want us to go do a little shopping."

"Yes, sir."

She waited, but the doctor said only, "I'm ready if you are."

"Yes, sir, I'm ready."

She followed Jeff out of the house and climbed into the carriage beside him. He spoke to the horses, and as they moved out of the back and down the narrow passageway that led to the street, he said, "Just beginning to learn my way around the city. Have you ever gone shopping here with Miss Damita?"

"Yes, sir, I have."

"Good. Then you direct me, and we'll go to the places that have shops that sell clothes. All right?"

Charissa nodded, then said, "You go right down over on Rampart Street. There are some fine shops there."

"Miss Damita buys a lot of her dresses in there. I don't think they have clothes for gentlemen." Charissa had directed Jeff to a line of stores. He pulled up in front of one, and the two had gotten down. Now she stood uncertainly, not knowing if he expected her to accompany him or not. She had assumed that he was buying for himself.

"We'll try this one right here." Jeff walked to the door, opened it, and held it for her.

Once again, Charissa did not know how to react. Her face grew warm, and she ducked her head and slipped through the door, murmuring, "Thank you, sir."

When they were inside, an older woman with silver hair, dark brown eyes, and a friendly face approached. "May I help you, sir?"

"Indeed you might. This young lady needs to be completely outfitted: dresses, undergarments, nightgowns, shoes, hats. At least one very nice outfit suitable for going to church. Day dresses—well, I'll leave it all to you."

The clerk's face did not change. She assumed at once that this tall man had taken the young woman for his mistress. This was a common occurrence in New Orleans, and she had fulfilled requests like this before. "Yes, sir, I will see to it."

"Charissa, I'll come back in about an hour. I'll expect to see you wearing something very nice. Oh, I'll need some luggage. A small trunk for the new clothes, and perhaps an overnight bag. Where might I find those?"

"Tyrone's, right across the street, has some very nice things."

"Thank you very much."

The next hour was like a dream to Charissa Desjardin. She had never bought anything in her life, never tried on dresses in a shop. The woman, who said her name was Mrs. Williams, was tactful. She took Charissa to a back room to try on fresh undergarments without commenting on the ragged quality of the ones she wore. Charissa, of course, had helped Damita dress and knew what a lady would wear, but never had she imagined wearing such fuss and finery herself. She tried on several dresses and surprised both herself and Mrs. Williams by having very definite tastes, refusing some dresses and liking others immediately.

The hour passed quickly, and Charissa put on one of the new dresses. It was made out of a light-blue cotton percale with a tight-fitting bodice and short, puffy sleeves; white and pink embroidery decorated the front and the hem. A white ribbon tied around the waist. To complete the outfit, she wore a pair of pink satin shoes and a bonnet with white feathers.

Mrs. Williams joined her at the mirror. "You look beautiful, my dear. Dr. Whitman is here."

Charissa found Whitman waiting near the door. His eyes opened wide, and she saw admiration in them.

"Why, you look very nice, Charissa! You pick that out yourself?"

"She certainly did," Mrs. Williams said. "She has fine taste, and she's a perfect size. The dresses fit exquisitely."

"I brought the luggage, so if we can pack these in there, we'll be ready to go."

Mrs. Williams neatly packed the clothing in the small trunk. Then Whitman asked, "How much will it be, Mrs. Williams?"

Mrs. Williams named the price, and Charissa gasped with dismay. She looked at Dr. Whitman, expecting him to protest, but he simply said, "That sounds fair enough." He took out a leather billfold and paid for the clothes.

Mrs. Williams asked, "What shall I do with your old things?"

"Throw them away," Dr. Whitman said, then turned to Charissa. "Are you ready?" He picked up the trunk, and she moved quickly to open the door for him. He put the trunk in the carriage, then turned, saying, "You'll need other things."

"What, Dr. Whitman?"

"Things that women use. Special soaps, I suppose, or makeup."

Everything seemed unreal. Without a word, she followed as he strode to another store she had visited with Damita. Dr. Whitman instructed her to select all the items she needed—and not to worry about the prices. He then said, "I'll be back in a few minutes to pay for them."

Twenty minutes later, they had purchased everything. "We'll put all these in the small suitcase," he said, carrying the packages to the carriage. Once he'd packed the parcels, he turned and held out his hand.

Charissa stared at him, wondering what he wanted. "Yes, sir, what is it?"

"I was just going to help you into the buggy," Whitman said, surprised. "That's what gentlemen are supposed to do, isn't it?"

Charissa flushed. She had seen this courtesy many times, but no one had ever extended it to her. She reached out, her face burning, and felt his big hand close about hers. She stepped up into the buggy, and he released her at once. "Thank you, sir."

"You're very welcome." He climbed into his seat. "Now, it's time we got a bite to eat. Let's go home and see what Rose can stir up for us. This shopping is hard work."

"Dr. Whitman—"

"Yes, what is it?"

"I don't understand. Why are you doing all this for me?" She knew well enough the history of men who took mulatto and quadroon girls and made them their mistresses. She wanted no misunderstanding. "I appreciate all of it, but I hope you don't think that I—" She could not say any more but looked at him squarely.

Jeff Whitman shook his head. "Don't worry. You don't ever have to worry about me—or my father—bothering you in any way, Charissa. I swear it on my honor. Do you believe me?"

Suddenly, Charissa Desjardin knew that she had met a man who was truthful. His warm brown eyes were mild, and she saw in them honesty and strength. He sat loosely, almost disjointedly, beside her, a taller man than she had never met before.

"Yes, sir, I believe you."

"Good. Then we won't have to talk about that anymore. Get up, boys. Let's get home."

The engines of the *Miranda* began to shake, and Charissa was fascinated by the big paddle wheels on each side of the vessel beginning to churn the water. She had never been on a boat before, although she had often watched them making their way up and down the river.

"Come along. We'll find where we're going to stay."

Charissa glanced at Whitman and followed him along the deck. He asked one of the stewards for directions, then led her to a corridor. He quickly located the assigned cabin, opened the door, and stepped back. "This is it, I suppose."

Charissa stepped in and looked around. It was a small room, but there was a set of bunk beds, one chair, and a small washstand.

He saw her eyes go to the beds and said, "My room ought to be right next door. Why don't you get settled in? Then, I always like to go up in the front of the boat and watch as we travel. We've got a long way to go—all the way to St. Louis."

"Yes, sir."

"I'm anxious for you to get home and meet my father."

"You have no other family?"

"No, it's just the two of us."

"You tell me he's been ill for a while?"

"Yes, I'm concerned about him." A frown darkened Jeff Whitman's face. "He's been very good to me."

Charissa wanted to question him further, but he left, saying, "I'm going up to the front. When you're ready, come on up, and we'll do some sightseeing."

They had left the Debakky house that morning, and Dr. Debakky had warmly bid Charissa to come back for a visit. He had shaken hands with her, which gave her quite a shock. Now, as she stood in the small stateroom, she felt a sense of joy. *Can it be true that my new master is truly kind and decent?* she thought. *He's been so good to me, and he even gave me my own cabin on the ship!*

She left the stateroom and found Whitman leaning on the rail of the deck. He talked about steamboats and Charissa, delighted, watched the shore disappear. The ship paddled to the middle of the channel, where the wind blew more strongly. The breeze blew off her small hat, and she grabbed for it. Whitman was quicker than she. He chased it down, snatched it up, and strode back, saying, "I think you have to pin these things on."

"Yes. I didn't do a very good job."

Whitman smiled down at her. "Women have more trouble keeping themselves pulled together than men. Ladies are always having to arrange things."

"Don't call me a lady, please, Dr. Whitman. I'm not a lady."

Whitman's face grew serious. "You are a lady," he said. "You've had a hard time, Charissa, but things are going to be different now. You're in a new world."

"Who sent you to get me? And why does he want to help me? Why did he want to help me and my mother?"

"I can't tell you that now, Charissa, but I will say this. You shouldn't worry about the one who sent me. He means nothing but good for you. Please let me ask you one favor."

"Yes, sir, what is it?"

"Let's just have a nice trip on the *Miranda.* We'll enjoy the scenery. We'll eat in the fine dining room. We may even get off at a few ports when the boat stops and do a little exploring. But please, don't ask me any more about why I came looking for you. You'll know soon enough, I think. Will that be all right?"

"Yes, sir, that will be all right." The earnestness of Jeff's eyes gave Charissa confidence. She looked down and smiled. She did not know what was happening to her, but somehow she felt that it was good.

"Charissa, this is Mrs. Shultz. She's our housekeeper. Mrs. Shultz, I would like you to meet Miss Charissa Desjardin."

The older woman smiled and said in her thick, German accent, "Yah, it is gute to have you here."

"Will you show her to her room?"

"Yes, indeed, sir."

"How is my father?"

"He's somewhat better."

"Thank the Lord for that. Charissa, you go along with Mrs. Shultz."

"Yes, sir," Charissa said as she turned and followed the housekeeper.

"Did you haff a good journey?" Mrs. Schultz asked.

"Yes, ma'am. It was very nice. I had never been on a boat before."

Mrs. Shultz was obviously curious about her, but she asked no more questions. The room to which the housekeeper took Charissa was every bit as beautiful as the one at Dr. Debakky's. It was a large room with two floor-length windows along the far wall, and a small desk and chair between them. The room had dark green and white wallpaper with illustrations of trees and birds, and wall-to-wall carpet of a light brown color. The furniture was made of shining wood, and a canopy floated over the bed enveloped in dark green velvet curtains.

"Such a lovely room!" she exclaimed to Mrs. Shultz.

"Yah, it is. I vill leave you alone now. Marcus vill bring up your tings."

"Thank you, ma'am."

"You can call me Olga."

"Yes, Olga."

As soon as the housekeeper left the room, Charissa studied the furniture more closely. She opened the drawers on the big chest and saw that they were empty. *Plenty of room for my new things.*

She sat on the bed, then walked to the window and looked outside at the street. A knock sounded at the door, and she moved to open it.

Dr. Whitman greeted her. "I'd like for you to meet my father, if you would."

"Yes, sir." Charissa was very interested in this man. She followed Jeff down to the first floor, into a big bedroom, and found, to her surprise, a rather small man. He was wearing a white linen suit and sat in a chair beside the window. He stood slowly, and she saw the signs of illness on his face. *Why, he looks nothing like Dr. Whitman!*

"This is my father, Dr. Irving Whitman. Father, this is Miss Charissa Desjardin."

"I am so happy to meet you, my dear."

The old man bowed to her, and Charissa curtsied as she had seen ladies do. This was indeed a strange new world.

"I'll leave you two to get acquainted."

"Thank you, Jeff," Dr. Whitman said. When the door closed, the old man said, "Please, I haven't been too well lately, and I need to sit down." They both took seats in chairs by the window.

Charissa sat nervously. Dr. Irving Whitman was watching her carefully, and he had a strange expression on his face. He asked her about her trip, and while she spoke, she saw that he was staring at her. He was clearly a troubled man. He fidgeted, clasping and unclasping his hands.

"Is something wrong, sir?"

"No . . . no, of course not. It's just that I was thinking of other things and of someone else."

Charissa realized that this was the man at whose bidding Jefferson had come. "Please, Dr. Whitman, I don't understand what's happening. Did you send your son to find me?"

"Yes, I did."

"But why? It has something to do with my mother, doesn't it?"

Irving Whitman sighed heavily and nodded.

"Won't you please tell me? I need to understand what I'm doing here. It's all so—it's all so strange."

Irving Whitman had imagined this moment for a long time. When he had gotten word from Jeff that Bethany had died, he had felt grieved that he could not make up some of his wrongdoing to her. Then all of his attention had turned to his daughter. He knew that she was, for he saw traces of Bethany, but also some of his own features in her. Finally he said, "I want you to do me a great favor, my dear young lady."

"Yes, sir. What is it?"

"I want you to listen to everything I have to say without saying a word. Please don't leave. Don't speak until I have finished. Then you may say anything you wish."

Mystified by this, Charissa said, "Yes, sir." She trembled as the old man began to speak. He rambled at first about his youth, how he grew up, what sort of a man he was, and she could not imagine what was coming. When at last he began to speak of the beautiful young mulatto girl who served in his household, truth began to dawn upon her. Her lips parted, and her eyes widened as he spoke of how he had taken advantage of the young woman.

"I think, my dear, you can guess the rest of it. I behaved badly. I persuaded my father to sell your mother. She left, and I thought that was the end of it. Then, when I sent Jeff to find your mother, of course, he didn't find her, but he found you."

The old man's eyes held pure misery, and he shook his head sadly. "I suppose all of us would like to go back and change things. I don't know if I would ever have had the strength." He whispered, "Your mother was a lovely woman in every way. I'm so sorry, my dear. So very sorry."

Charissa saw that he had finished, and she asked quietly, "But—why am I here?"

"Charissa, I want to try to make up for the wrong I did your mother. You're my daughter. I know I don't have too many years left to live, but what time I have, I want to do my best to help you. Can you ever forgive me, do you think?"

Charissa felt numb.

"I know this is a shock for you, and I won't ask you to speak now. But when you've thought it over, if you can find it in your heart to forgive me, you would make an old man very happy. Why don't you go now, and think this all over?"

"Yes, sir." Charissa tore her eyes from Irving's and left the room. Her mind was whirling. Without thinking, she moved toward two French doors that led to a side garden. She stepped outside and stopped. Jefferson Whitman, who had been sitting on a cast-iron bench, stood. She said, "Your father has just told me about . . . about my mother."

"He's very grieved, Charissa. He's an old man and sick, and he's doing all he can to make up for the wrong he did your mother. I know you're confused, but in time, I hope that you'll forgive him."

Charissa was silent for a minute. Then she turned and looked up into his face. "I'm your half-sister?"

"Not really, Charissa. You see, I'm adopted. Dr. Whitman is not my real father, so we're not related by blood. But Dr. Whitman wants you to have all the rights of a daughter."

Charissa found her hands were trembling. Jeff saw and reached out and took them. "I know this is so hard for you."

"I don't know what to do. I can see your father is a good man."

"He's the best man I've ever met. He made a terrible mistake, but he wants to make it right."

Charissa looked down. His hands were large and strong, and they gave her a sense of comfort. "I don't think I can do it, sir."

"Of course you can," Jefferson smiled. "I'll help you."

Charissa studied his eyes. "Will you, sir?"

"Not 'sir.' Just Jeff. We're brother and sister, after a fashion, and I'd like for you to think of me as an older brother. Yes, I'll help you.

You know," he said with a crooked smile, "I think it would be rather fun, having a younger sister."

"Fun?"

"Oh, yes," he said. He released her hand and stood loosely before her, a tall, lanky man with a homely face and a kindly light in his eyes. "When your suitors begin to come, Charissa, I'll be *very* stern. I'll scare them to death and run most of them off. Yes, I'll be very particular about the man who comes calling on my sister!"

Charissa suddenly thought about the first time she had seen him. "I hated you when you first came."

"I realized that," he said dryly. "I believe you would have shot me, if you had had a gun."

"I thought you were like all the other men who had tried to use me. But you're different. I don't think you'd ever hurt anyone."

Jeff released her hands and put both of his on her shoulders. Ordinarily, she felt tense and afraid when a man did this. But she felt no fear of this man who stood before her. He held her glance for a moment, then said, "You've come home, Charissa, and I'll take care of you."

Charissa Desjardin knew he meant exactly what he said. After years of fighting and struggling and building walls, she had come to this. She smiled then at the tall young man, a full smile, and said, "I'm glad to be here, Jeff."

PART THREE

· 1834–1835 ·

Jeff

Chapter thirteen

A yellow beam of sunlight shone from the window as Charissa stirred the saucepan. She turned toward it, noting the dust motes dancing, and the sight pleased her. *No one could count those tiny things—but if Papa is right, God knows every one of them.*

"It's April the first—April Fool's Day, the Americans call it." Olga Shultz had entered, and, coming over to stand beside Charissa, she bent and sniffed the food simmering. "That smells gute," she commented, "but it should be. I haf been teaching you for two years now how to cook!"

Charissa smiled. When she had first come to live with her father two years earlier, she wasn't sure she liked the older woman. Olga had a stern manner, and several months had passed before Charissa learned that she was a kindly, generous woman. Now the two were friends.

"The doctor seems happier these days. I think part of it is your doing." Olga always referred to the older Whitman as "the doctor." "And that is gute! You know that man lives for you, I tink. Your coming here vas like a medicine to him."

"It was for me, too, Olga. I'd never known anything like contentment before I came here." Charissa chewed her lip thoughtfully and shook her head. "Papa isn't doing as well as I'd like. I'm afraid for him."

"You just haf to trust the gute Lord, Charissa."

At that moment, Jeff entered the kitchen and smiled at the two women. "You're fixing me something good to eat, I trust." He wore his work suit, and his face was rosy from the razor.

"No, this is for Papa."

"Are you going to be able to come in and help later on? I need you at the hospital."

"Yes. I'll be there as usual."

Jeff put his arm around Charissa and squeezed her. "You've become a fine nurse, but a better sister."

Olga Shultz, standing off to one side, watched the scene with careful scrutiny. She saw that Jeff was careless as always, quick to give Charissa a hug or a pat—but she saw the look in Charissa's eyes, and the thought came to her as it had often. *She cares more for Jeff than he knows. He knows nothing about vimmen!*

"You know, it's a good thing to have a baby sister." He touched her cheek. Then he headed for the door, saying, "I'll see you later at the hospital."

Olga watched as Charissa stared after Jeff, then heard her mutter between clenched teeth, "I am *not* your sister!" Then Charissa shook her head. Picking up a bowl, she poured it full of broth and put it on a tray along with a napkin and silverware. "I'll take this in to Papa."

When Charissa entered her father's room, she found him still in bed. His eyes brightened and he said, "I'm lazy this morning."

"You don't have to get up. I brought breakfast to you. Here, I've come to see that you eat all of this." She put the tray down so that he could reach it easily and then waited until he said grace, which he always did. Then he took a big bite and almost choked.

"That's hot!" he said.

"Of course it's hot. That's what's good for you." Charissa busied herself about the room as he ate and then said, "I'm going to shave you this morning. I'll go get the hot water." When she came back with a basin full of steaming water, she put it down, then pulled the shaving mug from the cabinet and expertly worked up a lather. "Are you through?"

"All through."

She moved the breakfast tray, then leaned over him. She lathered his face quickly and picked up a clean cloth, put it over her left arm, and picked up a razor. "Now, be still. Don't wiggle."

Irving Whitman sat quietly, leaning back as the young woman began to move the razor over his face. Her hands were sure, and she shaved him far more efficiently than any male barber ever had. As she worked on him, he studied her face, marveling at how she had changed since she had come to live under his roof. She had been sixteen then, almost seventeen, and now, in a few more days, she would reach her nineteenth birthday. Those two years had brought a miracle, as far he was concerned. She had been an adolescent then, but now she was a woman. Her eyes mirrored a kind of wisdom. And there was a rich store of vitality within Charissa that reminded him of her mother. She had blossomed indeed since coming to live in St. Louis, and not only physically; living without fear, she developed a sweetness and a strong spirit that pleased him greatly.

"There," she said, wiping off the last of the lather and feeling the smoothness of his cheeks. "If I ever have to make a living, I can become a barber."

"There are no lady barbers," Whitman protested.

"There should be. Women are better at it than men."

Irving laughed softly. "I expect you're right about that. Sit down and talk to me."

The two of them spoke quietly together for twenty minutes. One of the high points of Irving's day was having Charissa simply spend time with him. "Jeff got a letter from Damita yesterday," he said. "It's a little strange to me, and I suppose it is to you."

"It surprises me."

Indeed, Charissa had watched the development of a relationship of some sort between Jefferson and Damita Madariaga ever since she had been there. She knew it had begun with a simple letter from Jeff telling Damita how well Charissa was doing. Damita had written back, and Jeff had shared the letter, at least the parts that expressed an interest in Charissa. Other letters had followed, and Jeff made two trips to New Orleans, giving for a reason his desire to spend more time with Elmo Debakky.

"What kind of a woman is she, Charissa? Jeff seems more interested in her than he has been in anyone for a long time."

The question was hard for the young woman to answer. "I can think of her only as a harsh slave owner."

Whitman saw displeasure written on Charissa's face. "I suppose that's inevitable," he said. He was silent for a moment, and when she did not speak, he said, "What about you? That young Bradford fellow who called on you for a while doesn't come around anymore."

"No, he's engaged to Emily Stratton."

"You let her take him away from you? I'm surprised at you, Charissa."

Charissa laughed. "I wasn't interested in him. He was one of the most boring men I've ever met."

"He was kind, though."

"Yes, but boring."

For a time the two were silent, and then Whitman reached over and took the young woman's hand. "I'd like to see you marry before I go," he said quietly.

"Please don't talk like that!" Charissa did not like to hear about the possibility of Irving Whitman's death, although she knew it could come at any moment. She had become so very fond of, and was so very grateful to, this good man that she could not bear to think of losing him.

"Why, I can't think why you feel like that, Charissa. It's a natural thing. I'll hate to leave you, but at least God has enabled me to do something for you."

"Something?" She leaned forward and took his hand in both of hers. "You've done everything for me."

"I'm glad you feel that way." He squeezed her hands and said, "The one thing I'd most like to do for you is to introduce you to the Lord Jesus." He saw her face change and said quickly, "I know you've got some memories that are very dark, but someday, you're going to find out that Jesus is the best friend you could ever have."

The two subjects that Charissa could not discuss with Dr. Whitman were his own precarious life and the matter of her feelings toward God. She had watched him, Jeff, and even Olga Shultz, and she saw in them an honest religion, but her early years had hardened her heart. She stood and said, "You need to get up now. I'll lay your clothes out. Maybe we can go for a walk in the garden. It's beautiful today."

"All right, daughter. I think you're right."

The young man who lay on the table was not badly injured, but he had suffered a deep gash on his right forearm when he had crashed his buggy. His name, Charissa knew, was Howell Peters, for she had heard one of the doctors speak of him before Jeff had come in to stitch his wound. "Peters is a playboy," Dr. Simpson had said as Charissa followed him down the hall. "Family's got all the money in the world, but he's a wild sort."

Charissa had helped to prepare the patient, and he was groggy from the laudanum that she had administered to kill some of the pain. He evidently had a tough constitution: the medication knocked most men out. He was a tall young man, well built, with blue eyes and blond hair.

When Charissa had cleansed the wound, Jeff entered. "This will sting some, Mr. Peters." He prepared to sew the wound.

"Go ahead, Doc. I'll try not to cry." He turned then and looked Charissa full in the face. "When a fellow gets hurt, it's nice to have a handsome nurse." When she did not answer, he said, "Are you married?"

"No, I'm not."

"Oh, that's good. Then I'd like to ask if I can come calling on you."

"You'll have to ask my brother."

Peters winced as the needle bit into his flesh and then grinned. "He must be a sour old fellow, but I'll chance it. Where will I find him?"

"He's putting the stitches in your arm, Mr. Peters."

Peters's eyes flew open, and he studied Jefferson's face. Jeff met his gaze steadily, which caused the young man to flush.

Peters could not speak for a moment, but then he grinned. He looked back at Charissa and saw that her eyes were dancing. "Dr. Whitman, I'd like permission to call on your sister."

Jeff continued sewing but said, "Are you a drinking man?"

"Sir?"

"I asked if you drink."

Peters swallowed and said, "Yes, of course, in moderation."

"How are your morals where women are concerned?"

Charissa began to mildly feel sorry for the young man. Jeff peppered him with questions about his behavior and attitudes, and it amused her to see young Peters squirming under the interrogation.

"What's your pastor's name? I'll have to have a word with him before I can give you permission to see my sister."

Peters stared at him and shook his head. "I don't have a pastor."

"Why not?"

"It's just not in my line."

Jeff put the last stitch in, clipped it with the scissors, and said, "You can put a dressing on this now, Nurse." Then he turned and said, "Until you have more stability, I would not feel inclined to grant you permission to call on my sister. Be careful with this arm. Come in and get the stitches out when the nurse tells you." He left the office, and Peters stared after him.

"Do you think you'd still like to come calling on me?" Charissa smiled as she began to dress the wound.

Peters laughed. He was a good-humored fellow. "I know you are trying to put me off, and you have a rather stern brother, but I *will* be calling."

Charissa shook her head. "You'll feel differently when you recover from that laudanum you've taken." She finished the dressing, gave instructions about changing it and when he should return to have the stitches out. As she left the room and turned down the hall, she ignored Peters, who called out, "You'll be hearing from me, Nurse."

She did not have a chance to talk to Jeff privately until later in the afternoon, when they had finished their work and were in the buggy, headed for home. Jeff was silent for a time, and then he asked, "You didn't want that insolent puppy calling on you, did you, Charissa?"

"Why not? He's very handsome."

"I don't like him."

Charissa studied Jeff's profile. She did not know at what point she had begun to feel herself drawn to him. When she had first come to live with the Whitmans, she had been cautious and lifted a high wall between herself and the young doctor. He had been unfailingly kind and cheerful; he had been instrumental in making her into a different kind of woman. He had hired tutors for her, taught her the social graces, and asked her if she would care to study something about nursing and find a career there. She had eagerly accepted, and the two had worked together closely.

"Why don't you like him?"

"He's just not good enough for you."

Charissa stared at him. "Which of the young men who have asked to call on me have you liked?" She well knew the answer.

Jeff cleared his throat and said, "I just want the very best for you, Charissa. You mean more to me than you can imagine."

His words were bittersweet. She knew that she loved him, but he had no such idea about her. He was protective of her, always gentle and courteous, and there was a streak of humor in him that popped out at odd moments. He was not handsome, but that didn't matter.

"You don't really want him to call, do you?"

"Not really."

Jeff nodded and heaved a sigh of relief. "That's good. He's not the kind of man I'd like to see you with."

Charissa suddenly asked, "What about you?"

"What do you mean, what about me?"

"Why haven't you ever married, Jeff? You could have married a dozen times. You'd better take what you can get—you're not handsome, you know." This was a familiar course of conversation for the two.

"I never thought I was."

"No, I give you that, but you're young, and you have a promising career. You have money. You have your moments, too." She teased, "Even if you are a homely brute, women like you."

"I think you're wrong about that."

Charissa took a deep breath and said, "I was talking with Papa this morning. He thinks you might care for Damita Madariaga."

Jeff blushed. "We've been writing some."

"And you went to New Orleans to see her twice."

"Really I went to see Debakky."

"Jeff, don't lie to me. You went to see Damita, didn't you?"

"I suppose in a way I did. She's such a beautiful woman, but she could never care for me."

"No, she couldn't. She'll never care for anyone but herself."

"I wish you could stop feeling bitter toward her. It's the only harsh thing I see in you, Charissa."

"You don't know her the way I do, Jeff. She's selfish to the bone. She always will be."

"People can change. But it doesn't matter. She'd never marry a fellow like me, anyway. Why, suitors line up, begging her father for her hand."

Charissa was weary of the conversation. She looked at the road, but her thought was, *He would marry Damita in a minute if she would have him!*

Charissa sat straight up in bed. The knock on her door was insistent. Throwing the covers back, she leaped up and pulled on a robe. When she opened it, she saw Jeff, dressed himself in a bathrobe. One look at his face and she knew everything. "What's wrong with Papa?"

"He's had a severe heart attack."

"Is he—alive?"

"Yes, come along. He's conscious, and he wants to see you."

Charissa felt numb as she followed Jeff down the stairs. When she entered the bedroom and saw her father's pale face, she knew somehow that death had entered the house. She walked over to him, took his hands, kissed his cheek, and asked, "Papa, can you hear me?"

Irving Whitman opened his eyes, and he tried to smile. His voice was very faint, just a whisper. "Daughter?"

"Yes, I'm here."

"It's time for me to be going. I'll see your dear mother again, and I'll tell her what a fine girl you are and how I loved you."

Tears gathered in Charissa's eyes. She held his hand while he went back to sleep. She felt his pulse, and it was beating faintly and erratically. Pulling up a chair on one side, she looked at Jeff, seated on the other side of the bed. Their eyes met, and the young doctor shook his head.

The minutes passed into hours. Irving held on to life, and when the dawn had just begun, he regained consciousness. His voice was even weaker, and he reached over and took Jeff's hand and blessed him. "You've been a fine son, Jeff. No man ever had better."

"You've been everything to me, Father—everything." Jeff's voice was husky.

Turning to Charissa, the old man saw the tears running down her face and said, "I have to go, and I'm not afraid. Only one thing troubles me."

"What is it, Papa? Tell me."

"It troubles me that you don't know Jesus."

At that moment Charissa's eyes were so full she could hardly see, and her throat was thick. "I've seen Jesus in you, Papa, and in Jeff."

"You have? That pleases me." He was silent, but she felt his hands squeezing hers. "It's easy to become a child of God, daughter. All you have to do is tell the Lord that you're a sinner, and ask Him to save you. It would please me greatly if you felt ready to do that."

Charissa was struggling. She remembered many painful moments, and she knew she had not lived perfectly. But this man who lay dying had given her so much! She lay his hand against her tear-stained cheek and sobbed. As she did, she felt the yearning of both men; she saw in Jeff's eyes that he was pleading with her.

At that moment, Charissa Desjardin knew she had to make a decision. She had reached a place in her life where she needed help. Her father would be dead. She would be without parents, and besides, she could not ignore the lives that these two men had led. She had found honor and truth in both of them, and each had always stressed that it was the Lord who made him live as he did.

And so, Charissa took a deep breath and lifted her head. She reached across to Jeff, and when he took her hands, she whispered, "Pray for me, both of you."

She heard Jeff begin to pray, and she closed her eyes. She heard Irving praying also, and she cried out in her spirit, "Oh, God, I don't know You, but I believe that Jesus died for me, and I have seen You in these men. I ask You to make me a different woman. Give me Your forgiveness."

The daylight finally came, and Irving lay still in the finality of the last sleep. Jeff laid his father's hand down and went and knelt beside Charissa's chair. He put his arm around her and whispered, "I'm so glad that Father knew your trust in Jesus. Glad for his sake and glad for yours."

"Jeff, I'm so—I don't know. I'm so alone."

"No, you have the Lord now, and you'll always have me."

"Do I really, Jeff?"

"Always, Charissa. I promise."

Chapter fourteen

Damita stared at the letter, a frown on her brow. She looked up at her father, who had brought the mail in and was reading one of his own pieces of correspondence. "Papa, I can't believe what's in this letter."

Alfredo Madariaga looked up. He appeared worried and weary. The past two years had put lines on his face. He was a proud man, and financial difficulties had shamed him. "Who is it from?"

"It's from Jeff Whitman in St. Louis—Dr. Whitman, I suppose I should say."

"Indeed? Why is he writing you, my dear?"

Damita flushed slightly and said breezily, "Oh, we've kept in touch since he went back to St. Louis. He came to see me twice when he was in town for business." Alfredo had been too absorbed with the family business to notice when Dr. Whitman came by.

"I can't think you two would have a great deal in common."

"We don't—except for Charissa, of course. Charissa was a slave here, but she's an heiress now, according to this letter."

"An heiress? How could that be?"

"I told you, Papa, but you forgot. Charissa was the natural daughter of Jeff's father, Dr. Irving Whitman."

"Why, yes, I do remember you told me that." He smiled. "It would be strange for you to meet her now, wouldn't it?"

Damita bit her lower lip. "I may have the chance to find out," she said, looking down at the letter. She hesitated, then said, "I never told you, Papa, but Jeff has become interested in me."

Alfredo looked surprised. "Interested how?"

"As a suitor."

"When did this all start?"

"He's a fine letter writer. He wrote to tell me how Charissa was doing, and I answered his letters."

"You don't mean to tell me the man's fallen in love with you by means of letters!"

"I'm not sure if he's serious. He's rather a shy man, but we've been writing for two years."

"I'm surprised at you, Damita," Madariaga said. He studied her for a moment. "How do you feel about this man? Surely you're not interested in him!"

Damita looked angry, then shrugged. "The last two years haven't been much fun, Papa. All the men who were after me when we had money have mysteriously disappeared."

"They weren't after your money."

"You think that if it makes you happy," Damita said in a strange, tight voice. "But I know better. It's been quite an education, watching so many men who practically fought over me suddenly discover that I wasn't such a prize."

"You're a beautiful woman, daughter," Madariaga said quietly.

Damita looked at the letter for a long time, then lifted her head. "That's evidently not enough for some men."

"Would you be pleased if Whitman came, seeking your hand? But of course, he has not done so."

Damita smiled and tapped her chin with her forefinger. "I've gotten to know Jeff pretty well over the past two years. He'll come to see me. You can be sure of that." She stood and smiled up at her father. "Don't worry about me, Papa. I'll not be an old maid on your hands!"

"Charissa, would you come into the study for a moment, please?"

Charissa had been passing the open door of the study when Jeff's voice caught her. Entering, she saw that an enormous pile of papers covered the large desk. The young doctor wore an anxious expression on his face, and she asked, "What is it, Jeff?"

"Come over here and sit down." She did so, and Jeff pulled his chair opposite hers. "You look tired," he said. "You haven't been sleeping well since Father died."

"Oh, I'm all right," Charissa said. This was not exactly true, for during the six weeks that had passed since the death of her father, she had not been sleeping or eating normally. Though she had tried to conceal it from Jeff, both he and Olga knew that she had taken the death hard. "I suppose I'll get over the loss of Papa sooner or later, but it's difficult. You see, Jeff, I never really had anybody except Mama. Now I've lost both of them."

Jeff leaned forward and put his hand over hers. "I know this is especially miserable for you, but it was a good way for him to go. He had lost interest in his professional life since he couldn't work anymore, and he threw himself into you for the last two years. You did so much for him, Charissa."

Charissa's lower lip trembled, and she turned away so that he wouldn't see. "I miss him every day," she whispered.

"Just think, though," Jeff insisted, "he's with the Lord now." He studied her face and then said more cheerfully, "And he got what he wanted most of all: to see you become a believer. It made him very happy, just as it does me."

Charissa forced a smile. "The Lord has been good. My heart was so bitter." Indeed, during the past few weeks Charissa had marveled at how her life had changed. Shortly after the funeral of her father, she had presented herself for membership at the Baptist church where Jeff belonged and been baptized. Then she began to study the Scripture as intently as she had studied nursing. "I can't tell you, Jeff, how helpful you've been in teaching me this new way of life."

"It's always a joy to see someone going into the kingdom, especially a family member—a sister," he added. He smiled, patted her hand, and then suddenly got up and went to the desk. He shuffled through the massive pile, found a certain sheaf of papers, and returned to his chair. When he sat down, he had an odd smile on his face, and his eyes were dancing. "I have a surprise for you."

"What sort of surprise?"

"This is Father's will. It took a little time to get it put together, and I was surprised at the size of his estate. He was a good businessman as well as a good doctor, and he made some wise investments." He handed her the document, and she looked at it but shook her head.

"I can't understand any of this."

"You can understand this." He turned over a few pages, then put his finger on a number with a dollar sign before it. "This is what he left you."

Charissa gasped. "But—that's impossible, Jeff!"

"It's what's he wanted you to have."

"It's too much. It should all be yours."

"No, he left me plenty. He wanted you to have this, and he put it into a trust fund so that you'll get a check every month. That's this figure here."

Charissa looked at the monthly figure and whispered, "Why, I could never spend that much money."

"Oh, I don't know," Jeff said. "You may have a talent for it. Just think of all the clothes you can buy. You can have a new carriage and a matched set of bays. Rings, bracelets. Whatever you want."

"Jeff, I don't really care for those things. You know that."

"I know you don't, but you can do lots of good with money, Charissa. You were talking about that mission work in Africa that you wanted to support financially. Look, you can send anything you like now."

Charissa brightened. "That would be wonderful!"

Jeff passed his hand over his face for a moment and shook his head. "There's one bad thing about it, though."

"What's that, Jeff?"

"You've had these young puppies wanting to call on you. They'll be coming by the dozens, now that you're an heiress."

"I don't think you need to worry about that."

Jeff said, "I know I don't. I was only teasing. I know you want a good, sound Christian husband, and God will send one too. Just you wait and see."

While Jeff talked, Charissa's mind filled with this change in her life. She thought back to just two years before, when she had been a slave, penniless, afraid, ignored, and now she was an independent woman of property. She was so busy with her thoughts, she did not notice that Jeff, after he had replaced the papers, had come back and was standing over her. When she glanced up, she saw that he was troubled. She had learned to read his moods, and she asked, "What's the matter, Jeff?"

"You know, Charissa, you have money enough to do anything you want. You could travel. You wouldn't have to stay here."

He was avoiding her question, so she asked again, "What's wrong, Jeff? There's something you're not telling me."

"It's nothing bad, Charissa. It's just that, well, I've decided—" He stopped, cleared his throat, and ran his fingers through his thick black hair. "I have decided to make a change."

"What sort of change?"

"I'm going to leave my practice here in St. Louis."

Instantly Charissa knew what was coming. "You're going to move to New Orleans, aren't you?"

"Why, yes. How'd you guess that? I'm going into partnership with Elmo Debakky."

The partnership was real enough; Charissa understood that. But she also understood that he had another reason for moving to New Orleans. *He's infatuated with Damita. He doesn't know her. He's such a fool where women are concerned.*

"I wish you'd go with me, Charissa," Jeff said hurriedly, stumbling over the words. "I know you have some bad memories of that city, but it could be a good move."

"I don't think I'd care to do that, Jeff."

Jeff started to speak again but stopped. He had learned that Charissa Desjardin had an enormous certainty in her, almost a stubbornness at times. He saw that in her now, in the tight line of her lips and the cold expression of her eyes. "I was afraid you'd feel that way," he said. "But at least think about it, will you?" He hesitated, then said, "I . . . I don't want us to be apart, Charissa."

Charissa felt such a heaviness she could barely speak. "I'll think about it, but I don't believe I would do such a thing."

For almost a month after Jeff informed her of his decision to move to New Orleans, Charissa felt troubled. The thought of living apart from him was more painful than she had imagined. She had admitted to herself before this that she cared for him, and she carried hope that one day, he would look at her the way a man looks at a woman he loves. That hope now seemed destroyed. She knew that he would not rearrange his life and move to New Orleans unless he was determined to court Damita.

Two weeks after his announcement, Jeff said, "Charissa, I won't sell the house if you want to stay here. It's really as much yours as it is mine, but I keep hoping that you'll change your mind."

After that conversation, Charissa began to pray frequently. She knew little about prayer. She had heard a sermon on it, had read in the Gospels and Paul's writings about the power of prayer, but she had not experienced it herself. Now she prayed passionately, asking God to do *something*. She did not know exactly what, but she knew that she was about to lose someone she treasured. At times, she cried out for God to change Jeff's mind and make him see her as a woman, but this did not happen. She grew despondent, and in the middle of July when Jeff was making his final plans, she grew desperate. She had read of fasting, and for two days she did not eat a bite and prayed almost constantly.

Late that Thursday night, she was on her knees, seeking God, when she suddenly seemed to collapse inwardly. Her face was pressed against the bed where she knelt, and she felt that she had done all she could. She said, "Oh, Father, I don't know how to pray any more, but I know that the Savior asked that Your will be done. So, that's what I pray: Let Your will be done." She stayed on her knees for a time, then rose, walked to the window, and looked out into the darkness. "Your will be done," she said. "And, Lord, I'm asking You to give me some sign about what I should do. I'm weak. I can't make this decision. If You want me to go to New Orleans with Jeff, I ask You to send somebody to tell me so."

As soon as she had prayed this, she shook her head. "That's a foolish prayer," she muttered. She crawled into bed and tried to sleep.

Charissa stayed in her room most of the day. She had broken her fast but continued to say the simple prayer, "God, Your will be done." After supper, she listened as Jeff explained, with some excitement, the great things the practice in New Orleans held for him. She tried to show interest but was glad when he rose to go to his study.

"I wish you were going with me, Charissa," he said. He went over, and as he often did, he put his hand on her head. He admired her hair, so black and sleek. He held his hand there for a moment and then turned abruptly and left the room.

Charissa went to bed as well, but at ten o'clock she grew thirsty. The pitcher was empty on her washstand, so she took it down to the kitchen. She was filling it up with cool water when Olga came into the room. "You're up late, Charissa! I thought you had gone to bed."

"I did, but I got thirsty and didn't have any water."

Olga waited until Charissa had filled the pitcher. She said, "You know, I tink all the time about how gute you were for Dr. Irving."

"He was the one who was good."

Olga hesitated, then put her arm around Charissa. She had never done this before. Charissa saw that the older woman was worried, and she asked, "What is it, Olga?"

"Oh, nothing. But I haf learned to loff you, too, during the time you've been here. I know—" She shook her head. "I know you're vorried about Jefferson leaving. I don't meddle in people's lives, Charissa, but when I vas praying for you tonight in my room, the strangest notion came into my mind."

Charissa stood still. "What was that, Olga?"

"I feel that God wants you to go to New Orleans."

Shock ran through Charissa. She could not speak.

"How you must hate it when people tell you what to do."

"No, no, that's not so. Olga, let me tell you what I've been praying."

Words tumbled out, and she ended by saying, "And so, God has given me exactly what I need."

"So, you vill go to New Orleans?"

"Yes, I will."

Mrs. Shultz stepped back then, but she took Charissa's hand. "Tell me—you loff Jefferson?" When she saw the girl drop her eyes, she said, "Oh, he does not know it. Men are stupid, but I haf seen it. Ve vill pray, you and I, that God vill open his blind eyes and see what a pearl has been hidden here." She put her hands on Charissa's cheeks, and her eyes burned with an unusual light. "And when he sees this pearl, he vill sell all he has to get it!"

The next morning, as soon as Jeff walked out of his bedroom, he met Charissa. She was smiling, and her eyes were bright with hope. He asked, "What in the world is it, Charissa?"

"I've come to tell you something. I'm going to New Orleans with you, Jefferson."

"You are? That's splendid!" He suddenly reached out, put both arms around her, and picked her up off the floor. He swung her around several times until she grew dizzy and then put her down and kissed her on the cheek. "You've made me so happy, sister!"

"I am not your sister, Jefferson."

Jeff was too excited to hear her comment. "We'll leave as soon as we can find work for the servants. I've already got a buyer for the house. Tell you what: Let's go shopping and buy you some outrageous clothes."

"And you, too, Jeff."

"All right. If you say so." He was almost giddy. He took her hand and said ecstatically, "We're going to bust New Orleans wide open, sister—" He shook his head and laughed. "I mean Miss Charissa Desjardin."

"You're here at last!" Elmo Debakky exclaimed. He had opened the door to find Jeff and Charissa standing outside. He grabbed Jeff by the hand, pulled him in, and then turned to Charissa and took her hand as well. "Welcome to New Orleans."

Jeff and Charissa had discussed living in Debakky's house. In truth, it was an enormous house, but Charissa felt it might present problems. Jeff, however, had convinced her, and now Debakky's delight was evident.

"I'm glad you're here. I've rattled around this old barn so long by myself, it'll be good to have someone to have fuss with. We might as well have our first one right now."

"It's a bit soon, isn't it, Dr. Debakky?"

"Just Elmo, Charissa, when we're all alone. Later on, when people are around, we'll be a little more formal. No, it's not too soon. I always say, have an argument as quick as you can, and get it out of the away. Then we'll all kiss and make up."

"What are we going to argue about?" Jeff smiled. He was pleased to be in New Orleans. He had been in such a turmoil, getting affairs closed up and then making the move, but now that he was there, he was happy to see his friend and felt that he had made the right choice.

"There's a ball tonight, one of those fancy affairs that I usually hate, but I got a new suit, and I'm going to wear it, and you two are going with me."

"Oh, I'm sure Charissa's too tired for that. It's been a hard trip," Jeff protested.

"Nonsense. She looks fresh as the morning breeze. If you don't have a dress, we have time to go buy one."

"I have a dress, Elmo," Charissa said, "but I'm not sure I should go."

"Of course you should go. We'll break in those new clothes we bought at home," Jeff said.

"It's not the same in St. Louis. Nobody knew me there. But I've got a past here."

"Forget the past!" Elmo shouted. He was pacing, rubbing his hands together. "I'm introducing you two to New Orleans tonight." He punched Jeff on the shoulder and said, "I'll introduce you as my new partner, the second-best physician in New Orleans." He turned to Charissa and said, "And I'll introduce you as Miss Charissa

Desjardin, the toast of St. Louis now come to grace the city of New Orleans. It'll be a ball to remember!"

The mayor of New Orleans sponsored the ball, and he spared no expense. The ballroom itself was a marvel. It was a large, grand room painted a brilliant white, with a high ceiling that featured three huge crystal and gold chandeliers. Enormous white columns encircled the room, and the white, highly glossed marble floor showed tiny, sparkling flecks of gold. On every wall behind the columns were floor-length windows that were covered with dark crimson drapes, and finely upholstered chairs had been set along two of the walls. At the far end of the room, a small orchestra was playing soft, enchanting music, and the rustle of women dancing in their brilliantly colored dresses made an inviting sound.

Damita was having a wonderful time. She was waltzing with Lewis Depard, and the admiration in his eyes was pleasing to her. He had been pursuing her rather steadily for some time, and once, she knew, he had almost mentioned the word *marriage.* But Lewis Depard had escaped many "permanent arrangements." As they spun around the floor, Damita was happy that he seemed to be more enamored of her than he was of his usual pursuits, though this did not mean much.

"You look beautiful, Damita."

"Thank you, Lewis. So do you."

"Oh, don't be foolish!"

"You *are* beautiful. You're a handsome man. I think when I get married, I want to marry someone just like you." Damita laughed when she saw the expression freeze on his face. "Don't worry, Lewis, I'm not pursuing or proposing to you. It would be fun, though, if I could bring a suit of breach of promise. Why don't you ask me to marry you, and give me that opportunity?" She laughed again at his expression and said, "But wait until there are witnesses."

"You are a minx, Damita! I never know how to take you. I suppose that's why I keep coming back for more."

The two continued their dance, and then Damita exclaimed, "Why, look, it's Jefferson Whitman! Come along. He wrote me he was coming back to New Orleans, but I didn't expect to see him here tonight."

The two left the dance floor, making their way between the dancers, and Jeff stepped forward, his eyes lighting up. As Damita held her hand out, he took it and held it as if he didn't know what to do with it. "You're supposed to kiss my hand, Jeff."

Jeff did so awkwardly. "I guess I'll have to take lessons in New Orleans manners now that I'm here."

"It's wonderful to see you. May I present Lewis Depard?"

"Good to meet you, Mr. Depard."

"And you, Doctor. So, you've moved to New Orleans. There's always room for another doctor. Maybe you can stop this yellow fever from killing so many people."

"I don't claim to have that kind of skill, but I certainly want to do my best."

Suddenly, Jeff seemed to remember something. "Oh, I'm so sorry. I have someone with me you will remember, Damita." He turned and said, "Charissa, come here." She had been standing slightly behind him, watching the scene, and now she advanced.

Damita stared at Charissa. She would never have known her. She had seen her only in the rags of a slave girl, a sixteen-year-old one at that. This woman—this lovely woman—was mature and refined in every sense. She managed to say, "Welcome to New Orleans, Charissa."

"Are you going to introduce me?" Lewis asked. The beauty of the woman had impressed him, and he smiled with anticipation.

"I'm sorry," Jeff said. "May I present Miss Charissa Desjardin. This is Mr. Lewis Depard."

Charissa curtsied, and Depard bowed from the waist in a skilled fashion. "I am happy to welcome you. Is your family in New Orleans?"

"Dr. Whitman is my brother," she said.

"Oh, I see. In that case, I will ask his permission to dance with you."

"Of course," Jeff said. Lewis led Charissa to the dance floor and swung her around gracefully, saying, "Will you be staying with your brother?"

"Yes, I will, Mr. Depard. I work with him, as his nurse."

"You don't say! I never had a nurse who looked as pretty as you."

Charissa moved around the floor lightly, listening as Depard flirted with her. He was so obvious about it, but then most men were. *He came after me as soon as he saw me,* she thought. *I wonder what he would do if I told him I was the former slave of Damita de Salvedo y Madariaga. She'll tell him soon enough, and then we'll see.*

Damita had watched the two walk away, and then Jeff said, "It's so good to see you."

But Damita was staring at Lewis and Charissa. "You didn't tell me she had grown up to be such an attractive young lady."

"She is, isn't she? I hope you'll be able to forget the old times and treat her as a friend."

"That will be difficult, Jeff, for both of us."

Jeff shifted his weight and started running his fingers through his hair, but Charissa had warned him sternly about this and he stopped. "I'm such an awkward fellow, Damita."

"An awkward doctor?" Damita smiled. "That could be dangerous, if you were cutting someone open."

"Oh, I don't mean that way. I mean with women. I just have never learned the knack of dealing with them."

"I'm surprised at that."

"You know how we Americans are," he said, "Pretty rough-hewn."

Damita glanced once again at the couple on the floor. It was hard for her to concentrate on what Jeff was saying. She could not get over the sight of Charissa Desjardin.

"What I'm saying is—would it be all right if I called on you, Damita?"

Damita was not at all surprised. On his two trips to New Orleans, he had attempted to court her. She had given him little enough encouragement, but he was a stubborn young man. Though his letters had been nothing like love letters, as she looked up at him and saw his eagerness, she smiled. "Of course. We are living in our town house, Jeff. Come to dinner next Wednesday."

Jeff could hardly keep still in the buggy, but Charissa was quiet. She had danced every dance, because the young men were drawn to her.

Lewis had danced with her three times and tried his best to get permission to call on her. She had simply said, "You'll have to ask my brother."

Jeff was drumming his fingers on his knees, a sure sign he was excited, and he said, "That young man Lewis, what's his name—Depard? He's a wild fellow."

"Yes. He asked if he could call on me."

Jeff stopped smiling. "What'd you tell him?"

"I told him he would have to ask you." She smiled demurely.

"He asked me, as a matter of fact."

"What'd you tell him?"

"I didn't have time to tell him much, but he said he'd call on me later and get my permission. You don't need a man like that."

"He seems very nice."

"He's more or less a rounder. Damita has told me about him."

"She seems to like him very much."

"He's a womanizer," Jeff said bluntly. "I'll have to tell him what the limits are."

Charissa stared at Jeff. "What are the limits, Jefferson?"

"The usual. You know. I can't have a man who isn't honorable going out with my sister."

Charissa shook her head in wonder. "Why don't you just find a man who meets all of your standards and then bring him to me, instead of the other way around?"

Jeff opened his mouth to answer, then saw that she was kidding. "I'm sorry if I'm too stuffy. It's just the way I am. You know that."

"I know that."

"Damita asked me to have dinner with her family next week. I think you might like to come."

"Did Miss Madariaga request my presence?"

"No, she didn't, but I'm sure you'd be welcome."

Charissa laughed. There was something ludicrous about Jefferson Whitman. For all his skill as a doctor and all his kindness as a brother, he was like a child in some ways.

"Jeff, the Madariagas would be horrified if you brought a former slave to their house to sit down at their table."

Jeff reacted as if she had struck him in the face. "You must be wrong about that."

"I'm not wrong. I'm sure you'll have a fine time. You go and enjoy yourself."

Chapter fifteen

"You look good enough for me to take you out, Charissa."

Charissa had entered the foyer of the house. She turned to smile at Debakky, who was looking at her with admiration. "Why don't you ever ask me out, Elmo?"

"Oh, I'm a confirmed old bachelor. And besides, you wouldn't go out with a simple fellow like me. You're moving in high circles now."

Indeed, for the two months that she and Jeff had been staying with Debakky, they had worked hard at the practice, both of them. But they had also plunged into social life in a way that Charissa would not have thought possible. It had been her confirmed opinion that once Damita had let the word out that she had been a slave, all social activity would end for her. Evidently, Damita had not breathed a word of this, nor had any of the Madariaga family. And Charissa had attended several balls and operas with Lewis Depard and enjoyed herself. She smiled at Elmo and said, "One day a woman will steal your heart."

"As soon as I find one as rich and beautiful as you, I promise to fall as hard as any callow youth. What is it tonight?"

"Oh, it's one of those Creole balls."

"You're going with Lewis?"

"Yes."

"What does Dr. Jefferson Whitman say about that?"

"I haven't told him yet."

"He won't like it. He's very possessive."

Charissa gave Debakky a strange look. "I know. He's very possessive of his 'baby sister.'"

"He loves you a great deal."

"Yes," Charissa answered flatly, "I know all about that."

Debakky was a shrewd man. The pair had not been in his house for a week before he had discovered that Charissa was in love with Jeff. He had watched to see if the young doctor returned her affections, but he saw nothing but the love a man would give his sister.

Jeff entered, resplendent in a suit of new clothes that actually fit him. Debakky had taken him to his own tailor, and Jeff looked well indeed. "You're going out, Charissa?"

"Lewis is taking me to the Creole Ball."

Both Debakky and Charissa saw Jeff's face change. He looked reproachful and said, "I don't really care for that fellow. I wish you wouldn't go out with him."

Charissa could not restrain herself. "You've gone out with Damita Madariaga three times in the last two weeks! I'd rather you didn't go out with her."

"That's different."

"How?"

Jeff merely pursed his lips.

Charissa looked at Elmo with discouragement in her face. "How can you argue with a man who gives you an answer like that?"

As she walked down the hall and into the parlor, Elmo said, "I think you're fighting a losing battle there, old boy."

"What does she see in the fellow?"

"Aside from the fact that he's witty, charming, handsome, and rich, I can't see a thing to attract a woman."

"He's a womanizer."

"I have no doubt he is. He's quite a swordsman, too, and a fine pistol shot. I think he spends most of his time getting ready for the duels that he intends to provoke."

"He's a fool!"

"New Orleans is full of fools, and so is the world, I suppose. Are you taking Damita tonight?"

"I didn't know that Lewis Depard would be taking Charissa, or I wouldn't have agreed to go."

Debakky started to say something but stopped. He shook his head, looked sadly at Jeff, and turned away without word.

What's the matter with him? Jeff wondered. *He's a smart man. He should see how wrong it is for Charissa to spend time with Depard.* He stood irresolutely for a moment, considering whether to try to persuade Charissa to stay home, but he knew that was hopeless. Instead, he left the house and headed for the ball, thinking, *Sometimes I wish we had never come to this place.*

As he climbed into the carriage, he thought about how his life had changed in such a short time. Mostly he thought about Damita. She seemed far out of his sphere; handsome young men of wealth courted her constantly. He was intensely jealous of Lewis Depard and said suddenly, "I wish the fellow would fall off a building and break both of his legs! That would stop his dancing and his dueling and his chasing women. Get up, horse!"

Alfredo strolled along the aisles of the cotton exchange, stopping from time to time to speak with the men who were the heart of New Orleans economy. Cotton was king in the South, and in New Orleans more than anywhere else. Most of the cotton grown in the southern United States found its way in the form of huge bales to New Orleans. Much of that went to England, but ships bore it all over the world.

The air was filled with talking, shouting, and laughter as Madariaga moved along. Almost every man, it seemed, smoked cigars, and the air was hazy. Madariaga removed one from his own pocket, bit off the end, lit it, and took a puff. He did not visit this section often, but he had wanted to see the agent about the world market. October was upon them, and the cotton was stacked up in bales on the wharf until it looked like a huge fortress. Madariaga had held on to his, hoping the price would rise, but to his dismay it had fallen. When the world agent reported this, the news had crushed Madariaga. Worry had become almost habitual with him; his debts were large, and everything depended upon the crops. He was one of many aristocrats in the area who rose or fell according to the price of cotton. No one knew exactly how this price was determined, and sometimes Alfredo thought that some small group of men simply decided, on the flip of a coin, what to do with it.

Puffing on his cigar, Alfredo was about to leave when he glanced into one of the offices and stopped abruptly. "Well, upon my soul!" he exclaimed and entered the office. "My dear friend! What are you doing here? I didn't know you were employed in New Orleans."

Yancy Devereaux rose from the desk and smiled wryly. "It's not by choice, sir, I assure you."

Madariaga asked, "What's happened? I thought you had bought a ship and gone into business in Savannah."

"Come in and sit down. It's a long, sad story."

Madariaga saw lines of fatigue around the man's mouth, and he sensed a lackluster spirit in him that he had not seen before.

"I did buy half-interest in a ship with a friend. He was a good man. He was going to be the captain; I would do the work on shore, getting cargoes. Never go into that business, Alfredo."

"What happened?"

"The ship went down off the coast of Africa, loaded with cotton. A hurricane hit it and we lost all hands. Also lost was every penny I had in the world."

"Oh, that's frightful, Yancy! I'm so sorry to hear it. Do you need any help?" Madariaga put his hand in his pocket, but Yancy put up his hand.

"No, I'm all right. I'm not likely to starve."

Alfredo was relieved; he had little to share. "How long have you been here?"

"Oh, about a month. It's just a job. I've decided to leave New Orleans."

Madariaga was grieved. He had never ceased to be grateful to Yancy for saving his daughter, and he said, "Perhaps I could introduce you to someone who might help you find a better position."

"No, but thank you for your offer. I'm going back to Shreveport. I know quite a few people there. I shouldn't have too much trouble finding something to do."

The two men talked briefly, and when Alfredo stood to leave, he shook Yancy's hand. "Why don't you come out and visit the family? They'd be so glad to see you."

"I will, if I don't leave right away."

"Don't leave until you come at least once. Our family owes you a great deal."

Alfredo left the cotton exchange feeling concerned. He thought about Yancy Devereaux all the way home, and when he arrived, he found that Jeff Whitman had arrived to take Damita to a ball. He greeted him absently, then turned to Damita. "I had quite a shock today, daughter."

"What was it, Papa?"

"At the cotton exchange, I ran into Yancy Devereaux."

Damita looked shocked herself. "I didn't know he was in New Orleans."

"It really troubles me." He told of Yancy's misadventures and shook his head. "Our family is in his debt. You wouldn't be with us, Damita, if it weren't for him."

"That's true enough. I'm so sorry to hear it."

Jeff listened quietly, standing off to one side, since it seemed to be family business. He watched Alfredo, and he noticed that the older man was rubbing his chest and flexing the fingers on his left hand. This was an alarming sign. "Are you having a problem in your chest, Mr. Madariaga?"

"Oh, probably just indigestion."

"What about your hand?"

Madariaga held up his hand and made a fist. "Oh, it's nothing. Just a little numbness in my fingers now and then." He shook his head and said, "Now, don't start trying to doctor me. I'm all right."

Damita looked worried. "You really should let Jeff look you over, Papa."

"Yes, we'll have to do that sometime." He turned to go but said, "I'm worried about Yancy. I'm going to see if I can find something for him to do."

As soon as her father left, Damita asked, "What do you think is wrong with Papa?"

"Probably nothing. You know how doctors are. We spend all of our time listening to symptoms. Sometimes we begin to see them when they're not there."

Damita knew that Jeff was being evasive. "Tell me the truth. I want to know."

"Probably nothing, but I wish he would come in and let Debakky examine him. He has some very mild symptoms that could mean a heart problem."

"Is it dangerous?"

"Oh, I've seen men who take care of themselves live many years with heart problems. Most of them even live longer than people without heart conditions, because they take better care of themselves."

"But not always?"

"Not always. Sometimes they go very suddenly." He reached out and took Damita's hand, something he rarely did. "I think you should try to persuade him to come into the office. Debakky has a great deal of experience in this sort of thing, much more than I have."

"I'll talk to him, Jeff."

Damita did not enjoy the ball. She was preoccupied with thoughts of her father and his symptoms. When she saw Yancy Devereaux standing against a wall, drinking out of a crystal glass, she was startled. But she walked over, and when he saw her, he put the glass down and smiled.

"Damita, it's good to see you."

"It's good to see you, too. I didn't know you were in New Orleans until today. Papa told me he saw you at the cotton exchange."

"Oh, how the mighty are fallen. Did he tell you about my bad luck?"

"Yes. I'm so sorry."

"Oh, it doesn't matter. I've got my health, and I'll be able to recoup."

Damita saw that Yancy was tired, and despite his words, he was not as optimistic as he tried to sound. She recalled their last meeting and asked abruptly, "Do you ever think of when the ship sank?"

"Certainly! How could I forget that?" He considered her expression, then said, "We nearly died. I still can't see how we survived. As a matter of fact, I've had bad dreams about it."

Damita eyes grew wide. "I have, too."

"But we did survive. I've never been very religious, but I've thanked God many times for saving us."

"I didn't behave well to you at all the last time we met, Yancy. I'm sorry."

"Nothing to be sorry about. It was a tough time."

Damita had never forgotten how she had offered herself to him—and how he had spurned her. She looked into his eyes and whispered, "I was very foolish. I've never stopped being ashamed of—" She could not finish and dropped her eyes.

"Don't even think about it, Damita. Under stress, we all behave abnormally." He saw that she was troubled and asked cheerfully, "Would you like to dance?"

"Very much."

The two whirled out on the floor, and Damita tried, as tactfully as she could, to find out what Yancy's prospects were. He shrugged off her questions, saying, "I'll find something. I always do. Maybe I'll become a Mississippi riverboat gambler. All you need is a fancy vest, lots of hair oil, and the ability to cheat at cards."

Damita laughed, but then she shook her head, saying, "My father would like to help you."

"He said so, but I'm a big boy now, Damita."

She did not speak for a time. Being near him again turned her thoughts to those few days on the ship, and she said, "I've thought so often about the McCains. I can't get them out of my mind."

"I think about them, too. You know, as long as we remember them, they're still here, Damita."

She looked at him with surprise. "What do you mean?"

"I mean that as long as people think about us, and talk about us, we still exist somehow. I remember them so well. I think they were more in love than any couple I've ever seen."

"I know. She told me one day me how much she loved him. She said she was afraid she idolized him, which bothered her a little. That surprised me. I didn't know a woman could love a man too much."

He smiled. "I don't think one can."

The dance ended, and the pair walked to the refreshment table. Damita asked, "Did you know that Charissa is in New Orleans?"

"No. What's she doing here?" He listened as she spoke of the change that had taken place in Charissa's life. "It's really quite miraculous," Damita said. "She's over there, dancing with Lewis Depard."

Yancy said, "Who's the tall fellow there? He looks as if he'd like to break her partner's back."

"Dr. Jeff Whitman. In a way, he's responsible for her, I understand. His adopted father was really Charissa's father. It's all rather confused."

The two were watching, and Yancy said, "That looks like trouble, Damita."

Jeff had approached Lewis Depard and said something to him. Depard's face was flushed, and clearly a quarrel was brewing.

"Come on. Lewis challenges everybody. I'll have to try to stop him."

Yancy followed Damita and saw that, indeed, both men were angry.

"I resent your words, Dr. Whitman, and I must take exception to them."

"Take whatever exception you want to, Depard, but you are going to be respectful of my sister."

"Jeff, he didn't mean anything," Charissa protested.

"I think he did," Depard said. He had been drinking. "I'm afraid I will have to ask for satisfaction."

"No, Lewis, don't say that!" Damita said. She took his arm. "Come away. It's all right."

"No, it's not all right. I've been insulted!"

Charissa said to Jeff, "If you just tell him you're sorry, that's all that is necessary."

"I won't say any such fool thing. I'm not sorry."

Both women urged the men to break off the fight. Yancy watched. He had seen Depard in action before. He took pride in his dueling ability, and Yancy knew that he would not be pacified.

"I'll have my man call on you, Doctor. Even an American can't refuse a challenge."

"Send whomever you want!" Jeff was furious.

Depard bowed and walked away stiffly.

"You can't fight him, Jeff," Damita said.

"I'll have to."

"He'll kill you," Charissa said. "He's already wounded several men."

Yancy watched as the two women tried to calm the tall man, but it was hopeless. Jefferson Whitman was a stubborn fellow. *If he had any sense, he would simply laugh at the man, as I did once.*

As if reading his mind, Damita said, "Yancy, tell him how foolish it is."

"Who is this?" Jeff demanded.

"Oh, I'm sorry. This is Mr. Yancy Devereaux."

"You're the man who saved Damita's life," Jeff said, relaxing at once.

"I was able to help her, but let me join my voices with these young ladies'. It would be senseless to fight a man like him. He's not worth it."

But all the arguments of the three could not turn Jeff from his plan, and he finally said, "Come along, Charissa, I'll take you home."

Damita watched him and Charissa walk away. "Yancy, do something! You know about things like this."

"All right." Yancy quickly caught up to the pair and said, "Dr. Whitman, it's customary in duels to have a second. If you have no one else, I've had a little experience."

"That's generous of you, sir. I know nothing about duels."

"Then let me take care of all the preliminaries."

"Thank you very much."

As Damita approached, Yancy leaned over and said, "Don't worry. He'll be all right."

"How can you promise that?"

"As I said, I've had a little experience in things like this."

Charissa had begged, pleaded, cajoled, but Jeff was adamant. "I couldn't let him insult you like that."

"It wasn't an insult, Jeff. He's that way with all the women."

"Then he needs to learn to have better manners with women."

"Jeff, I can't let you do it."

"I have to."

"Please! For my sake?" she asked desperately.

Jeff looked at her in surprise. "I couldn't think of myself as a man if I refused a challenge like this."

Charissa stared at him and shook her head. "Jeff, you're being ridiculous."

"I probably am. Most men are. But I'll not tolerate his arrogance."

Damita visited the cotton exchange and found Yancy in his office. He invited her in and closed the door, and she said, "We can't do a thing with him, Yancy. He's going to get killed."

"Damita, I told you: No, he's not."

"How can you say that? Haven't you heard what an expert Lewis is with a sword or a pistol?"

"Yes, I know all about that. I can't say as I care for all this nonsense, but it's become a way of life here among you Creoles."

"I know it, and it's awful!"

Indeed, New Orleans had produced a band of swaggering hotheads, who went about looking for excuses to fight duels. They had developed provoking fights into a fine art. They spoke constantly of their "honor" and demanded "satisfaction" at every opportunity. Manuals of dueling etiquette had been published, books about how one was to offend or to be offended. Those manuals decreed that a man must deliver insults according to rigid instructions; the insult might be verbal, or it might be just a flick of the glove in the face. Custom also fixed the places for dueling, usually in the outskirts of the city. Duelists and their audiences gathered regularly at a certain grove of trees outside New Orleans to watch the show.

Yancy saw that Damita was still worried, and he asked, "Do you love this man, Damita?"

"I don't know, Yancy. He's a good man. A fine doctor."

"But do you love him?"

"No, I don't," she answered, shaking her head. "But I respect him. He's a gentleman, Yancy, and I don't want him to die."

"Listen to me." He held her by the shoulders. She saw that his face was serious, and a resolved light shone in his eyes. "I've offered to be his second. I promise you that nothing will happen. Will you believe that?"

Damita felt the strength of Yancy's hands. She saw in his face a fierce determination and an honesty that made her whisper, "Yes, if you say so, Yancy, I'll believe it."

He smiled and released her and said, "Just leave it to me."

The October dawn brought chilling winds. Jeff shivered despite his bravado and said to Yancy, "I should have worn a heavier coat. I'm shaking, but it's not because I'm afraid."

"Aren't you?"

"To be truthful, Yancy, I am. I'm scared to death."

"Remember that the next time. This is foolishness. You can still get out of it by simply offering the man an apology."

"I won't do that."

Yancy sighed. "I knew you wouldn't. Well, you stay here. I'll go arrange the pistols. I'm glad it's pistols instead of swords."

"Why?"

"It's much safer. Remember what I told you now: Turn sideways. Gives him less to shoot at." He marched over and met Lewis's second, a tall, cadaverous-looking man named French. "I suppose we may place our men."

"Yes, I think all is well." He opened up the case he carried and said, "You may choose either one of these."

"It doesn't matter. I'd like to load them."

"Of course," French said, but his eyes were doubtful. He watched carefully as Devereaux loaded the pistols, putting in the powder, the balls, and the small wads that kept the balls from rolling out. "You have done this before, sir," French noted.

"More often than I'd like to think about. Is this satisfactory?"

"Yes."

"I'll take this one, then, for my man. Are we ready?"

"Yes, I think so."

Yancy walked back and handed Jeff the pistol. "It's cocked, ready to fire."

Jeff nodded as he took the pistol. "What happens now?"

"We'll meet, and there'll be talk of a last chance to apologize."

"I won't do it," Jeff said again.

"Of course you won't. You're too smart for that. You'd rather die than admit you're wrong. Come along."

The two combatants and their seconds met. French said, "An apology would be accepted, sir."

"You won't get it!" Jeff said stubbornly.

Lewis smiled. "You would be wise, Doctor. This is not your game."

"I won't do it! You were wrong, and I was right to stop you."

"I suppose we're ready, then," Yancy said.

The seconds arranged the men back-to-back, and French said, "Each of you will take ten steps as I count. You will turn and fire as you will. Is that satisfactory, Mr. Devereaux?"

"Perfectly."

Yancy stepped back alongside French. French's voice rang out, "Are you ready? Then, one—two—three—"

Yancy watched as the two men paced slowly away from each other. *By George, the doctor's an awkward fellow, but he's got nerve. I'll say that for him. For his first time out, he's holding up well.*

"Eight—nine—ten!"

Both men turned, and the shots were instantaneous. Both dropped their arms, and French exclaimed, "Missed! They both missed!"

"That's all," Yancy said. He walked forward and motioned the two men together. "Your honor is now satisfied."

"The doctor may feel that another shot is necessary," Lewis said.

"I thought you were more acquainted with the dueling code," Yancy said. "If you want satisfaction, sir, I am here to give it to you, sword or pistol."

Lewis Depard sucked in his breath, as Yancy suddenly appeared much larger than he remembered. He had never refused and was about to accept when French said, "You are entirely right, Mr. Devereaux. Lewis, be sensible, man! You're wrong."

Lewis dropped his eyes. "You're right. I apologize."

"Good enough," Devereaux said. He said to Jeff, "Come along. Let's get away from here, Doctor."

As they were walking, Jeff commented, "I understand how I missed, but I thought he was a dead shot."

"Even dead shots miss sometimes. Try to remember what you learned from this."

"I will never forget it. I thought I was a dead man."

At Yancy's house, Damita was incredulous. "You mean they both shot and both missed?"

"That's what everybody says."

"But Lewis *never* misses." She stared at Yancy and saw that he was trying not to laugh. "What's going on?" she demanded. "They could have been killed."

"No, they couldn't."

"What do you mean? Men get killed all the time in these foolish duels."

"Not when I handle it."

Damita knew that Devereaux had a sense of humor. "What did you do, Yancy?"

"What did I do? I took some dough, and I rolled it up into little balls about the size that a pistol takes. I cooked them in the oven and then coated them with oil. When I loaded the guns, I palmed the real musket balls, and put toast in. It was a pretty neat piece of work, Damita. Lewis's second was watching me like a hawk, but I'm a very shifty fellow."

Damita stared at him, and he broke out laughing. "They shot each other with toast!"

Relief washed through Damita. Without knowing she did it, she reached out and put her hand on his chest. He covered it, she began to smile, and then she began to laugh heartily. "Oh, that's so funny!"

"You must never tell anybody about this. The fools would try to kill each other again."

"I won't. But, Yancy, I didn't know you were so clever."

"Oh, I'm a slippery man. One time back in Shreveport—" At that moment a servant entered the room and said, "There's a man to see you, Miss Madariaga." She turned and saw Charles Devere, her family's butler, come in, his face stiff and pale.

"What is it, Charles?" she said.

"It's your father. He's ill. You must come home at once."

"What is it?"

"I think it's his heart."

"Is the doctor there?"

"I went for Dr. Debakky and Dr. Whitman. They should be there by now."

Damita started to follow Charles out of the room, but at the last minute, she turned and said, "Thank you for helping, Yancy."

"I hope your father's all right."

"Thank you," she whispered, but her eyes were filled with terror.

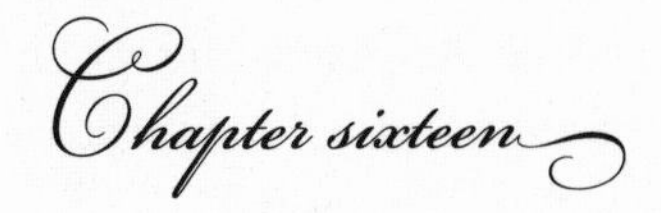

Chapter sixteen

As soon as Damita stepped inside the house, she met her mother. She was weeping.

"What happened, Mama?"

"Oh, Damita, he just gasped and fell over. I'm so afraid."

"Where are the doctors?"

"They are both with him. They'll be out in a few minutes."

"Come and sit down, Mama." Damita led her into the parlor and sat beside her on the sofa.

"He had just come in from the city," Elena said, her voice quavering. "We were in the drawing room, talking about repairs for the house, and he seemed perfectly normal. Suddenly, he grabbed his chest. He had the most awful look on his face, Damita. It was as if someone had shot him! He fell, and I could tell he was in terrible pain."

"Did he say anything?"

"He whispered to get the doctor, so we put him in bed, and then I sent Charles."

"But have the doctors said anything? Have they been out?"

"Dr. Whitman said that it looked very serious, but he said there was always hope. Oh, Damita, what would we do without your father?"

Damita suddenly realized the enormity of what was happening. She knew her father was not the wisest of men, but he was always available when she had any needs. He loved his family better than anything on earth. A great emptiness filled her, and the fear tasted like brass in her mouth.

The two tried to comfort each other while they waited for word from the doctors. When they heard the sound of a door closing, they stood up. Jeff Whitman and Elmo Debakky appeared.

"Doctor, what is it? Is he all right?" Elena asked.

Debakky spoke for the two of them. His face was very serious. "I'm afraid we must prepare ourselves for the worst, Señora Madariaga."

"Oh, no, don't say that! There's got to be something you can do!"

"In cases like this, we doctors are almost helpless," Debakky said. "Dr. Whitman tells me he's had symptoms recently."

"Yes, he complained about his chest and numbness, but he wouldn't see a doctor. You remember, Dr. Whitman."

"Yes, I do. I wish he had come, but even that might not have helped. We just don't know."

Jeff was watching Damita and saw how pale her face was, and suddenly she began to collapse. "Damita!" He helped her over to the couch, and she sat down. "Just lower your head," he said.

In a minute, Damita straightened up, and her face showed a little more color. "Can I see him, Jeff?"

"It will do no harm. As a matter of fact, I think it would be wise if both of you went to see him." He looked at Debakky, who nodded.

Damita and her mother entered the room where Alfredo lay. The two doctors stood silently at the doorway. Elena went to one side of the bed and Damita to the other. Damita could hardly speak for the tightness in her throat. Her father was lying absolutely still, his hands crossed over his chest. His face was rigid and pale. She thought for one awful moment that he was dead, but then his eyelids fluttered, and she cried, "Papa! Can you hear me?"

The answer was very faint. "Yes, daughter."

Elena took his hand. "You must be quiet. You are very ill, Alfredo."

From where he stood, Jeff could see Damita's face. He had seen it often express joy and excitement, but now he saw only grief. *Poor girl. She's never had any real problems, and now she's going to have to learn to cope without her father.* He glanced at Debakky and shook his head.

Damita leaned close to her father as he began to whisper, "I regret not—"

"What is it, Papa? Don't worry about anything. You'll be all right."

Alfredo knew better. There was terror in his eyes, and both Elena and Damita could see it. "Don't worry, Papa. You'll get well."

"No, I'm dying. I wish I had served God better than I did."

"You've been such a good man. Always good to us," Elena whispered.

"But I have not served God as I should."

The dying man's voice grew weaker. He took Damita's hand and said to his wife and daughter, "Serve God."

The two sobbed. With his last bit of strength, Alfredo Madariaga said, "Elena, I have loved you." She leaned over and kissed him, and then he turned his eyes on Damita. "Daughter," he said, "take care of your mother. She needs you."

Jeff wanted to speak up and pray for the man, but it was too late. He saw a sudden stiffness, and Alfredo's body arched, then relaxed in a terrible and sudden looseness.

"Papa, don't die! Don't leave us!" Damita cried, falling over the body.

Debakky took Elena by the arm and whispered, "He's gone, my dear Señora Madariaga."

Jeff pulled the young girl from the bed. "Come, Damita," he whispered. "There's nothing more you can do for him."

Damita turned to him blindly and threw herself against him. He put his arms around her protectively. "Oh, Jeff," she wept, "we've lost him!"

Jeff Whitman could say nothing.

Her father's death struck Damita harder than she could have imagined. As a matter of fact, she had never given a thought to the death of a member of her family. And when it came, it brought her to a state of nervousness and loss she was powerless to fight.

On a cloudy Thursday afternoon, she went to visit her father's tomb. She wore a black cloak with a bonnet covered with black crepe. As she passed through the tombs, she was aware that other mourners had come to visit loved ones' graves. Many of the burial sites were graced with funerary ornaments, some of them flower emblems fashioned of wire, beads, and glass, which were called *immortelles.*

When Damita reached the grave, she began to arrange the immortelles on the tomb, which was already ornately decorated. Then she leaned against the tomb and pressed her face to the cool marble. She was given easily to tears since the loss of her father, and now she wiped them away and whispered, "Oh, Papa, why did you leave us?" She finally rose and left. The immortelles that adorned the tomb of Alfredo Madariaga caught the late afternoon sun and made a gay appearance, in stark contrast to the tombstones surrounding it.

"Damita, Mr. Pennington is here."

Damita looked up from where she sat in the parlor. She had been reading, and her mother had entered abruptly. "Mr. Pennington? Who's he?"

"The man from the bank."

"Oh, yes, I remember." Damita stood. "What does he want, Mama?"

"I don't know, but we'll have to talk to him."

"All right. Where is he?"

"In your father's study."

The women left the drawing room and walked down the hall. When they entered the study, Mr. Pennington rose quickly to greet them. Both women nodded and noticed that he seemed rather nervous. "Won't you sit down, Mr. Pennington?" Elena said.

"Thank you, Señora. I believe I will." Pennington took his seat and cleared his throat.

As she looked at him, Damita remembered that she had seen him when she had gone with her father to the bank. She also remembered that he had come to the house one time, but she didn't know why. His obvious apprehension made her ask, "Is there something wrong, Mr. Pennington?"

"I'm afraid there is," Pennington answered. He seemed to struggle to find words.

"What is it, sir? You seem troubled," Elena asked.

"This is a most distressing errand for me, ladies. Your father and I did business together for many years, and I know that he never burdened you with financial matters."

"No, he didn't. He took care of those himself," Elena said.

Pennington shook his shoulders slightly, then straightened up. He opened a large case he had brought with him. "I've brought here quite a few papers. They're complicated, and I think you might do well to turn all this over to your attorney."

"What are those papers, Mr. Pennington?" Damita asked.

"These are records of your family's dealings with our bank. I'm sorry to tell you that they are in very poor condition. Your business affairs, that is."

Something seemed to close around Damita's heart then, and she saw that her mother was worried also. "Father mentioned more than once the loans that he had from the bank, but we've tried to help by cutting back on expenses. You remember that we sold off some of the slaves."

"Yes, I have that record here, but I'm afraid that the situation has grown even more critical."

Elena swallowed hard. "Can you explain it in simple terms, Mr. Pennington?"

Pennington ran his hand over the leather case that held the papers. Looking down, he said, "I'm afraid you are facing bankruptcy."

"Bankruptcy!" both women exclaimed. "Surely not!" Elena said.

"I'm afraid so. The papers are all here, and as I say, I think you should have your lawyer examine them. I've gone over them myself, Señora Madariaga. I realize this is a terrible time to tell you this, but even if your husband had lived, this meeting would have taken place."

"What does it all mean?" Damita asked in a whisper.

Pennington shook his head. "Your attorney will go over the figures, and he will tell you that this town house and the plantation will have to be sold."

"No, that can't be possible!" Damita cried. "Surely some arrangement can be made."

"I've explored every alternative, Miss Madariaga. Your father was an honest man and a good man, and I've done the best I could for him. As a matter of fact, for years I've tried to get him to further economize, but he was hopeful that cotton prices would rise again. Unfortunately, the price of cotton has plummeted and stayed low, and all of these notes, some of them ten years old, are now due. You understand, it's not my decision. My board instructs me."

Elena cried, "But where will we live? What will we live on?"

"I will work with your attorney to try to realize enough money from the sale to set up a fund. It will be very small, but at least it will be something—enough for you to rent a small place and cover the necessities."

Pennington saw that both women were devastated. "I'm so sorry," he said. "I will leave these papers with you. Contact your attorney and have him come to the bank, and we will do the best we can for you. I'm so very sorry." Pennington picked up his hat from a chair and hurried out.

Damita looked at her mother and saw that she was helpless. Her mother had always been totally unaware of anything related to business, but then, so had Damita. Elena was trembling, and Damita put her arms around her and said, "Don't worry, Mother."

"But, Damita, what will we do?"

Damita said as strongly as she could, "We will find some way to save the plantation. There must be a way, and you and I will find it."

The young doctor stirred the food on his plate but didn't eat it. Charissa startled him when she asked, "What's wrong with you, Jeff?"

Looking up from across the table, he saw that both Charissa and Elmo were watching him. "I guess I'm off my feed a little."

"You have been for weeks now," Elmo said. "Is it physical?"

"Oh, no, I'm healthy as a horse."

Charissa exchanged glances with Elmo, and she said, "Both of us have been worried about you."

Jefferson Whitman was not a man who shared his problems easily, but he put his fork down and shoved his plate back. "I'm worried about the Madariagas," he said.

"What's their position?" Elmo asked. "I've heard that they are financially strapped."

"It's worse than that, Elmo. They're destitute."

"I can't understand that," Charissa marveled. "I always thought they were rich."

"That's an illusion with some of these New Orleans folks," Elmo said. "They own a lot on paper, but as a rule, they owe more than they own. You remember the Baxter family. I thought they were millionaires, but they filed for bankruptcy. Came as quite a shock."

"That's what's happened to the Madariagas," Jeff said moodily. His eyes were troubled, and he nervously pushed his knife around with his finger. "I've been trying to think what I could do to help. I'm going over there again this afternoon."

"What do they say when you visit them, Jeff?" Charissa asked. He had offered little detail of those visits, but it was at the beginning of these trips that he had begun behaving rather peculiarly.

"They won't talk about it much, but they're worried sick. As it is, they stand to lose everything. They have a lawyer who's fighting it out with the bank, but I can tell they don't have much hope." He suddenly stood and said, "I think I'll go now."

He left the room without another word, and Elmo glanced at Charissa. "I hope he doesn't do anything foolish."

"Foolish? In what way?"

"Jeff's infatuated with that woman. I've tried to talk him out of it, but he won't listen. And after all, it is none of my business."

"I know that."

Charissa said, "He may well do something foolish, Elmo. He's more than infatuated—he's in love with her."

"You think she loves him?"

Charissa said evenly, "No. I think she loves only herself."

Damita saw that Jeff was nervous the minute he arrived at the town house. "You seem troubled, Jeff. Is something wrong with your practice?"

"Oh, no, not in the least. It's going very well, indeed. As a matter of fact," Jeff said, "I'm worried about you."

Damita forced a smile, saying, "You've been a comfort, Jeff. We found out that some people we thought were friends were not, but you've been steadfast."

"Damita, I don't have any smoothness or any way with words, so I'll just say what's on my mind."

"Of course, Jeff. What is it?"

"Damita, I want you to marry me."

Damita had, of course, seen that Jeff cared for her. At one point, his obvious infatuation had amused her. She had even teased her mother about it, saying more than once, "I may marry that Kaintock. Would that make me a Kaintockess?"

Later on, she had realized that he was truly a good man, but now as she faced him, struck by his proposal, she could not answer.

Jeff saw her hesitate and reached out and took her hand. "I know I'm not the kind of man you think of as a husband. My manners aren't refined. I'm not handsome. I'm not a lot of things that a woman like you would want, but I love you, Damita, and I'll try my best to make you happy. And I would take care of your family."

His words moved her. "Jeff," she said gently, "you do me honor, but I don't love you. Not in the way a woman should love a husband."

"I know that," Jeff answered, "but I think you would come to feel something for me in time."

At that moment, Damita felt a tremendous compulsion. She had slept little the past weeks, ever since Pennington had first informed them of the impending tragedy. She had racked her brain, trying to think of a way out. *How easy it would be just to marry this man and let him take all the worry!* She studied his face, and the temptation was stronger than she would have believed possible. But at the same time, something in her would not permit this. She said quietly, "Jeff, you must give me time to think this over, and I want you to think it over, too. A man should never marry a woman who doesn't love him. I know you think I'd change, and I might, but there are no guarantees."

Jeff kissed her hand. "All right," he said. "I won't change my mind, but I hope you will. I would like nothing better than to take care of you, Damita."

Chapter seventeen

Charissa left the clinic early. Upon reaching the house, she walked into the kitchen, pulled off her hat, and sat wearily on a tall stool next to a counter. "Rose, could I have a cup of tea, do you think?"

"Of course, Charissa." Rose put on the kettle on the stove, then asked Charissa about her day at the clinic. Something in Charissa's tone caught her attention. When the kettle boiled, Rose made the tea, poured it into two china cups, put them in saucers, and sat down beside the young girl. "You look tired," she said.

"I suppose I am, a little bit."

"You work too hard. I'm going to tell Dr. Jeff to give you more time off."

"No, don't do that, Rose. I enjoy the work." Picking up the teacup, Charissa sipped, then gasped, saying, "This is hot!"

"Can't get a cup of tea too hot," Rose said, smiling. She was an attractive woman with coal-black hair almost as dark as Charissa's, but she had startling light-blue eyes.

As the women drank their tea, Rose saw that Charissa remained tense. She asked casually, "What do you think about Dr. Jeff's asking Miss Madariaga to marry him?"

Charissa grimaced. "I didn't know you knew."

"You can't have secrets in a house, even one with as few servants as this one." She waited for Charissa to answer her question.

When she didn't, Rose's face grew serious. "You're troubled about it, aren't you?"

"Yes, I am. You have to remember, Rose, I know that woman. I was her slave, and that's a powerful way to learn about people."

"Is she really that bad?"

"She had me beaten for something that was her own fault—spilling some wine on her dress. She was only seventeen at the time, but she hasn't changed."

"I wonder why Dr. Whitman can't see that."

Charissa shook her head, and a wry bitterness filled her voice. "He's blind where she's concerned, but I suppose most people are."

"I think somebody needs to shake him. If his father were alive, perhaps he could do it."

"I doubt it. Nothing can change the way he sees her."

"Have you tried to talk to him?"

"I've talked to him constantly, but I can't go up and say, 'You shouldn't marry that woman. She's a witch,' can I?"

Rose smiled faintly. "I suppose not."

Charissa finished her tea, then gave Rose an apologetic smile. "I am sorry I'm such poor company."

"I think we're all worried about him. I know Dr. Debakky is. I wonder if he's talked to him."

"He tried, but it didn't do any good." Charissa rose and said, "I think I'll lie down awhile before dinner."

"Good. Why don't you take a hot bath? That'll relax you."

"I don't think so now. Maybe later."

Charissa left the kitchen and climbed the stairs to her room. She reached the door, and when she put her hand on the knob, she stopped. An idea grasped her mind. She stood straighter. Her eyes narrowed, and her lips drew into a thin line. *I can't talk to Jeff, but I can talk to Señorita Damita Madariaga. She'll probably have the butler throw me out of the house. It would be just like her. But I've got to try.*

She whirled, ran down the stairs and out the front door, slamming it behind her.

"Who do you say is here, Charles?"

"Miss Charissa Desjardin."

Damita stared at the butler in disbelief. "All right," she said. "Where is she?"

"I put her in the parlor, Miss Damita."

"Thank you, Charles."

Damita stood slowly. Thoughts raced through her mind. She walked to the parlor, and when she entered, she saw her former slave standing in the middle of the room. "Hello, Charissa," she said.

"I'm sorry to trouble you, but I'd like to talk with you."

"Of course."

"Would you mind closing the door? It's a private matter."

Damita, curious, closed the door. She walked over to her guest and asked, "Would you sit down?"

"No, I don't think this will take very long."

"There's nothing wrong with Jeff, is there?"

"Yes, there's something wrong with him."

"You mean he's sick?"

"No, I don't mean that."

Damita thought, *The last time we were in this room together, she was a slave, and I owned her. Now no one would ever know that from looking at her.* She saw the determination in Charissa's face and said, "Just say what you have to say."

"I came to say that you'd make Jeff miserable if you married him."

Damita was incredulous. "That's hardly your business, is it?"

"Yes, it is. He's been very kind to me, as his father was before him. I'd hate to see his life ruined."

"And you think I would ruin it?"

Charissa smiled slightly. "Do you forget how well I know you, Damita?" It was the first time she had called the woman by her first name. "He's not like the young men who chase you around to parties and balls. He's a serious man, and you'd make him very unhappy."

"He doesn't seem to think so."

"He doesn't know you. As a matter of fact, he doesn't know anything about women."

Strangely enough, Damita was not angry at Charissa, and this puzzled her. Ordinarily, if a former servant or slave had spoken to her on such a personal matter, she would have been furious. She marveled at her sense of calm. Suddenly, an idea occurred to her. She leaned forward slightly, and her eyes narrowed. "I see how it is."

Charissa saw something in Damita's eyes that made her ask, "What is it you see?"

"I see why you don't want me to marry him."

"I've told you why. You'd make him unhappy."

"What you don't say is that *you're* in love with him."

As soon as Damita said this, a rich color suffused Charissa's face. Something like guilt washed across the young woman's countenance, and she had difficulty speaking. Charissa stammered, "That's . . . that's not so."

"I think it is."

"No, you're wrong," Charissa said loudly. "He's my brother."

"No, he's not your brother."

Charissa had expected anything but this. She would not have been surprised to see Damita fly into a rage, but the young woman showed a composure that was disturbing. The accusation, true as it was, was one that she could not bear to hear Damita speak. "No, it's not so!" she cried. "You mustn't say things like that."

Damita felt a sudden compassion for the girl. "I'm sorry," she said. "It's very obvious that you are."

Charissa whispered, "It would be a tragedy if you married Jeff. Thank you for seeing me." She strode to the door, opened it, and fled.

Damita watched her go. *What a strange thing,* she thought. *But Jeff would never care for her, except as an object of pity.*

She walked over to the window and watched Charissa as she climbed into her carriage. When the carriage disappeared from view, she whispered, "I'm sorry for her, but I'll do anything to save my family." She turned from the window, and a resolution that she had made earlier became stronger. *There's* got *to be some way to solve this financial mess. If I could get the bank to agree to just one year, we sold this house, and we had a good crop, I'll bet we could at least hang on to the plantation.*

She went to her room and put on a traveling dress and a bonnet. On her way to the front door, she told her mother, "I'm going out to the plantation."

Elena showed surprise. Thinner since her husband's death, the widow now had new lines of worry in her face. "Why are you going there?"

"I'm going to talk to Napier."

"What in the world for?"

"I've been wanting to talk to him about the plantation. If we rearrange things there so that we're assured of cutting expenses, and if we get an extension from the bank, I'm hopeful we'll be able to save the place. Don't worry, Mother. I'll probably stay overnight. I'll be back in the morning." Kissing Elena, she turned and left the house.

"You don't know what you're talking about, Miss Damita," said Claude Napier, the overseer of the Madariaga plantation. He was a strong, bulky man with blunt features, small hazel eyes, and a mouth like a catfish, usually twisted in a sneer. He had listened as Damita explained what she wanted, but now he was impatient. "Do you think we haven't tried all them things before?"

"But this is an emergency, Napier. If we don't do something, we'll lose this plantation. Then you'll be out of a place just as we will."

Napier looked down at Damita with disdain. "You never gave the plantation a thought until now. In all these years, what do you think I've been doing? I've been struggling to make it pay, and all the time your father was out gambling money away."

"Don't you speak of my father!" Damita snapped, her eyes flashing. "I won't hear a word about it."

Napier said, "Have it your own way, but I'm telling you right now that there's no way to make this place pay enough to get it out of debt."

"I'll have to see what I can do myself."

As she was leaving, Napier called out, "What do you think you can do? You don't know the first thing about growing cotton."

This was a forceful truth, but Damita did not turn to answer. She climbed into her carriage and said to the driver, "Take me back to the city, please."

As the carriage started with a violent jerk, she was thrown back but did not even rebuke the driver. All the way back to the city, her mind worked, trying to find some way of escape. She felt small and helpless and vulnerable, and fear was a coldness that filled her from head to toe.

I may have to marry Jeff. She closed her eyes and tried to think of another way. No ideas came, and she began to wonder what it would be like to be married to the doctor. *He's a good man. He's not handsome, and he's certainly not the kind of man I've always wanted, but he wouldn't be a cruel husband. It would be good for Mama to have the security. And he would take care of all of us. With his financial support, we'd be secure for life.*

All the way back to New Orleans, Damita thought wildly about her options. She instructed her driver to take her to the wharf. She knew little enough about how business was conducted there, but she knew she could ask Yancy about the price of cotton.

Getting out, she told the driver to wait and walked toward Devereaux's office. As she stepped inside, she saw Yancy speaking with an attractive young woman with curly brown hair and twinkling blue eyes. He saw Damita and smiled. "Miss Madariaga, I would like for you to meet a good friend of mine from Shreveport. This is Mrs. Lucy Adcock."

The two women exchanged greetings, and Yancy said, "Mrs. Adcock needs to get to the depot, and I can't leave the office. Would you possibly be able to show her the way, Miss Damita?"

"Of course, it'd be no trouble at all."

"I wouldn't dream of putting you out."

"It isn't far. Yancy, I'd like to see you for a moment when I come back."

"I'll be here all day." He turned and said, "It's so good to see you. You tell Howard that I appreciate his offer."

"I hope you'll take him up on it."

Yancy shrugged. "Who knows? Take care, Lucy."

The two women left the office, and Damita said, "My carriage is here. Why don't we go in that? It's only a few blocks, but it's cold today."

"That would be very nice."

The two women climbed into the carriage, and Damita gave the instructions. As the carriage moved forward, she asked, "Have you known Yancy for a long time?"

"For quite a while. You see, my husband and I bought his plantation just outside of Shreveport."

"Oh, I see! Is it a large place?"

"Very large. Yancy never told you about it?"

"No, he never has."

"It's really quite a story. Yancy took over the place when he was a very young man. I don't know how he scraped together enough money to make a down payment. The plantation had gotten rundown, but it had possibilities." Lucy Adcock shook her head. "We didn't know him in those early days, but later on, we found out that he had worked night and day, year-round, never taking a vacation. And he made a fine place out of it. I wish you could see it."

"You and your husband bought it?"

"Yes, we did. Yancy worked like a slave to pay it off, and as soon as it was in the clear, he put it up for sale. It's beautiful." Lucy Adcock's eyes sparkled. "He not only worked on the land, but he made the house a showplace. Howard and I have been so happy there."

"I didn't know Yancy was that skilled—running a plantation *and* restoring a home."

"Oh, there's nobody like him!" The woman hesitated, then said, "As a matter of fact, I came to see him about coming back and managing the place for Howard."

"Managing it?"

"Yes, we heard about his bad fortune. He made little of it, but it hurt him to lose everything he had. So, Howard and I talked about it, and we thought how wonderful it would be if he'd return and just take over. Howard works too hard, but with Yancy there, he and I would have lots of freedom. We could even travel abroad."

"Do you think Yancy will come?"

"I don't know. Howard has offered him a most lucrative position, but Yancy has bad memories of all those hard, lean years when he worked like a slave. He did some of the plowing himself. He was more of a slave than any of the black people who worked with him. Those were difficult days for him, but I hope he moves back to Shreveport. Have you known him long?"

Damita answered, "For quite a while. I think it's wonderful that you made him an offer like that."

Chapter eighteen

March had come to New Orleans, a warm, early spring that drove out the cold breezes. Damita had ordinarily welcomed the season's change, but now, with the crisis she woke up thinking about every day, she took no joy in it. She struggled constantly with the question of what to do, and the conversation she had had with Lucy Adcock stayed with her.

Jeff had been insistent, but she had put him off as gently as she could. Now, early one Friday afternoon, she was walking nervously about the house, remembering Jeff's visit the night before. He exerted more pressure this time. Moving to the window, Damita thought about how he had urged her, saying, "Damita, I want to take care of you and your family. I think we ought to marry at once."

Now, looking out blindly at those who passed by on the street below, Damita knew that things could not go on as they had. She had met with Asa Pennington several days prior, and he had admonished her more stringently than ever before. "Something has to be done, my dear young lady. It's not just the bank, but other creditors."

Damita had asked him the question that had been on her mind lately. "Suppose we had a good manager for the plantation. Is there any way that the bank could arrange to give us more time?"

Pennington had been rather negative, but Damita had seen something in his eyes that had encouraged her. Turning, she put on her coat and hat and left the house. She had her driver take her to the cotton market, where she found Yancy working on papers in his office. He smiled and stood to his feet. "A welcome relief from these dull things."

"Yancy, I need to speak to you."

"Go ahead."

"Isn't there someplace we could go, where we won't be interrupted?"

Yancy looked puzzled. "I suppose so. Nothing very urgent this afternoon. I can close early." He picked up his coat, put it on, then settled his white hat with the broad brim on his head. "Come along. We should be able to find a quiet corner. Have you ever been to Luigi's?"

"No, I don't think so."

"It's a small place. It'll be empty this time of the day, but they make good *café au lait.*"

She accompanied him down the street, and he turned into a small café. A compact man with a broad smile greeted them. "Ah, Mr. Devereaux, you're early for a meal."

"Just *café au lait* for both of us."

"I will fix it myself."

"Right over here, Damita."

There was only one other couple at the other end of the room. The sun shone in, lighting Yancy's face as he sat down across from her. She studied him carefully. There was a looseness about him, and his face was smooth and tan. His body was angular and strong-looking—the body of a man who made his living with his muscles.

Suddenly she realized she knew very little of this man. He was smiling faintly, but she knew that behind that smile was a hunger and a loneliness and a temper that could sweep a woman away. She knew that his nerves were not easily touched by small things, but as she watched him, she sensed that he was somehow troubled by deeper issues.

After the waiter had brought the coffee, she ignored it and leaned forward, saying, "I've been thinking of something ever since I met your friend Mrs. Adcock."

"She's a fine lady, and her husband's a fine man."

"She told me about your early struggles to make the plantation pay. She said you worked harder than any man should have to."

Yancy turned his head slightly to one side and studied her. "Why did she tell you about all that?"

"Because she was so anxious for you to come and manage their plantation. Are you going to do it?"

"I don't think so."

"Why not?"

"I guess I worked myself too hard when I was building that place up. I still have bad dreams about it. I don't suppose you have any idea of what it's like, working until you can't speak properly, and falling into bed, too tired to eat. Those years took something out of me. If I had it to do over again, I wouldn't."

"I'm sorry to hear that, Yancy."

Her words startled him. "Why should you say that? What difference does it make to you?"

"Because I'm going to ask you to do something, and now I know you won't."

Yancy picked up his cup, sipped the coffee, then said, "Why don't you ask me, and let me make up my own mind about what I'm going to do?"

A tiny ray of hope flickered inside Damita. She said quietly, "I want you to come and manage our plantation."

He was surprised and showed it. "Why would I want to do that?"

"There's no reason. I know you hate farming. I know it would be hard for you, but it's the only hope we have. I've been down to talk to the banker, Mr. Pennington. I believe that if a good man were there to take over, he would give us one year. It would be a terrible year, about like those early years for you in Shreveport, but I'd give up everything and so would my mother, if we could only hang on to the place."

Yancy was almost distracted by the beauty he saw in her face, in the rich curve of her lips and the ivory shading of her skin. He put these thoughts out of his mind and studied her more closely. "I know you've been having difficulty."

"It's more than that. It's the end of everything for us. We won't have anything, Yancy."

"I ran into Dr. Debakky the other day. He told me his partner had asked you to marry him."

Damita was startled. "He . . . he has."

"That would be an easy way. Doctors have lots of money. The bank would do anything for him."

Damita felt thoroughly uncomfortable. She held her head high and said, "I have been tempted, but I just can't do it." She hesitated, then asked, "Would you please do one thing for me? Come and look at the plantation, and then look at the figures, before you say no."

Yancy suddenly smiled. "All right. I can do that, but no guarantees."

"I understand. Thank you, Yancy."

When she arrived back home, Damita explained her plan to her mother, and Elena said excitedly, "Oh, if he could only help us, Damita!"

"Don't say a word to him, Mother. We mustn't pressure him."

Four days later, Damita stood outside her father's study. The door was closed, and she stared at it as if it held some answer for her. Yancy had accompanied her to the plantation. She had introduced him to Claude Napier, who had been boorish as usual, but Yancy had spent two days walking over the grounds and lots of time talking to the slaves. This displeased the overseer, and he said in a surly fashion, "There's no way to save this place. I done told her that."

Damita also knew that Yancy had visited Mr. Pennington, although he had not revealed the results of his meeting. Now he had been all day in the study, pausing only long enough to eat a light lunch. Damita had sent it in by one of the maids, for he had demanded to be left alone.

As she stood by the light of the lamp that lit the hallway, she thought, *What will I do if he says no?* The thought frightened her. She reached out and knocked firmly on the door. When she heard his voice, she entered.

"Hello, Damita." Yancy was in his shirtsleeves, standing beside the window. She saw nothing in his face that indicated his intentions.

"I couldn't wait any longer, Yancy. Can you tell me anything?"

Yancy walked over to the desk, which was covered with papers. She could see that he had filled up many pages with figures and notes. "It's not going to be easy."

His words renewed Damita's hope. "You mean you'll help us?"

"Damita, it would take a miracle, but I'll try. I'll try, if that's what you want."

"Oh, yes, Yancy! That's what I want!"

She walked toward him and put out her hand, but he shook his head. "Wait a minute. Let me tell you the rest of it."

"What is it?"

"If I come, I must have complete authority over all money and everything that goes on at the plantation. You will have to sell this house. You might realize a little money on it. I've talked to Mr. Pennington, and he'll let us have just barely enough to make a crop, but we'll have to sell off some of the slaves. We'll work with a small crew. If we get a good cotton crop, he will give us another year. Two good years would do it, but it's going to be nothing but misery."

"I don't care about that."

"That's what you say now," he said. "But you've never had to really do without, Damita. This means no new dresses, no new shoes, no running around to the opera every time you take a notion. And the same is true for your mother. It'll be poor doings."

"Do you think you can save us, Yancy?"

"I don't know."

"I'll do anything to keep a place for my family."

Yancy suddenly reached out and pulled her close. Damita did not resist but looked in his face. She saw something in his eyes that reminded her of those moments when she had almost given herself to him, and now she whispered, "What are you doing, Yancy?"

"I know you once had something in your heart for me."

"Please, don't put it on that basis. Don't talk of love."

"I can't promise that."

Damita put her hands on his chest and tried to free herself, but his grip was too strong.

Then Yancy released her and said quietly, "There's a real woman somewhere in you, and I'm hoping sometime, when things get bad enough, you'll turn that woman loose." He laughed and said, "And I hope I'm there when it happens."

PART FOUR

· 1835–1836 ·

Yancy

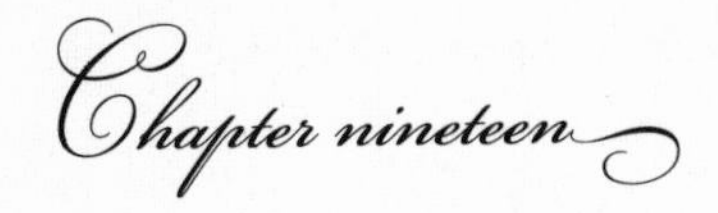

Chapter nineteen

As Jeff stepped out of the house and walked across the yard to the carriage shed, a movement overhead caught his attention. He looked up to see a flight of swallows divide the air in evanescent shapes, making a kaleidoscopic pattern. He watched them with a sense of delight and longing; since moving to New Orleans, he had spent little time in the out-of-doors he loved. He had promised himself that he would go hunting and fishing, but the workload had been so great that he was never able to do it.

Now, as he stood still, a butterfly fluttered across the flowers that Rose had planted. It was a red admiral, and its wings made a delicate lens for the sunlight to pass through. The butterfly moved like a flake of color glittering in the air. The beauty of the tiny creature created a mood in Jeff Whitman, and he suddenly wished for some simplicity in life. He'd had that once, but now everything, personal and professional, was complicated. He shook his shoulders with an angry motion and hurried to his buggy.

Jimmy Bledsoe, who handled the horses, had hitched up the bay. "Mornin', Doctor."

"Good morning, Jimmy. Got 'im all hitched, I see."

"Yes, sir." Bledsoe was a small, wiry fellow of eighteen with red hair and blue eyes whom Debakky had hired recently. "You want me to drive you, Dr. Whitman?"

"No, Jimmy, I'm not going far today." Getting into the buggy, Jeff took the reins from the young man, then commented, "I'd like to be going fishing today."

"Why don't we go, sir?" Jimmy asked eagerly. "Nothin' I'd like better than some good redfish."

"I'd like to, but too much to do. See you tonight."

Jeff spoke to the horse, who picked up into a fast pace. He had intended to go straight to the hospital, but he changed his mind and drove instead to the Madariaga house. He found a place for the buggy, tied the horse, patted him on the neck, and walked to the front entrance. As he passed through the iron gate, Jeff could hear voices and the sounds of furniture being moved. Knocking on the door, he waited, and it was opened by Yancy Devereaux.

"Hello, Doctor. Come in."

"Hello, Devereaux. What's going on?"

"We're in the middle of a sale."

"What are you selling?"

"All of the furniture."

Jeff stared at Devereaux, who was in his shirtsleeves and evidently had been working; sweat shone on his brow. The April sun was rising and brought heat to the city. "What's the purpose of that?"

"We've got to make some money, Jeff."

Jeff then saw Damita. She had a displeased look on her face, and he removed his hat, asking, "Selling everything?"

"Well, almost," Yancy answered for her. He exchanged glances with Damita, who seemed upset. "I guess I'll get the items in the blue room ready to go."

"We're not selling that washstand that belonged to my great-grandmother."

Yancy looked at her for a moment with a calm expression. "We'll talk about it later," he said and left the room.

"What in the world is this? What's going on?" Jeff said.

"I haven't had a chance to tell you about it, Jeff." Damita looked weary and frustrated. She picked up a newspaper and began to fan herself. "I've asked Yancy to take over the plantation and try to make a paying proposition out of it." She explained the details and added,

"Yancy says we have to sell all of our belongings here in the town house. I didn't realize how attached I could get to things, but almost every item in this house has some sentimental value."

Jeff was shocked at the turn of events. "Is all this really necessary, Damita?"

"Yes, it is. It's the only way to save the plantation, and Yancy's the only man who can do it."

"But I thought he was a clerk of some sort."

"He is now, but he took an old plantation in Shreveport from nothing to one of the finest places in the county. I'm praying he can do the same thing with this one, but it's hard. I had to agree to let him make all the decisions."

"Surely you're not going to let him sell items that mean something to you!"

Damita gave him a desperate look. "We have to do it. He's our only hope, Jeff. I get upset with him, but I promised that he could have full control."

"Damita, if you'd marry me, we could save this house and the plantation, too. I don't like to sound like a braggart, but my father left me well-off."

Damita smiled wanly, reached out, and put her hand on his arm. "You don't know how much I'd like to do that, but I just can't, Jeff. I don't love you like that."

Just then, Yancy came back into the room, followed by Elena, who was in tears. "Yancy, we can't sell that bed! It's a family heirloom."

"I'm sorry, Mrs. Madariaga, but we've got to have cash."

"How much is the bed? I'll buy it," Jeff said impetuously.

"Oh, no, Jeff, you can't do that," Damita insisted. She saw his intention. "You can't buy all of our furniture."

"Certainly I can!"

Yancy shrugged. "If you pay the top dollar, you can have it."

"Is there no sentiment in you, Yancy Devereaux?" Elena cried.

Damita walked over to her mother and suggested, "Mama, go out to the plantation. This is too hard on you."

"That would be a good idea, I think," Yancy said quickly. "As a matter of fact, why don't you go with them, Damita? I can take care of this."

"No, I'm going to stay here and help you."

"You mean," Yancy grinned, "you're going to stay here and argue with me over every piece of furniture."

Jeff Whitman watched the two and suddenly felt anger, and he knew it was foolish. He had made his offer, and Damita had refused it. He reiterated, "Damita, anything you really want to keep, I'll buy and store it until you can use it."

"Thank you, Jeff, but I can't let you do that."

Jeff sighed and asked, "When will you be moving to the plantation?"

"Today," Yancy said. "The new owner of this house is coming tomorrow, and we have to be out of it."

"After you get settled in, I'll come out and visit." Jeff departed, feeling somehow left out. Yancy Devereaux had taken over, and this gave him an uneasy feeling. *That fellow has no sensitivity,* he thought. *I don't know why Damita would want his help rather than mine.*

He drove to the hospital, and when he arrived, he found that Charissa had preceded him. "You're late," she said as he entered the surgeon's room where the doctors kept their street clothes.

"I went by Damita's. You know what they're doing?" He changed his coat and explained the Madariagas' plan. He ended by saying angrily, "That fellow Devereaux—she's given him full authority."

"It sounds like a good plan to me. If he's a skillful overseer, maybe he can save the plantation for them."

"I don't like it. It was painful to see them having to sell their furniture like beggars."

"It may do them some good."

Jeff turned and faced Charissa, his eyes wide with surprise. "What do you mean by that?"

"They've never had any real needs, Jeff. Want tends to mature people. You don't learn from good times but from bad. Maybe this will make them view others a little differently."

"You just don't understand, Charissa. They're not used to this sort of thing, and it's unnecessary. Why, if she'd marry me, it would solve all their problems."

Charissa shook her head. "No, it wouldn't," she said quietly and left the room.

Jeff stared after her and tried to understand what she meant. *That young woman is an enigma. She just doesn't understand how it is with me, how much I love Damita.*

~

Damita stepped down from the carriage, and a strange feeling overtook her. She looked over the fine, old home, then ran her eyes across the fields that spread out in every direction. *I've taken all this for granted for years. It was just here, and now that I might lose it, I realize how much it means to me.*

Yancy had tied up the horses, and now he said, "We've got a lot of work to do, Damita."

"I know."

"I know you think I'm a miser, but we have a long way to go before we make this place into a paying proposition."

"I know." She turned and faced him. "I know I'm spoiled, and I've never had to work. None of us have. You'll just have to be patient with us."

"Patient as Job. By the way, I'm going to have a talk with Napier. I think you ought to be there."

"He's an unpleasant man. I've tried to talk to him, but I've never been able to like him."

"When I was here, I talked to the slaves, and . . . I might as well be blunt. He's forced himself on some of the female slaves."

Damita stared at him. "I didn't know that."

"It's a common thing, but it's going to stop. He's also too free with that whip of his. That's going to stop too. Come along. You want to change clothes, or go as you are?"

"These will be all right."

The two walked past the main house, past the line of cabins where the slaves lived, and to the shack where Napier lived alone. He was sitting outside and stood as the pair arrived.

"Need to talk with you, Napier."

Claude stared at him without expression. "What is it?" he growled.

"Things are going to be different around here from now on,"

Yancy said. "We need to get it straight. I want you to hear it from Miss Madariaga."

"Hear what?"

"That I'm in complete charge of this plantation."

Napier glared at him. "I've been the overseer a long time!"

"You still are, but I'm the overseer of the overseer. Isn't that right, Miss Madariaga?"

"That's right, Napier. You must obey any orders that Mr. Devereaux gives you."

"The first order I'll give you is this, Napier: You will not take advantage any longer of the female slaves. The first time I hear of it, you are off the place."

Napier shot a glance at Damita but then said truculently, "Who's been telling you tales?"

"You haven't been too careful to hide your tracks. I'm not arguing about this. Do you understand what I'm saying?"

"Any more orders?" he asked, sneering.

"Lots of them, and here's another. You've beaten some of the slaves. That's all over."

"You can't work field slaves without discipline."

"I'll do the disciplining, but if I catch you whipping anyone, we'll have more than words. Now, what are you doing here? You don't have enough work to do?"

Damita was standing slightly behind Yancy. She saw the huge muscles in Napier's arms and shoulders tense, and for a moment she was afraid he would attack his new boss. He was a brute of a man, and she had heard about how he had beaten men senseless.

"If you've got anything to say, say it now," Yancy said coolly. He was facing Napier, standing loosely with his feet slightly spread and his arms at his sides.

"You'll see quick enough that babying these slaves won't do," he answered. "But now I've got work to do out in the east field." He turned and walked toward the stable, and rebellion showed in the set of his straight back and the way he held his head.

"I don't know why Papa kept him on so long. He's a cruel man."

"He'll have to toe the line or get out. As a matter of fact, I've got half a mind to run him off now. It'll come sooner or later, I think. But there's something else that we've got to talk about."

"All right, Yancy. What is it?"

"We've got to get rid of about half of the slaves. My plan is to keep the best ones, treat them well, and encourage them so that they'll work hard. When I took a look, I saw a lot of field hands just loafing. Some of them were too old to be in the fields. Slavery's a bad system, and I see the worst of it here."

"If that's what you think, then I'm sure it must be done."

"I'm going to be busy, so I'm giving you the chore of deciding which ones to sell."

"Me? Why, I can't do that! Some of these have been with us for years."

"I'm sure they have, and you've always been interested in their welfare!" Yancy said sharply.

Damita's eyes flew open at his statement. It was true. She had never given any thought to the welfare of the slaves, and she knew he was thinking about the beating that she arranged for Charissa. "I can't do it."

"You'll have to. I can't do everything. First, decide which ones we really need. Then go to your rich friends, people you know who will treat them decently. They'll be glad to do you a favor, won't they?"

"I'd be like a beggar."

Yancy grinned. "That's what you are, Damita. We all are, in one way or another. I don't think you've understood yet how hard this is going to be. It'll be a miracle if we make it through the next two years, so let's settle it right now. You've agreed to do what I've said, and now I'm saying to help me get rid of half of these slaves. Yes or no?"

Damita's face flushed. She hated to take orders, but as she looked at his face, she understood that he expected her to refuse. Stubbornness rose in her, and she said, "All right, I'll do it then."

Yancy was somewhat surprised but nodded with approval. "Try to keep the families together," he said. "I've seen babies taken from women, and men and women who lived as husband and wife torn apart, without a thought. Do your best for them."

"All right," Damita said, suddenly resolved to do this thing well. "I will."

Damita returned home exhausted. The entire month had been trying. She had struggled over her task of thinning out the slaves, and it had been more difficult than she could believe. She had discovered that she knew almost nothing about them or their personal lives, and now that she did, letting some go had been grim business. She had visited all of her friends, asking them to buy the slaves, and the task had been humiliating.

The rigors of the first month at the plantation weighed heavily on Damita. She herself had worked as she had never thought possible. When she wasn't out trying to get someone to buy the slaves, she was helping Yancy, because he always had something more for her to do. She once had had no idea of the enormity of work necessary to keep a plantation running, but she knew it now!

As she entered, she heard her mother's voice and called, "Mama, where are you?"

Elena stepped quickly into the foyer, her face anxious. "Damita, I'm so glad you're home. Yancy's been looking for you."

"Do you know where he is?"

"He's at the blacksmith's shop," Elena answered. She looked at her daughter. "I'm worried about you. Are you getting enough rest?"

Damita smiled and said, "Of course I am." She left the house and walked to where the blacksmith worked. From a distance, she saw Yancy shoeing a horse. She stopped and watched. He was stripped to the waist and sweat glistened all over his body. She had never seen him like this. He was a strong man, and the years he had spent doing hard physical labor showed.

She walked into the shop. "Hello, Yancy."

Yancy looked up and grinned. "You come to help me shoe horses?" He put the horse's hoof down, patted him, then picked up his shirt and put it on. "How did it go?"

"I managed to sell them all at last."

"You've done a good job."

"I've hated every minute of it."

"I can imagine. You've got a good heart. Hard-hearted people wouldn't have thought a minute about it."

Damita suddenly smiled. "You're paying me compliments. You must want something."

"Just a drink of water. Come along, and tell me all about what you've been doing."

The two walked over to the well, and he drew water from the bucket. Both drank from the dipper, and he listened as she described, with some pride, how she had placed the last four slaves that morning.

"Who bought them?"

"I went to Lewis. His family has a very large plantation. He was glad to take them off my hands, and for a good price, too." She laughed. "I raised the figures you gave me."

"You're getting to be a steely businesswoman."

It was pleasant standing in the sun, and now that the job of selling off the slaves was over, Damita felt relieved. She looked at Yancy and said suddenly, "I hate slavery. I found that out."

"So do I. You know, Damita, it does something to a person to own a slave. Once you own one, you're saying that a man or a woman is no more than a horse or a dog. When you 'own' another person, you put yourself in that position."

"I never thought of it like that."

"I've always thought slavery was a horrible mistake. We'll pay for it someday."

"Some say that the South will pull away someday and become a separate nation."

"The North will never let that happen. If you listen to—"

A young black woman suddenly interrupted: "Mr. Yancy, come quick!"

"What's wrong?"

"It's Mr. Napier—he's whippin' my daddy!"

Yancy's face darkened, and without a word, he ran toward the barn. Damita followed with the young girl. When they reached the far side, she saw a slave stretched out on the ground and Napier whipping him savagely. She saw the blood and the lash marks on his back, and it sickened her.

As Napier drew back to strike again, Yancy grabbed the whip and ripped it from Napier's hand. Then he grasped the man's arm and whirled him around, his voice brittle with anger: "I told you, Napier, never to whip a slave on this place!"

"You keep out of this! This boy was uppity."

"Get up, Jake," Yancy said, not taking his eyes off Napier's face. "You can go now."

Napier's fury boiled. "Give me back that whip!"

"Here's your whip. Now take it, and get off this place."

Napier took the whip, and his hazel eyes glittered with hatred. "You think you're somebody, don't you?"

"I know who you are—you're nobody. Now get off this place!"

Napier suddenly threw a clumsy blow that caught Yancy in the chest and drove him backward. He cursed and threw the whip back to strike Yancy with it. Damita cried out, "Look out, Yancy!"

But the blow was never delivered. Yancy threw himself forward and struck the big man squarely in the mouth. The big man roared and countered with a punch, and the two men began to exchange blows. Damita could not move. She had never seen such a thing. It was a brutal display; both men were strong and able, and both had obviously been in brawls before. One blow caught Yancy low on the jaw and drove him to the ground, and Napier ran forward, aiming a kick, but Yancy grabbed his foot and twisted it. Napier fell to the ground, and Yancy jumped to his feet. Blood dripped from the faces of both men.

Napier took a direct blow to his temple and started to collapse. Yancy rained blow after blow on the man's face and body, and finally Napier fell, crying out, "Enough—I've had enough!"

Yancy's shirt was ripped to shreds, and blood poured from a cut over his eye and from his lips. "Get off this place now!" he said.

Napier got to his feet, groaning, and staggered away.

"You've got thirty minutes to disappear. If you don't, I'll shoot you."

Damita ran to Yancy and looked up into his face. "You've got to get something cold on those cuts." She quickly led him to the big house and into the kitchen. Fortunately, her mother was not there at the moment, and Damita nervously dipped cloths in cool water and wiped Yancy's face.

He murmured, "I thought I'd given up all this, but he didn't leave me any choice."

Damita was sponging away the blood. "You've got a cut over your eyebrow. I don't know if it should be stitched or not."

Yancy ran his fingers over it. "No. Just get some plaster and pull it together."

Damita's hands were trembling as she worked over his wounds. He had taken some hard blows. His right eye was almost closed already, and his lips were puffy.

"Nothing like a good, rousing beating to make a man realize how small he is."

"He was a beast! I wish you had shot him."

"I should have gotten rid of him before this." He reached up and caught her hand, the one that held the cloth. "You make a pretty good nurse."

"I . . . I haven't had much practice."

Damita stood, his hand holding hers, looking into his battered face. "I wish things like this didn't have to happen."

"We've all got to eat our peck of dirt, as someone said. You know, if you married Whitman, you wouldn't have to go through such adventures."

Damita didn't answer but pulled her arm loose and dipped the cloth again in water. "Hold this over your eye for a while. Maybe it'll help." She gently touched his cheek. Her eyes were tender. "I know you're not doing this for money, but for us. I didn't mean for you to get in a fight."

Yancy grinned, then winced. "I'm too old to cry, and it hurts too much to laugh. We've got a long way to go, Damita, but I think we'll make it."

"Yes," Damita answered, studying his battered features, "we'll make it, but I wish you didn't have to bleed in the process."

Charissa leaned back in the carriage, listening as Matthew Denton spoke of the sermon that they'd just heard. From time to time, she glanced at him, noting the strong jawline and the healthy glow of his face. He was not handsome but roughly attractive, and as he spoke, she thought of how strange it was that she should be riding along in a carriage—she who had not been a Christian only a year ago—with such a devout man.

"So, I agree with the pastor that there is such a thing as election. I'm not certain that it's quite as prominent as he seems to make it."

"What's your opinion of election and predestination?"

"Well," Matthew said slowly, "I think God is sovereign. He can do anything He pleases, but I think He chooses certain people such as Paul, for example. The Scripture says that he was a chosen vessel, but the pastor seems to think that Paul had no choice at all, that God simply made him become an apostle. I can't quite believe that." He turned to her and smiled warmly. "I think we've all got wills of our own."

Charissa agreed and sat contentedly as the horses clopped along the cobblestone streets. She enjoyed Matthew Denton's company. He was the son of a prominent businessman, who owned a large hardware store and a plantation just north of the city. Charissa and Matthew had met after church services, and he had driven her home several times.

He was a straightforward young man; he always said what was on the top of his mind. Charissa could tell that he was contemplating something, and she asked, "What are you thinking about, Matthew?"

"I'm thinking about you."

"That's flattering."

"I'm wondering if you've ever thought about me as a man you might marry."

Charissa was stunned. She could see in his large blue eyes that he was serious. "Why, I never thought of it, Matthew."

"I'm asking you now to think of it. I've grown very fond of you, Charissa."

"But you don't know anything about me."

"I know you're a fine Christian young woman. I know you're smart, because you're a nurse. I know we get along real well."

"But that's not enough to make a marriage."

"I'm just asking you to think about it." He smiled and looked very boyish. "I'd make a good husband. You'd never know meanness from me."

Charissa took a deep breath and said, "Matthew, I need to tell you something. You may know it already, but if you don't, you should."

"Know what, Charissa?"

"I'm a quadroon, Matthew."

Denton looked at her, lifting his eyebrows. "I never knew that."

"You need to know also that I was born a slave. For a while, I was the property of New Orleans people. Their name is Madariaga."

"Alfredo Madariaga?"

"Yes, I was his daughter's maid for a few years."

"No, I didn't know anything about that." Denton held the lines loosely in his hands as the horses pulled the carriage along at a fast clip. "You don't look like it. Why, your skin is whiter than mine."

"I am, though. My mother was a slave. So, you see, that makes a difference."

"Not to me."

His guilelessness was both amusing and sad to Charissa. "It would make a difference to your family," she said.

Denton shook his head. "I don't think it would, but it doesn't matter to me."

Charissa felt affection for the young man, but nothing more. "In any case, I don't intend to marry for a long time—if ever. I may give my whole life to medicine."

"That wouldn't be good. You need to have a husband and a family."

"I'm not sure that will ever happen to me. Matthew, please, I wish you wouldn't speak of this again."

Denton was silent for a moment, then shook his head. "I can't promise that, Charissa. I've grown mighty fond of you."

"I had an offer of marriage yesterday, Jefferson."

Charissa was sipping her coffee after breakfast. Debakky had left early, and she and Jeff had lingered over the meal, talking about the work at the hospital. They had spoken for some time about the yellow fever that was relentlessly attacking the city. Charissa had not really intended to tell Jeff of Denton's words, and now she saw that her news affected him strongly. He sat up straighter, and alarm showed in his eyes.

"An offer of marriage? Who was it from?"

"Matthew Denton."

"Is he the one whose people own the hardware store?"

"Yes, and a very large plantation somewhere."

Jeff began to fidget. He picked up the saltshaker and rolled it around in his hand, staring at it. He was clearly troubled.

Charissa was mildly amused. She had not cared for any of the young men who had called on her, yet Jeff put them all through a strict grilling process. Many of them never bothered to call a second time.

"I'll make it a point to talk to him."

"Oh, I'm sure he'll meet all your standards."

"My standards?"

"Yes. You interrogate all my suitors, wanting to know if they're worthy of me or not."

"I'm going to continue to do it!" Jeff said almost stridently. "I have to look out for you, Charissa."

"I'm sure you'll find Matthew qualified. He's going to be one of the deacons in the church. He's already been chosen. Did you know that?"

"No, I didn't."

"He's very active on the mission board also. He's always in church. Never misses a service."

"That's a good thing."

"He's a savvy businessman too. His family's got money, and he's a hard worker. Would that meet your standards?"

"Don't talk as if I were some kind of a judge, Charissa!"

"That's what you are, Jefferson. You always question those poor young fellows like an ogre."

"I do not!"

"Yes, you do," she said calmly. "What if you wanted to court a young woman, and her father grilled you like that?"

"I'd admire him for it," Jeff said, holding his head up high. "It would be his duty."

"I think you'll have a hard time disqualifying Matthew. He's highly sought after by many young ladies—and by their mothers, I might add."

"What did he say to you?"

"I don't think I should reveal any confidence."

"Did you agree to marry him?"

"Not until after he passes his examination with you."

Jeff flushed. He realized that she was teasing him, which she often did. "Tell me straight out. Do you care for him?"

"I like him very much, but I don't want to marry him. Jeff, you're funny."

"I don't mean to be," he said stiffly. "The truth is, I just want the best for you, Charissa, and—" He hesitated, then smiled. "The truth is, I'd miss you if you were to marry. I'd hate that."

Charissa was silent for a moment, then asked, "What do you think will happen to us when *you* marry?"

Jeff stared at her. "Why, we'd go on, just as we are."

His remark was bittersweet. "You are so naive!" Charissa moaned, shaking her head. "I'm constantly shocked at how much you know about medicine and how little you know about people."

"What are you talking about? Of course we'd go on as we are."

"Jefferson, what wife would want a young woman around? I will leave when you marry."

Jeff considered her statement. He could not think of a thing to say, and Charissa said, "Just give me plenty of warning. That's all I ask." She smiled and saw that he was speechless. "For once in your life, you don't have any answers. Now I know how to handle you when you get rambunctious."

Later that morning, before they left, Jeff waited in the kitchen for Charissa to finish dressing and join him in the buggy for the ride to the hospital. Rose was working about the kitchen as he drank his coffee, and he told her, "Charissa had an offer of marriage."

"I'm not surprised at that. I'm just surprised she hasn't married already. She's such a beautiful young woman."

"I don't think she should marry him."

"Is he a bad man?"

"Well, no."

"Is he a good man?"

"From all I hear, he is."

Rose Bozonnier, the housekeeper, was an astute woman, and she saw that the doctor was troubled. She knew why. She remarked, "She's going to make a wonderful wife, Dr. Whitman. She's compassionate, she's smart, and she's good-natured. She's everything that a man could want. Why, she'd make a perfect wife for a doctor."

"I thought, for a time, that Debakky might be interested in her."

Rose looked at him with kind eyes. "He's not the only doctor in the world."

"She's met all of my doctor friends. She doesn't like any of them."

At that moment, just as Rose opened her mouth to answer,

Charissa came in, and Jeff said, "We've got to hurry. We're late. Good-bye, Rose."

"Good-bye, you two. I'll have a good supper ready for you tonight." She watched the pair from the window as they left and muttered, "Jefferson Whitman, open your eyes!"

In September, when the door to the Madariaga plantation house opened, Lewis Depard was surprised to see Yancy Devereaux. "Hello, Yancy," he said.

"Hello, Lewis. Come visiting?"

"Yes. Is Damita here?"

"She's here. Come on in."

Depard took off his hat and put it on the hall tree.

Yancy said, "Damita told me about your taking the last of our hands and giving them a good place. We both appreciate that."

"Oh, don't bother yourself. We have so many, four more won't matter."

The two were speaking when Damita walked into the foyer. "Lewis, it's so good to see you," she said. She offered her hand, which Lewis kissed.

"You look enchanting as always, Señorita."

"Come into the dining room. We're having *café au lait* and a cake that I made myself."

"You don't do all the cooking, do you, Damita?"

"Oh, no, but I'm learning. We had to keep a cook, or we all would have starved to death."

In the dining room, Damita served the coffee and cake. Lewis entertained them with stories of New Orleans, the balls, the latest opera, and Yancy sat back and watched the pair. He liked Lewis Depard, although the fellow was a fop, of sorts. He had no idea what Damita thought of him.

"Someone's at the door," Yancy said. "Let me get it. Are you expecting anyone, Damita?"

"No."

Yancy went to the door and opened it. Jefferson Whitman was there, and suddenly Yancy's ready sense of humor surfaced. "You've come to join the other suitors, have you, Doctor? Come in."

Jeff entered, took off his hat, and put it on the hall tree, noticing that another was already there. "Other suitors? What do you mean?"

"Come in. We're just having *café au lait.*" Yancy led the way, and when he stepped in, he gave Damita a wink. "The doctor's come to call, Damita."

Lewis turned to speak to Damita, but then his eyes fell on Jefferson. "Oh," he said and fell silent. An awkwardness filled the room. The the last time the two had met, they had been dueling. True enough, they had shot each other with toast, but neither of them knew that.

"Jeff, won't you come in?" Damita asked. She felt as uncomfortable as Lewis, but she saw that Yancy was enjoying himself. She gave him a reproachful look and said to Jeff, "I'm glad you called."

Lewis stood and walked around the table directly toward Jeff. Damita had a horrified thought that he was going to strike him, but instead Lewis said, "Doctor, I was too hasty at that ball. I want to offer my apologies."

Jeff was shocked. Everyone knew that Lewis Depard never apologized.

"Of course I accept your apology. And I offer mine." He put his hand out, and Depard shook it.

"Now, that's much better than trying to shoot each other," Yancy said loudly.

Lewis gave him an irritated look and then turned back to Jeff. "I must tell you, Dr. Whitman, that I am very serious about Damita. I intend to marry her."

"So do I, sir."

For one instant the electricity in the air seemed to crackle, and then Yancy remarked, "I hope we don't have another duel. Those things are terribly time-consuming."

"Yancy," Damita snapped. "Of course there's not going to be another duel. Come in and sit down, Jeff. Tell us what's been happening to you."

Despite all of her attempts, Damita could not bring the two to accept each other fully. They cast hard glances at one another, and it was obvious that neither of them had any intention of leaving. Finally she said, "I'm sorry, but I have work that must be done today. Errands to run. Would you both excuse me?"

She shook hands with both of them. Lewis said, "I will be back to visit when you have more time, Damita."

"So will I," Jeff said loudly.

As the two left, Yancy chuckled, and Damita stared at him coldly. "What are you laughing at, you fool?"

"At the comedy. This is better than a play."

"I don't see anything funny about it."

"You don't? You've lost your sense of humor. I'll tell you what you could do. You could marry both of them."

Damita glared at him. "What are you talking about?"

"They make a pretty good pair, if you put them together. I mean, you've got Jeff, who's sober and responsible and rather boring, and you've got Lewis, who is foolish and quite a bit of fun. You'd have one husband to be serious with and the other to go to balls and be foolish with."

"I think you're the fool, Yancy Devereaux! I never heard such nonsense!" Damita cried. She hurried out of the room, but Yancy ran after her and caught her arm. "Come along. Let's go look at the crop." She stopped and said, "I'm upset, Yancy. That was awful, having both of them here at the same time."

"It'll work out," he said cheerfully. "Come on, I want you to see the fields."

They walked along the rows, and Yancy pointed out things that she had never noticed before: the quality of the cotton, the snowy fullness of the fields. She was silent but interested. She had been around cotton all her life, but never had she watched it grow into a crop, step by step, and she still was shocked at the tremendous amount of labor it had taken. "I never knew how hard it was just to raise cotton."

"It's not a business for lazy men, but it's a fine crop."

"It is beautiful, isn't it? Do you think the price will hold up?"

"I hear that it's good. We'll hope so."

Damita reached out and plucked a bowl, then pulled the white fibers apart. "Who would have thought that something so light could bear the weight of saving a family from ruin?"

"We could lose it all, Damita."

Damita glanced up and saw that Yancy was staring at her in a peculiar fashion. "Don't talk like that."

"That's the way life is. Nothing's certain in this world."

"Nothing's going to happen," she said quickly. "It can't."

"I thought that about the ship I bought into, but it went down. We like to fix things so that they don't change, but they do." He resumed walking, and she joined him. "You remember the immortelles, those decorations that you put on graves?"

"Yes."

"That's just an attempt to fix things. I don't think those immortelles are really immortal. They'll wear out someday, too. You've seen them, old and broken. We're the only thing that's immortal."

"You really believe that? You never talk about religion."

"But I think about it."

"I remember you told me one time you were afraid of some things, of growing old, of being alone, and you said you were afraid to face God."

"I'm still afraid of those things, but sometimes I think making peace with God is the easiest thing. Nothing we can do about growing old, but we can do something about God."

"What do you mean?"

"I mean we can honor Him and love Him."

Damita was silent. She had never heard this sort of talk from Yancy before. She remembered the story about his mother and realized his faith had grown, though it was hard for her to understand what form it took.

Then he said, "But there's something else I'm afraid of."

"What's that?"

"I'm afraid of missing out on what's important in this life."

She stopped. "What do you mean?"

"A woman is important to a man—and children are too."

She saw that he was waiting for her to speak. "Family *is* important," she agreed quietly.

"It's important for a woman to find a man, too, isn't it?"

"Of course it is."

Yancy stopped walking and took her hands in his. "You have nice hands," he said. "Strong, smooth. Some women have ugly hands, but not you." He paused. "Be sure, Damita, that you desire the man you choose. Forty years in bed with a man you don't love would be a misery."

Damita pulled her hand back, her face reddening. "Don't talk to me like that."

"All right, I won't."

Damita did not know how to take his words. She felt angered that he would speak so inappropriately, and yet she was curious. "Why do you say a thing like that to me? It isn't nice."

"Because I know that at one time you felt something for me."

"That wasn't love," she said quickly. "It was . . . it was just wickedness on my part. You knew it—you turned away from me, Yancy."

"I didn't want to spoil things," he said simply. "If I hadn't felt something for you, I would have accepted your offer immediately."

Damita could not think how to answer him. He had put his finger on the thing that had troubled her for years. "Don't confuse me, Yancy!" she cried. She turned quickly and walked away, leaving him to stand alone in the cotton field.

The stalks blew lightly about him, and he watched her go. "You're already confused, Damita Madariaga."

Chapter twenty-one

Looking over the rim of his fine china cup, Elmo Debakky studied Charissa for a moment, then remarked, "It's amazing how men can make fools of themselves, when they really set out to do the job."

Charissa and Debakky had lingered after breakfast, and now Charissa looked steadily at the physician. "I suppose you're referring to Jeff."

"Yes. He and Depard are making fools of themselves, chasing after Damita. They've provided a mint of entertainment for the upper crust of New Orleans. People don't go to the opera anymore; they just gather to watch those two circle around each other." He sipped his coffee, then shook his head and said more soberly, "I hate to see Jeff chasing that woman."

"I'm just thankful he and Depard haven't had another stupid duel."

"Maybe it's just a matter of time. I don't know what makes men behave like that."

"At least the cotton crop was good this year, so Damita's safe from losing her plantation."

"That was good news, all right." Debakky glanced out the window and shook his head. "What's the date?"

"December twenty-eighth."

"It seems as if 1835 just sped by." He glanced at Charissa. She was wearing the simple gray dress that she always wore to work at the hospital. She seemed subdued. Debakky had learned long ago her secret, that she loved Jefferson Whitman, and had considered shaking Jeff to make him realize what he was missing. But he was not a man to interfere. Now he said, "I'll tell you what we ought to do. The society of New Orleans is getting up a New Year's Eve ball. The governor will be there, the mayor, and all the bigwigs. Why don't you let me take you?"

Charissa glanced up from her coffee and studied the doctor. He was not handsome in the least, but he was intensely masculine and one of the wittiest and smartest men she had ever known. "That would be nice, Elmo," she said. "I'll look forward to it."

Elmo grinned at her. "Why don't you fall in love with me, Charissa? It would make your life a lot simpler."

"What do you mean?"

"I mean, you could stop mooning around about Jeff. The man hasn't got good sense. He can't even see you."

"No, he can't. He never could."

"Not your fault. He's one of the best doctors I've ever seen. Too bad he's not as smart about women as he is about medicine." He saw that Charissa did not want to discuss it and said, "If you'd just fall in love with me and we got married, you wouldn't have to worry about anything."

"I'd have to worry about you."

"No, you wouldn't. Tell you what: Just give me a list of all the things you want in a husband."

Charissa laughed. Elmo always had the ability to lift her out of her mood. "And what would you do with such a list?"

Elmo looked at her with mock surprise. "Why, I'd convince you of how you could get along without all those things."

Yancy poked the fire and watched the sparks fly in myriad, tiny fragments up the chimney. He kicked a large chunk of firewood with his boot, and Damita said, "One of these days, you're going to catch yourself on fire. Take your foot out of there. You'll ruin your boots."

Yancy put the poker down, turned, and backed up to the fire, soaking in the warmth. "I love fires. I love everything about them—cutting down the trees, splitting the wood."

"You don't like carrying out the ashes all that much, I noticed."

Yancy grinned at her. "You're right about that. But for every pleasure, there's always a penalty to go with it."

"Is that some more of your deep philosophy, Yancy?"

"Oh, yes, I'm going to write a book one day. I'll call it *Yancy Devereaux's Guide to Perfect Living.*"

"That'll solve a problem for a lot of people," Damita said. She was sitting in an overstuffed chair directly across from the fire, sewing. Her hands moved nimbly.

Yancy asked, "What's the nicest dress you have?"

Surprised, Damita looked up. "What are you talking about?"

"Tomorrow's the fancy New Year's Eve ball. I've decided we're going."

Damita shook her head. "I told Jeff and Lewis I wouldn't go."

"Don't you want to go?"

"To tell the truth, I'm a bit tired of their attentions."

"I thought a woman liked that sort of attention."

"Oh, Yancy, it's foolish! I don't care for either one of them—not for a husband, at least."

"We're going to take in that ball. We've worked hard, and we deserve a break."

"I'd rather not."

"I'm not asking, Damita," Yancy said. "I'm telling you we're going to do it. Don't you remember? When I agreed to come here, you agreed to do everything I commanded."

Damita was so surprised she poked her finger with the needle. "Ow!" she said and stuck her finger in her mouth. "I didn't promise to go to balls with you!"

"Yes, you did. You said I could make every decision. My decision is that we need some foolishness." He pulled up a chair opposite and faced her. "I haven't mentioned it, but you've done a wonderful job of adjusting to this life."

Damita stared at him. "Why—thank you, Yancy." She never

expected compliments from this man who had suffered so in his own life.

"I know it was hard for you. I was used to tough living, but you weren't. And you've helped keep your mother from being miserable as well."

"You're the one who's had to do all the hard things."

"No, that's not so. But let's not argue about that."

Damita felt warmth at his praise. Only rarely did he offer it, although she often felt his eyes on her. "All right," she said. "Do you really want to go to the ball?"

"I think it would be fun. We'll go late," he said.

"What in the world for? I always like to go early."

"Not me," Yancy grinned. "I like to make a big entrance. Walk in about thirty minutes late, and people notice. You like that kind of attention yourself."

Damita made a face at him. "You say the most awful things!"

"Put on your prettiest dress. We'll show these New Orleans folks how it should be done. We'll be the best-looking couple at the ball."

"I really would like to go," Damita said, smiling, and her eyes were bright.

"Good. Then it's settled."

Charissa was enjoying the ball, which surprised her. Jeff had been gloomy enough, and she knew that Damita had refused to attend with him. He had finally decided to accompany Debakky and Charissa, and he had asked Charissa for a dance. She had been having a fine time, dancing mostly with Debakky, but she had also observed that Jeff and Lewis had met and simply stared at each other, bowing slightly. After their dance, she stood beside Jeff and saw that he was glaring at the young Creole.

"How does it feel to have New Orleans laughing at you, Jefferson?"

Jeff turned, astonished. "That's an unkind remark."

Charissa was sick of Jeff's behavior. She had attended the dance for pleasure, and now the alienation between the two men annoyed her. "Jeff, you look absolutely foolish!"

Jeff glared at her. "I haven't been ungentlemanly."

"You two are chasing around after Damita like mindless dogs."

Jeff blinked with surprise and reddened slightly. He looked down at her. "I wish you wouldn't talk like that."

"All right. I won't."

After their tiff, Jeff tried several times to make conversation, but Charissa answered in monosyllables. Then he asked, "Why didn't you let that young Matthew Denton bring you?"

"You know we're not seeing each other anymore. I asked him not to speak of marriage to me again. He'd be miserable with me."

"Don't be foolish! Nobody would be miserable with you. You have everything that a man needs."

"But you don't need me, do you, Jefferson?"

"Why, of course, I do. You know better than that." He hated to quarrel.

Charissa heard a commotion and turned to the entrance of the ballroom. Jeff followed her glance and watched as Yancy and Damita entered. "She told me she didn't want to come tonight!"

"They make a fine-looking couple, don't they?"

"Yes, I suppose so."

Damita had spotted Jeff and knew that Depard also was there. "I wish I hadn't come, Yancy," she whispered. "Lewis and Jeff will work themselves up into some sort of a disagreement."

"No, they won't. I have a plan."

Damita looked up at Yancy. "What kind of plan?"

"A plan so that you won't be bothered by Jeff or Lewis or any other fellow. You'll dance only with me tonight. Come on."

He pulled her to the floor, and they began to swirl amongst the other dancers. Yancy noticed all the eyes upon them and was pleased. "Everybody's here, and they're all looking at us."

"You have no humility at all, do you?"

Yancy tried to look hurt. "What do we have to be humble about? We're a handsome couple. By the way, I didn't tell you: You look beautiful tonight."

Damita smiled. "So do you. Yancy, how are you going to keep men from asking me to dance?"

"I can't keep them from asking," Yancy said with a grin, and humor flashed in his eyes as he added, "I can stop them from dancing with you, though."

"Men are touchy—you know that, Yancy. Don't forget that dueling is common around here."

"That's not my problem."

Damita remembered how his first encounter with Lewis Depard had led to the threat of a duel with broadaxes. "Be careful," she said. "Some of these men won't take jokes lightly."

"I'm not responsible for their deficiency of humor. Now, let's just enjoy the dance."

They swept around the floor, and as soon as the music came to an end and the couples applauded, a voice said, "I request the pleasure of the next dance, Miss Madariaga."

Damita and Yancy turned to see a tall man smiling at them.

"Oh, hello, Anthony."

Anthony Rivera was a wealthy businessman Damita had known for a long time. He was a widower, now in his mid-thirties, and he was reputedly looking for Wife Number Two. She started to agree, as was customary, but Yancy said, "I'm sorry, sir, but that would not be possible."

Rivera bristled. "And why not, sir?"

"Señora Madariaga asked me to chaperone her daughter. She made me absolutely responsible. I won't allow the young lady to dance with anyone unless I approve of him."

Rivera sneered, "You're a Kaintock, aren't you?"

"Yes, I am. And I'm proud of it."

"And you don't approve of me!" Rivera snapped. "May I ask why not?"

"I don't like your mustache," Yancy said. The people around the three had fallen silent and were listening carefully. "I never trust a man who wears one. Sorry."

A murmur ran through the crowd, and Rivera said, "I'm afraid I must take exception to your remark, sir."

"That's your privilege."

"I will have my man call on you."

"Not until after the last dance, if you don't mind."

Rivera smiled coldly. "After the last dance it will be, then."

Debakky had made his way through the crowd and listened to all this. "That's a dangerous fellow, Yancy."

"I'm afraid you'll have to be my second, Doctor, if you don't mind."

"I think this dueling business is foolish."

"It is, of course, but will you help me out?"

"I suppose so," Debakky said seriously. Then his tone lightened, "Perhaps I'll dance with Miss Madariaga."

"No, I'm afraid not."

"Why not?" He teased.

"You're a physician. I never trust that breed with women."

Debakky let out a belly laugh. The music started, and he found Charissa and repeated what had happened.

"He's going to have a duel with that man?"

"I don't think so. Yancy's a clever fellow."

"He's going to get himself in trouble. You know how touchy these Creoles are."

The music started, and Yancy put his hand out to Damita. She joined him in the dance and asked, "Have you lost your mind? What do you think you're doing?"

"Looking out for you, Damita. You can't be too careful in a place like this. Why, some of these men probably have impure desires in their hearts."

Ordinarily, Damita would have smiled at this remark, but she was worried. "Anthony is a fine shot. He's already killed one man in a duel and wounded several others."

"Don't ever worry about what's going to happen tomorrow."

"I'm worried about what's going to happen after the last dance. He'll be waiting for you."

"Don't think about that," Yancy said cheerfully. The two finished that dance, and instantly, another gentleman asked for the next one. His eyes were fixed on Yancy, who looked him over and said, "I'm sorry, sir. I couldn't possibly let Miss Damita dance with a man who wears foppish attire such as yours."

Damita gasped, and the man's face turned scarlet. "Very well then, sir. My man will call."

"Won't be necessary. After the last dance, we'll settle this business. Dr. Debakky will act for me."

"That will suit me exactly, sir."

Yancy winked at Damita and said, "Nothing like a little drama to enliven a dance, don't you think?"

Damita did not know what to think. She knew that Yancy's antics had become known throughout the ball, so that after every dance several men came by, asking for the next one. Yancy refused them all, and in each case, the disappointed man challenged him. Yancy simply said to each, "See my man, Dr. Debakky, over there. He handles all my dueling business."

Yancy's behavior became the talk of the crowd. Everyone's eyes were on him and Damita, and Jeff exclaimed to Debakky, "He's crazy! Why, he's been challenged at least ten times!"

"Don't worry about it. Yancy's a clever fellow."

Jeff turned to Charissa and said, "I always thought Devereaux was a savvy man, but this is suicide."

Charissa was smiling. "Look around you. Everybody's laughing. It's become a joke, which is exactly what he intended, I think."

"After that last dance, he'd better have a plan," Jeff said. "He'll need doctors if he fights all of these men."

"This is the last dance, Damita," Yancy said. His eyes were bright, and he smiled. "I'm so glad we came. I've never had so much fun at a ball."

"You have lost your mind, Yancy Devereaux." Damita was worried. "Some of these men are expert duelists. I know you're trying to make a game out of it, but that just makes it worse. Anthony Rivera has no sense of humor about these things."

"He's the first, is he? I get them all confused. Let's see, there must be at least fifteen or twenty of them now. You know, it would be great if we could make a little money off of this."

Damita stared at him as he whirled her around. "What are you talking about?"

"We could sell tickets. Yancy Devereaux's Famous Dueling Extravaganza! Ten dollars a ticket. Why, all of New Orleans would come out to see me get punctured by these hotheaded young fellows."

Damita shook her head. "I don't think it's funny, Yancy."

"You're too serious, Damita. Forget about it. Enjoy this last dance."

Damita tried to focus on the dance. She studied her partner. *He's really enjoying this,* she thought. *How could he? Doesn't he have any nerves at all?* "Please, Yancy, let's leave before it's over. Let's get away from here."

"Why, we couldn't do that. We'd disappoint all of your admirers."

"They don't admire me. They just want to shoot somebody or stick him with a sword."

"I'll have to give them a chance."

The music stopped, the danced ended, and the crowd began to whisper, every eye on Yancy Devereaux and Damita Madariaga.

Yancy said to her, "Come along. I see my foes are gathering around Debakky."

He offered his arm, and she took it. As they walked over, she noticed Lewis Depard staring at her, disbelief on his face. Jeff was standing back in the crowd with Charissa.

"Dr. Debakky, have you made the arrangements?"

Debakky's eyes were sparkling. He had a small piece of paper in his left hand. "I think I've got them all in order. I believe, Mr. Rivera, you are the first."

Yancy said, "Suppose we all retire outside, where such business as this is usually conducted. Will that satisfy you, sir?"

"Perfectly," Rivera said. His face was pale. He knew that Yancy was making light of something important to him. "Laugh while you can, Devereaux."

Yancy grinned at him, then asked Damita, "Will you wait here, dear? I have a few engagements."

Damita said, "No, I'm going with you."

"Why, ladies don't attend such things, Señorita Madariaga!" Rivera exclaimed.

"Then maybe I'm no lady, but I insist on going. I'm ready, Yancy."

Almost everyone who had attended the ball crowded outside to watch the spectacle. It took some doing to get a space cleared away for the duelists to carry out their business.

The night was bright and clear, with the stars and a full moon overhead. "Good night for shooting, eh, Señor Rivera?" Yancy asked cheerfully.

Rivera glared at him. "I'm willing to accept your apology."

"I'm sorry, but your mustache still offends me."

Laughter rose from the crowd.

"Dr. Debakky, I am acting for Señor Rivera," said a man named French, who often served as a second in duels. "We've chosen our ground, and I have the weapons here, if they would suit you."

"Let me see," Debakky said. He stepped forward and examined the leather case that French held open.

"These look very nice," he said. "What do you think, Yancy?"

Yancy was standing alone, but his eyes were scanning the crowd. He saw Damita watching him, her face pale in the moonlight, and he winked at her. "Just a minute," Yancy said. "I'm the challenged party. I have the choice of weapons."

"There'll be no duels with axes, sir," French said coldly. "We've heard of your frivolousness."

"No, firearms will be fine with me, but I'll choose which firearms."

"What did you have in mind?"

Yancy said, "Wait right here. I have them in my buggy." He strode to his buggy, which was parked nearby, and threw back a canvas cover.

"What's he got in there?" Charissa asked Jeff.

"Can't see. It looks like rifles."

Yancy brought back not rifles, but shotguns. Holding one in each hand, he said, "You may take your pick of these, sir. Both of them are in working condition, and your man may do the loading himself." He thrust one of the shotguns at French and another at Debakky, then reached into his pocket. "Here, this ought to do. Double-ought buckshot."

"What do you mean by this foolishness?" French demanded.

"Why, this is my choice of weapons. What we will do is this: You gentlemen will load the guns. Mr. Rivera and I will stand ten feet away from each other, aim, and at the count of ten, we'll fire."

A silence fell over the crowd. Yancy stared at Anthony Rivera. "I'm sure you wouldn't want to take advantage of a man, sir. You might be a better shot than I am, but with shotguns, accuracy is not a problem."

"This is foolishness!" Rivera cried out.

"Do you always have to have the advantage? Neither man has it with these. I'm the challenged party. These are the firearms. Let's get at it."

Rivera stared at him. "You jest! You wouldn't dare do a thing like that."

"Try me," Yancy said grimly, and the crowd murmured in disbelief.

The pressure was on Anthony Rivera. He could not believe that any man would suggest such a thing. Neither man could possibly survive the encounter. He challenged Yancy again. "You're bluffing."

"Try me," Yancy repeated.

Rivera said huskily, "Give me that shotgun!" French loaded the shotgun, handed it to him, and Debakky did the same for Yancy. Rivera said, "I'm ready." His voice was defiant, and he moved into position.

Yancy took the shotgun Debakky handed him and moved until he was ten feet away from his opponent. "I'm ready, too."

"French, start the count," Rivera said and lifted the shotgun, aiming it at Yancy.

Yancy coolly lifted his own shotgun. "I'm ready," he said. "You may begin, Mr. French."

The spectators hushed. Damita was having difficulty breathing. She cried out, "Don't do it! Don't do it, Yancy!"

Yancy paid no attention, nor did anyone else. He was taking aim with the shotgun, his eyes locked on his target.

French continued to count, "Three, four, five—"

Anthony Rivera was a man of cool courage. He had engaged in many duels with sword and pistol, but always he had a good chance of surviving. He still could not believe this crazy Kaintock meant what he said, but the cornflower-blue eyes stared at him down the length of the shotgun without blinking.

When the count reached eight, Rivera cried out, "No! Stop!" He found that his hands were trembling. He laid the shotgun down and said to Yancy, "This is murder! It's not dueling!"

"It's about as close to it as most duels are."

Rivera glared at Yancy, then turned and walked away, declaring, "I will have nothing to do with this foolishness. It does not follow the code."

Yancy called out, "Come again if you change your mind, Anthony." Then he asked, "Who's next?"

"I believe Mr. Leslie Thornton is next."

Leslie Thornton, however, quickly spoke up. He was a short, heavyset young man who immediately said, "I don't believe that I will engage in a shotgun duel with anybody."

"Number three. Franklin Towns."

Debakky continued to call off the names, but the mood of the crowd had changed. Obviously, no man in his right mind was going to stand up to a crazy Kaintock and exchange shotgun blasts from ten feet. Finally the doctor said, "That's the last. I guess we can all go home now."

Yancy handed the shotgun to Debakky, who whispered, "What would you have done if somebody had taken you up on it?"

"I'd have run like a rabbit, like any sensible man!"

Damita had been silent all the way home. Yancy drew up at a small creek that overflowed the road. "The horses are probably thirsty. We'll give them a drink."

Damita said, "Yancy, I don't understand you at all. I don't understand men. You could have been killed."

"Not much chance of that."

"Why, one of them might have taken you up on it."

"I didn't think so. Not much of a risk, really."

She said again, "I don't understand you."

"I like to have a little mystery about me. It's provocative to women."

The moon was round and silver overhead, and as they sat in the buggy, the only sounds they heard were the horses nuzzling in the water and far-off the cry of a bird.

Damita said quietly, "I was afraid."

"Afraid for me?"

"Why, of course. You could have gotten killed—I don't care what you say."

"But you were really afraid for me. I find that hard to believe."

"Why should you?"

"Why, we have done little but fight since we met."

"I know. But I owe you so much. You saved my life once, and now you've saved my home and my family." She turned to face him fully. "You'll never know how much gratitude I have for you."

He said, "We're good friends, then?"

"Yes," she said, smiling. "Very good friends."

"Don't you think good friends should express their feelings in a more tangible way? Something more than just words."

Damita felt the fear and the tension leaving her. She decided to play along with Yancy's unpredictable sense of humor. "What did you have in mind, sir?"

"Something like this." Yancy put his arms around her and drew her close. Then he bent his head and kissed her.

Damita returned his kiss. His lips were firm on hers, and his arms pulled her near him with strength. Something timeless brushed them both at that moment, and it somehow frightened Damita. Yet she held the kiss longer than she had intended.

He broke away first and said huskily, "You are all woman, Damita!"

"You make me afraid, Yancy."

"Afraid of me? You shouldn't be. You should know that by now."

"I don't trust—" She could not finish.

"You don't trust me, Damita?"

She laughed, reached up, and put her hand on his cheek. "No, I don't trust myself. Take me home, Yancy."

He laughed then and turned, speaking to the horses. "Get up, boys. This lady doesn't trust herself."

The horses picked up the pace, and Damita sat so close beside Yancy that she could feel the warmth of his body, and from time to time she stole a glance at him. She had never known a man like this. As they moved along under the bright moon, she could not help but wonder how she would handle him in the days to come.

Chapter twenty-two

As Damita Madariaga walked along the path that led from the back of the house to the line of cabins, she was carrying a heavy tray covered by a white cloth, and her arms ached from the weight of it. For some reason she thought of a passage in the Bible about Moses, who held up his hands until they grew weary, and then Aaron had to support them. *Wish I had him here to help me,* she thought grimly. *I'm going to drop this.*

The cabins were built in a double line, facing each other, and in the center a woman was boiling clothes in a huge iron pot, poking them with a stick. Damita said as she hurried by, "Hello, Matilda."

"Hello, Miss. Kin I hep you with that?"

"No, thanks. It's food for Hetty's family. Is she any better?"

"No, ma'am, not that I kin tell. But I'm watchin' her, and I keep checkin' on the kids."

Stopping in front of the last whitewashed cabin, Damita stepped through the open door. The window at the side threw a beam of pale sunlight across the floor and on the bed, where a woman lay. Damita put the tray down and glanced at Hetty's three children, sitting on the floor and watching her with big eyes. The youngest was no more than a year and a half old. "Hello," she said. "How are you today?" She got no answer, but then, the children rarely spoke to her. She turned and greeted Hetty. "Are you feeling any better?"

"Yes, ma'am, I believe I am."

"I brought you something for supper tonight. I brought some extra, too, so it should be enough for tomorrow's meals."

"Miss Damita, you is powerful good to take care of us like this."

"I just want to see you get well, Hetty. Can I do anything else for you?"

"We hain't got no water, ma'am. I'd get it myself, but I's powerful feeble."

"I'll take care of that."

Damita picked up the bucket, walked down the pathway to where a well with a stone curbing served the slave population, and filled the bucket. Once back inside the cabin, she filled the pitcher and then left the rest in the bucket on the table. "There you are, Hetty." She stood over the woman. "I'll come back to check on you tomorrow."

"Thank you kindly, Miss."

Outside the cabin, Damita blinked at the fading sunlight. The sun was sinking like a huge ball in the west, and for one moment she watched it, then turned and walked back down toward the house.

As she crossed the grounds, she heard the familiar noises of the plantation. She recognized the sound of an ax biting into a tree, and to her right, men's voices shouted from an open field. She could not make out the words, but she saw one of the slaves plowing in the field calling out to another one.

The life of the plantation had come to mean a great deal to her since she had thrown herself into its operation. She thought of Hetty and felt a pang. *I never would have even known Hetty was sick before. I wouldn't have bothered to learn her name. The only slaves I knew were those who served in the house. Now, I know the names of every one of them and most of their problems, too.*

She walked around the huge chestnut tree that sheltered a group of chickens, which clucked and fluttered at her approach. Damita considered how different life had been since Yancy had come. She no longer took everything for granted. Always before, when meals were put on the table, she never thought about where the eggs came from. Now she took a sense of pride in them; she often gathered them herself, and sometimes she even helped in the kitchen when Ernestine, the rotund cook, taught her the secrets and fine art of cooking.

She entered by the back door and paused for a moment, wondering what they would have for supper. She had made herself responsible for the menu, and she and Ernestine worked on it together. Her mother was not much help with this. She seemed to know nothing about domestic things. But she liked to suggest different meals.

Damita had started down the hall to find her, when Elena approached and said, "Mr. Depard is here, daughter."

"Where is he, Mother?"

"He's in the small parlor. He's been telling me about his journey to Europe."

When Damita stepped into the parlor, Lewis Depard was sitting on an old wooden chair, looking at a month-old newspaper. He stood and tossed the newspaper aside. "Oh, there you are, Damita."

"Hello, Lewis. Have you been waiting long?"

"Not long."

"I had to take some food to one of the slaves. She's had some kind of sickness."

Lewis Depard's face changed slightly. "Do you have to do things like that?"

"I do now. Sit down, Lewis."

Lewis took his seat and said, "It doesn't seem right for you to have to work the way you do."

"It hasn't hurt me at all. As a matter of fact, I don't mind it now. I did at first." She saw that the idea was completely foreign to Lewis. He had never done a day's work in his life, she supposed, and the idea of personally seeing to a sick slave was beyond his comprehension.

"Hetty's a good woman and a hard worker, but she's not able to take care of herself right now," Damita explained. "Her husband is Big Jake. They have three children. I can never keep their names straight. One of them, I know, is Henry. Another is Mason, and one is Jeb." She shook her head. "I was talking to Hetty yesterday. I'd never really talked to a slave before about anything personal. She told me how afraid she was that my father would match her with some man she hated. She had always favored Big Jake, and she was so happy when Papa put them together. I started thinking about how little they have in their lives, these slaves. Not much good."

"I suppose that's true."

Damita saw that Lewis was hardly listening to a word. He was usually cheerful and smiling, but today he wore a sober expression. "Why do you look so serious, Lewis?"

"I've been doing a lot of thinking, Damita, and I've come to ask you to marry me."

"Marry you! Why, Lewis, I'm surprised."

"Why should you be?" he asked, eyebrows raised. "You know I've always intended to ask you."

"You've pursued so many young women. I think sometimes you planned to romance the eligible young women in New Orleans in alphabetical order. You just worked down to me as a matter of course."

Lewis walked over to the sofa and sat beside her. He took her hand and said, "Don't be foolish, Damita. You think I have no feelings at all?"

For some reason, Damita could not take him seriously. "I think you have too many feelings, Lewis."

Lewis reached over, pulled her to him, and kissed her. "I want us to get married. It's time for me to settle down, and you don't need to be doing all this work. We can live here, if you please. I'll take over all the debts."

Damita pulled away from his grasp. "Yancy's doing well. We'll be out of debt next year."

Lewis frowned. "I know he's a good manager. Maybe we could keep him on."

"But I don't love you, Lewis."

Lewis paused. "You're not still interested in that Whitman fellow, are you?"

Damita realized at that instant that Lewis Depard was really a shallow, selfish individual, despite his good looks and his money. *He reminds me a whole lot of myself,* she thought, *as I used to be.*

"Lewis, I want us always to be friends, but please don't speak of this again."

Lewis sat silent and bewildered. He could not believe she was rejecting him. He had come as a matter of form, thinking all he had to do was say the words, but now his pride was hurt. "Well," he said, getting up, "I think you'll change your mind."

"I won't change my mind. Please don't mention this again."

"All right," Lewis said, his face flushed. "I won't. Good-bye, Damita."

"Good-bye, Lewis. Thank you for the honor you've done me."

Lewis stared at her, then whirled and walked out of the parlor. Damita heard the door slam and went to the window to watch him go. He mounted his big stallion, struck him with a whip, and shot off at full-speed.

"There goes my big chance," Damita said, feeling more amused than anything else. "Go on, Lewis. Chase all the other young women—but leave me alone." She turned to leave, but Elena entered. "Lewis left?"

"Yes."

"Why didn't he stay for supper?"

"I guess he wasn't hungry, Mama." Then she gave her mother a slight smile. "He came to ask me to marry him."

Elena straightened up with astonishment. "He did! That's fine!"

"It's fine because I'm not having him."

Elena Madariaga was not adapted to the hard way of life that her family now had to endure. Her brow wrinkled, and she said hurriedly, "Damita, you must think about that. Why, he could give you everything."

"No, he couldn't, Mama."

"Certainly he could! He has enough money to buy a place in town and to make this place pay."

"That's not everything, Mama."

Elena studied her daughter's eyes, then shook her head. "You've always had a romantic streak in you, but I'm worried about the future."

"We'll be all right. Yancy will see us through."

Elena sat down. This had come as a blow to her.

"It'll be all right, Mama," Damita said and sat down beside her. She put her arm around her mother and hugged her. "Yancy won't let us down."

Elena tried to smile. "I always thought you were more interested in Dr. Whitman, but he hasn't been out for a while. Have you quarreled with him?"

"No, but I expect he's very busy. The yellow fever's spread again in New Orleans."

"Mercy, I hope it doesn't get out here. That's one blessing of living outside of the city. We're safe in the country."

"I don't think that's exactly true. The Wilsons' cook is down with what they think is yellow fever. They're only three miles from here."

"Don't talk like that! I can't bear to think about that awful sickness."

"All right. I've got to go see about getting supper started. What would you like, Mama? Ernestine will teach me how to fix it for you."

"I'm so tired, you could scrape it off with a stick," Elmo Debakky moaned. He and Jeff Whitman had entered the house and now stood inside the foyer. They had both been working long hours to care for the yellow fever victims. The number of dead had risen throughout May, and it was still rising. Both of the men were depressed; they had lost fifty-nine patients that week. "There's starting to be a panic over this epidemic," Jeff said wearily. "People are leaving the city as fast as they can. I suppose they're wise."

Indeed, the population of New Orleans was leaving by the hundreds, on cart, wagon, horseback—any way they could flee. The very poor had to walk, leading their children by the hands and carrying what they could in their free arms. The streets were strangely quiet, for the cake sellers, the knife sharpeners, the fish peddlers stayed at home, frightened or sick. Slowly, the business of New Orleans was grinding to a halt, and even the bars, which were usually full to capacity at this time of the year, were deserted.

The two men filed into the kitchen, where Rose met them. "I fixed you something to eat," she said.

"I'm not hungry," Jeff said.

"Sit down and eat," Debakky said firmly. "You have to keep your strength up."

Jeff sat with Debakky and ate, but his thoughts were focused on how insidious the yellow fever was. It came on so gradually: just a little headache or just a slight chill. Then the body temperature began to rise, and very soon a fever struck. The patient's eyes grew bloodshot, and he suffered tremendous thirst. Often a victim experienced a false recovery, followed by an even worse bout with the sickness. The victim's face grew dark, blood oozed from his lips, gums, and nose, and he vomited a dark substance: the "black vomit" that was proof of the disease.

Rose hovered over the two men, urging them to eat more. "What can you do for these poor people?" she asked.

Debakky shook his head and said, "People are trying all sorts of crazy remedies. Some of them drink lime water."

"That's right. Some have even swallowed sulfur, and others put onions in their shoes," Jeff murmured. "All useless, of course."

"I've heard that some are being bled. Does that help any?"

"Of course not!" Debakky exclaimed. "It makes it worse."

Jeff said, "I suppose Charissa has gone to bed."

"Why, no, she hasn't come home yet."

Both men looked at Rose, surprised. "Hasn't come home?" Jeff repeated. "She left the hospital at four o'clock. I made her go home to take a rest."

"Why, I haven't seen her, Dr. Whitman."

"I suspect she's gone to help at the church," Jeff said heavily. "Quite a few of our members are down with this thing."

"She can't go on like this," Rose said. "She's a strong young woman, but she's pushing herself too hard."

Jeff did not even hear Rose. He sipped his tea, lost in his thoughts, then noticed Debakky rising to go to his room. Jeff bid him good night, stood, and walked into the parlor. He sat down in a plush leather chair and leaned his head back, weariness and ache in his bones. He didn't intend to, but he dropped off to sleep.

He awakened with a start. He realized someone was coming through the front door. Scrambling to the foyer, he met Charissa. "Where have you been?"

"I stopped by the church, and Pastor Harris told me about the

Johnson family. They're all down and have no one to help. I felt I should go."

"Is it yellow fever?"

"I'm afraid so—one of the children and Mrs. Johnson. Poor Mr. Johnson, he's worried sick."

Jeff listened as she described the situation and said, "I'll go by tomorrow and see what I can do. Come along. I'll bet you haven't eaten a bite."

"No, I meant to stop, but I didn't have time."

"Rose has gone to bed, but I'll scare up something." He took her arm, and they walked down the hall together. "You sit down there," he said when they entered the kitchen. He began to rattle around, gathering pots and pans, and Charissa smiled at him. The fine doctor was helpless in the kitchen, but he wanted to do it.

Once he had concocted a meal, he brought it to Charissa, sitting down across from her. She looked depleted, and he shook his head. "This is terrible, Charissa."

"We'll make it, Jefferson."

For a time he was silent, and when he spoke, his words surprised her. "I think I made a mistake in coming to New Orleans. We should have stayed in St. Louis."

"Why, are you unhappy here?"

Jeff shifted uneasily and ran his fingers through his thick hair. "I guess *unsettled* is a better word. Do you like it here, Charissa?"

"Not really. I always liked it better in St. Louis."

"I'll tell you what," he said, and his eyes brightened. "When this epidemic quiets down, let's go on a vacation."

"A vacation! Where?"

"How about England? I've never been there, and I've always wanted to go."

Charissa was astonished. He had been so caught up in his pursuit of Damita that he never thought about things such as vacations or traveling. But now he was plainly discouraged, and she felt compassion for him. At the same time, she felt a spark of hope. *If he got away from Damita, perhaps he could think clearly. She'd make the worst wife in the world for him, but he can't see that.*

"That would be very nice."

Jeff smiled. "Good! We'll talk about it later. Now, you go to bed. You're exhausted."

Two days later, Charissa returned early from the hospital. Rose met her at the door and said, "We have a visitor. It's Miss Madariaga. She's here to see Dr. Whitman."

"Did you tell her that he wouldn't be back tonight?"

"No, I didn't. I didn't know it."

"Thank you, Rose. I'll talk to her."

As soon as she entered the parlor, Charissa saw Damita sitting stiffly on the sofa. Something was wrong, Charissa knew, and when Damita rose, she asked, "What's happened?"

"It's Mama. She's very sick, and Yancy is, too." She bit her lip and added, "And three of the slaves. I'm afraid it's the fever. Is Jeff coming?"

"No, I'm sorry, he's not. He had to go see some patients over at Metairie. He said he wouldn't be back for two days. There's quite an epidemic there."

Damita seemed to shrink. "Is Dr. Debakky here?"

"No, he's working overtime at the hospital."

Damita whispered, "I'm so afraid."

"The doctors are all so hard-pressed with this thing," Charissa said quietly. "He'll come when he returns." She saw that Damita was pale and her hands were trembling. "If you'd like, I'll come and see what I can do. We'll leave word for Jefferson."

Damita stared at her, her eyes wide. "After what I did to you? Why would you do that?"

Charissa disliked Damita but knew that this was something she must fight. "It's what God's called me to do, to help the sick."

"You must hate me, Charissa!"

"I did once, but God is taking that away, a little at a time. Let me get my things together, and we'll go at once."

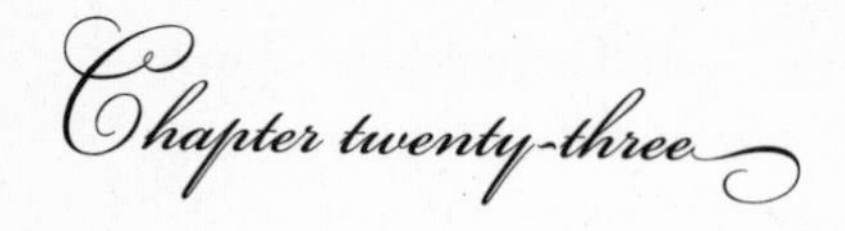

Chapter twenty-three

As soon as Jeff stepped inside the door, Rose greeted him anxiously. "Dr. Whitman, Miss Madariaga was here."

Jeff had taken off his hat and was about to hang it up. He stopped and turned. "When was this?"

"It was the day before yesterday. There wasn't any way to get word to you."

"What's wrong, Rose?"

"It's the yellow fever. Her mother and the gentleman who manages the plantation are down with it. And several of the slaves, I think."

"I wish I'd known that. Will you tell Miss Charissa that I've left for the Madariaga plantation?"

"Oh, she's already gone, Dr. Whitman."

"Gone where?"

"She went back with Miss Madariaga to help with the nursing."

Jeff put his hat on and said, "I'll have to go right now."

"Doctor, take something to eat."

"I'll get something there. Thank you, Rose. If anyone asks, you tell them where I am."

Rose followed him outside and watched him call out to the groom, "Hold it, Jimmy! Don't unhitch those horses."

Damita had been dozing slightly in a rocking chair, but a sudden noise awoke her. She straightened up and leaned forward to look at the figure on the bed. Yancy Devereaux's face was a waxen, yellowish color, and perspiration flowed from him. She laid her hand on his forehead. *Fever's up again.*

She dipped a cloth in the basin on the table and began to bathe his face. She thought about calling Charissa, but there was really nothing that a nurse could do. *Nothing a doctor can do either,* she thought grimly. A single sheet covered the powerful body. He had lost weight, she knew. She thought of how, at times, the chills shook him so violently that she was afraid, and she wanted to hold him on the bed to keep him from falling.

As she bathed his face, she heard him whispering. Pausing, she leaned down and put her ear close to his lips, but she could not make out the words.

Though Yancy remained seriously ill, Elena had made progress; she had not improved, but she had not worsened either. Damita had helped Charissa take care of the slaves as well as she could, and now, as she continued to bathe Yancy's face, she thought how strange it was that Charissa had come. She felt a strong sense of shame as she realized how unselfish her former servant had been. She had said to Charissa once, "It must be terrible for you, being in this city where you were a slave." Charissa had simply smiled and said, "I don't let memories tell me how to feel. If you do that, you're at the mercy of the past."

Her words had remained with Damita, and she recognized that she was guilty of such things. Looking down, she thought of how often she had remembered the shipwreck and how she had almost given herself to Yancy Devereaux.

Just then Yancy began to toss and turn, trying to throw off the cover. His eyes fluttered, and he spoke, but he was in a delirium.

Without warning a terrible fear came to Damita. She was not a young woman given to fears, but as she looked at the drawn face of Yancy and thought of her mother, the thought seemed to explode somewhere inside her: *They could both die—mother* and *Yancy!*

Chilled to the bone by the thought, Damita struggled to push the fear away, but it became stronger. *I'd have no one, not anybody! I'd be all alone!* She had never contemplated such a fate, for she'd always had her parents for support, but the very thought of being alone in the world was unbearable, and she clenched her hands together and closed her eyes. *Please, God—don't let them die!*

The prayer rose to her lips, but even as she tried to pray, she suddenly became aware that the fear of losing her mother and Yancy was not her only danger. I might die, too—I nearly died when the ship went down, and if I had, I would have been lost forever!

Damita groped her way to the chair and sat down, collapsed actually. She was suddenly weak. She had always taken religion more or less for granted, had trusted in the fact that she had been sprinkled as a child, had been fairly faithful to observe the habits taught by her church—but as she sat in the semidarkness of the room, she *knew* that all this was nothing!

How long Damita sat in the chair and struggled with her fears, she could never remember. Gradually, she thought of people she had known who had spoken of Jesus as a *friend*. She had never understood this, had doubted if it could be.

Now she suddenly knew that the form of religion was not good enough. A longing was born in her, and as it grew, she knew that she had to have God in her life. She had only a faint concept of how to find God, but she knew that somehow Jesus was the key.

God, I don't know how to pray—I'm afraid, and I've led a selfish life. But I want to change! How I want you, God!

She began to sob and said, "Jesus, help me! You're the one who died for sins—forgive me."

The struggle went on for what seemed like a long time—but it came to an end. Damita ceased to sob, and a sense of rest came to her. She never knew how to describe that feeling, but it was there.

Finally, she looked up and whispered, "Lord, I don't know how to serve You, but I'm going to try with all my heart to love You—and to love others!"

Damita was exhausted, but as she stood over Yancy, she saw his eyes seem to clear, and she whispered, "Yancy, can you hear me?"

A long silence, then "Yes. What are you doing here?" His lips seemed to be almost paralyzed. She instantly rose, filled a glass with water, and held his head up while he drank. "You must drink all of this you can."

Yancy gulped the water, some of it running out of the corners of his mouth and down onto the pillow. When he turned aside, she put the glass down and saw that he was looking at her.

"You shouldn't be here," he muttered.

"How do you feel?"

"Get away from here, Damita, before you get this thing."

"I can't go."

Yancy's eyes were again cloudy with the fever, but he understood her well enough. He licked his lips and moved restlessly. "How are the others?"

"Holding their own. Mother's still sick, but the slaves are coming out of it."

"I don't think I'll make it."

"Don't talk like that," Damita said. She put her hand on his forehead, pushing his hair back. "You're going to be fine. There are no new cases on the plantation."

He lay looking up at her, and she could not tell what he was thinking. She began to speak then of Charissa. "That woman shames me. I didn't know how selfish I was until she left her home to help us."

"Good woman."

"I'm going to try to get your fever down, Yancy. I'll be right back."

Damita had found that laying cold cloths over his body reduced the fever. She went out to the springhouse and brought in a bucket of water that she kept there. It was the coolest water to be had, but she wished for some ice. In Yancy's sickroom, she put the bucket down, dipped a large, thick towel in it, then pulled the sheet back and laid it over his chest. "That feels good," he whispered. "I hope I don't have any more of those chills."

Damita continued to replace the towel, which quickly grew hot from Yancy's fever. She heard a door open and close and turned to see Whitman enter the room. "Jeff," she said, "I'm so glad you came."

"Hello, Damita." He walked over and picked up Yancy's wrist and felt his pulse. "How are you feeling?"

"Rotten."

"You're able to complain. That's a good sign." He gave Yancy a quick examination and said, "What is this, the fourth day of it?"

"That's right," Damita said quickly.

"That's a favorable sign."

"Is it really, Jeff?"

"Of course." He looked at her and said, "You look exhausted, Damita."

"Make her go to bed, Doc," Yancy said hoarsely. "She's worn herself out, taking care of me."

"That's good advice, Damita. I'll be here now. You go rest."

Suddenly, weariness fell upon Damita almost like a blow. "All right," she said. She stood up and smiled weakly. "I'm glad you're here, Jeff," she said, then turned and left the room.

The doctor said to Yancy, "I know you feel pretty bad, but I think you're going to make it. I'll do the best I can."

"I'd appreciate it if you'd save my life. I saved yours once."

Jeff stared at him. "What do you mean, you saved my life?"

Yancy smiled a thin smile. As bad as he felt, he had a spark of humor in his eyes. "You remember that duel you had with Depard?"

"Of course."

"You weren't in any danger. I changed the musket balls for pieces of toast."

"What are you talking about?" Jeff demanded, thinking this was a hallucination. He listened as Yancy told him about forming the balls and painting them.

"Don't ever tell Depard. He'd want to do it all again."

Jeff laughed. "I was a fool then, a bigger fool than I am now, I guess. I've learned a few things." He looked down at Yancy and said, "I'll be here. Try to sleep."

"All right, Doc. You're the boss."

The time passed slowly for Damita. Jeff stayed for two days, then had to go back to the city, promising to return. The routine continued unbroken, and Damita was pleased to find that she was strong enough to handle each day as it came. She knew that Charissa was surprised, too, and once the two were taking a late supper when Charissa said, "You're tougher than I thought."

"I'm tougher than *I* thought," Damita said, pleased at the compliment. She looked Charissa in the eye and said, "I still can't get over how you left everything to come help us."

"It's my job, Damita."

Damita studied Charissa, marveling that even though she was exhausted, she still had an exotic beauty. Her thoughts turned to Jeff Whitman, and without meaning to, she said, "I've thought so much about you and Jeff."

Charissa stared at her. "What about us?" she said cautiously.

"It's very obvious that you care for him. Of course, he doesn't know that, does he?"

"No, he doesn't. He's in love with you."

"No, he's not."

Charissa started. "What do you mean by that?"

"He's infatuated. I've seen enough of it to know. I told him months ago that we'd never marry. I thought of him, for a time, only selfishly. I was afraid for the future. I was afraid I'd be poor. I couldn't imagine what would happen to our family." She looked up, and misery was in her eyes. "How you must have hated me for that. Nothing but a fortune seeker!"

Charissa said quietly, "It didn't endear you to me, Damita."

"Well, no more of that."

"It wouldn't make any difference, at least as far as I'm concerned."

"What do you mean?"

"He never thinks of me as a man thinks of a woman he might love. I'm always his sister. How tired I get of his saying that. He thinks it pleases me. He's not very sensitive, is he?"

"He's dumb as a post about women," Damita said bluntly. "But you'd be good for him. You're everything he needs in a wife. I'll tell him that."

"No, don't, please."

"I guess I couldn't. But I see a goodness in you, and I hope he does, too, one day."

Yancy woke with a start. He felt strange. He lay flat on his back, wondering what this sensation was. It finally came to him. "I feel good," he said aloud. He threw the cover back and sat up. He saw that the sheets were dry—he had slept all night without breaking into a sweat. *My heaven, I feel good!* He stood up, swayed, and then sat back down so abruptly he nearly fell over backward. *Whoa,* he thought. *I'm not all that strong. But I'm getting out of this bed.*

Carefully, he stood again and took small, cautious steps to where his clothes were folded across a chair. He dressed, sitting down, and when he had pulled his boots on, he stood and went over to the window. It was a beautiful day. *Just feels good to be alive.* Thanksgiving rose in him, and he found himself saying, "Lord, I'm not much for praying, but I want to thank You for pulling me through this."

He smiled to himself. *Maybe I'm getting religion in a big way,* he thought. But then he added, "Do the best You can for me, Lord. I'll not forget this." He slowly left the bedroom and walked downstairs, holding on to the banister. When he turned into the kitchen, he saw Charissa standing at the window, looking out. She turned, and her eyes widened when she saw him.

"Yancy, what are you doing up?"

"Couldn't stand that bed. I didn't have any fever at all last night—but I'm weak as a kitten."

"Here, sit down. What you need is some good food. How about something light? How does scrambled eggs and toast, and maybe some hot tea and milk, sound?"

"I could eat a bear, I think."

"You can't have bear."

Charissa cooked a quick breakfast, then sat down and watched Yancy eat with gusto. She reached over once and held his wrist, testing his pulse. "Slow and steady," she said with a smile.

"Where is Damita?"

"I don't think she's awake yet. She was up most of the night with her mother."

"I can't get over," Yancy said thoughtfully, "how much she's changed."

"Yes, she has changed more than I would have dreamed possible. I believed she was selfish to the bone and would die that way, but she's not now. You've done that for her, Yancy."

"Me? I haven't done anything."

"I think you have. You saved her life this time, just as surely as you did when you pulled her out of that shipwreck."

Yancy sipped his tea. "Don't quite see that," he said.

"Don't you remember how afraid she was when her father died? She didn't have anyone to cling to. Her mother's helpless," Charissa said, shrugging, "in business matters, at least. But then you came along and took over and gave her hope. I've seen it in her since when you came."

Yancy changed the subject to the plantation's upcoming crop, and the two chatted for a few minutes. Then Charissa smiled wearily and said, "I'm about worn out myself. I think I'll go lie down."

"You've both worked too hard," Yancy said.

Charissa stood, turned, and suddenly began to sway.

"What's wrong?" he asked with alarm.

Charissa turned around, and he saw that her lips were pressed tightly together. "Just a dizzy spell," she whispered.

Yancy looked more closely at her. "You don't look well."

"Oh, I'll be all right. I'm just tired. I'll go lie down awhile."

Yancy had walked slowly to the porch and sat down in a cane-bottom chair. It was such a pleasure, simply to watch life from some vantage point other than a bed. He heard footsteps, and Damita stepped outside. She looked astonished.

"You shouldn't be up, Yancy!"

"Yes, I should," he answered, smiling. "I didn't have any fever last night, and I feel great. Just weak yet."

"I'm glad to hear it! Where's Charissa?"

"She was worn out. She didn't look too good to me. She went to lie down."

Damita sat down beside him. "She's worked herself almost sick."

Yancy was silent for a time, then said, "Damita." When she turned to face him, he said, "I guess this is when I tell you how grateful I am for all you've done for me."

Damita flushed slightly. "Why, Yancy, that was nothing."

"No, it wasn't." He laughed shortly. "When I got out of bed, you know what I did first? I began to thank the Lord for pulling me through."

"Oh, I've done the same thing. Mama's doing fine, too."

He put his hand out, and when she put hers in it with a look of surprise, he squeezed it. "In any case, I owe you."

"No, it was my turn."

"What do you mean by that, Damita?"

"I mean it's a little down payment for what you did in pulling me out of the wreck—and for saving our plantation."

Yancy held her hand firmly. "So, we're even now?"

Damita hand was relaxed in his grasp. He looked so good—his face was ruddy, his eyes were clear, the yellow tinge had gone. He had been so sick, and now she saw the returnings of strength. "I don't think people ever even up for things like that."

"I reckon you're right, but when I was sick and you were always at my bedside, I remember thinking, even when I was too ill to speak, how glad I was you were there—that you hadn't left me."

"That's what I felt when the ship went down. We were clinging to that board, and your arm was around me, and I was scared out of my wits. But you held me so tightly, and I knew you wouldn't let me go."

Yancy did not speak. Damita put her free hand over his. "Thank you, Yancy, for not letting go of me at that terrible time."

Yancy studied her eyes, then said, "I couldn't bear the thought of losing you, and I still can't. I don't know how to say this any better, but I love you, Damita. I always will."

Damita remembered something a friend of hers had said once:

"It's funny. Sometimes a fellow bends over to tie his shoe, and when he straightens up, the whole world has changed." She knew at that moment exactly what he meant; when Yancy spoke those simple words of love, she realized that the truth had been with her all the time, for a long time, and now she knew what it was. She stood and pulled him to his feet. He looked at her with surprise, and she lifted her arms and put them around his neck. "Yes, you must never let me go. I've been selfish all my life, Yancy, and I still am."

"No, you're not selfish."

"Yes, I am," she said, and her eyes were bright, her lips trembling. "I want you in the most selfish way you can imagine." She pulled his head down and kissed him on the lips, his arms went around her, and she buried her face against his chest. "I love you, Yancy. I've been the biggest fool in the world, and I suppose I will be again, but you'll have to take me as I am."

Yancy stood in wonder, amazed at the woman in his arms. He laid his cheek against the top of her head and whispered, "Don't worry. I'll hold you so tightly you'll never be able to get away, Damita."

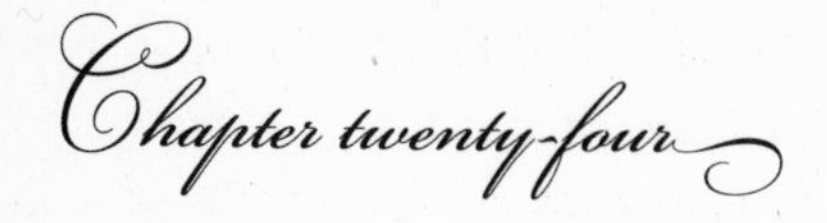

Chapter twenty-four

As soon as Jeff opened the door and saw Damita, he recognized strain in her face. "Is something wrong?"

"It's Charissa, Jeff. She's very sick."

Jeff's looked as if she had struck him. "Sick?" he asked hoarsely. "Is it the fever?"

"I . . . I don't know, but I think you'd better come."

"All right. I will."

"Jeff, wait. I know this is no time to speak of this, but let me tell you one more thing."

Jeff stared at her, his mind occupied only with Charissa. "What is it?" he asked impatiently.

"I wanted you to know that Yancy and I are going to be married."

Jeff stared at her. "I guessed that might happen, Damita."

Damita shook her head. "You and I have both been confused, but now the important thing is Charissa."

"I'll follow you back. Let me get my horse," he said.

Charissa felt a hand on her forehead and stirred slightly. Her head ached, and a cough seemed to tear her in two. A voice asked, "Charissa, can you hear me?"

Charissa pulled herself out of the sleep that had wrapped itself around her. For a moment, a face was blurred before her, then it cleared, and she whispered, "Jefferson?"

"Yes, it's me."

"How long have you been here?"

"I came as soon as I heard."

Charissa began to cough, and he held her hands until it subsided. "That sounds terrible."

"I feel terrible."

"I can give you some good news. You don't have yellow fever. You've got some kind of congestion and infection."

Charissa fully awoke then and licked her lips. Jeff gave her water, then sat down beside her.

"How did you know I was sick?"

"Damita came and got me."

"You can't stay here. There are too many sick people."

"Yes, I can," he said, almost roughly. He reached out, took her wrist, and felt her pulse, then put his hand on her forehead.

Charissa lay quietly, watching him. He said nothing, but she saw his concern.

Abruptly he said, "Charissa, Damita's going to marry Yancy."

"Oh, Jeff, I'm so sorry."

He looked at her strangely, then forced a grin. "Don't be sorry. I could never have made her happy, and she couldn't have made me happy, either."

"I know you feel bad about it, though." She coughed again, but then she smiled and said, "You know, it's good to have a brother to take care of me."

Jeff stared at her sternly. "I am *not* your brother, Charissa."

Charissa looked at him with surprise.

"I wish you'd stop calling me your brother. It bothers me."

Charissa suddenly felt buoyant. "Why does it bother you, Jeff?" she asked in a weak voice.

"I don't know, but please don't say it again."

Charissa was aware of the warmth of his hand as he held hers, aware also that life had somehow changed for her. She smiled at Jeff fully and completely, and he reached out and put his hand on her cheek. "You're going to be fine, Charissa. You have to be."

"You're a masterful doctor."

"Am I?" He smiled, leaned forward, and kissed her head. He stroked her hair back from her face and said, "You must get well very quickly. I can't have my—" She knew he almost said sister, but he changed his mind and said, "I must have my *best friend* feeling perfectly well again. Will you do that?"

"Yes, I will, Jefferson."

Jeff was getting ready to leave the plantation, and he was speaking with Yancy and Damita. "She doesn't have yellow fever, of course. It's just some sort of respiratory infection. I think she's over the worst of it, and she'll be fine." Jeff shook hands with Yancy and nodded to Damita. "I'll be back tonight. I know you'll take good care of her."

The pair bade him good-bye, and as soon as he was out the door, Yancy turned and said wryly, "I was afraid he might challenge me to a duel for taking you away from him. If he does, I think I'll choose cornstalks for weapons."

"He didn't seem too broken up about it, did he? I suppose I should be upset about that. Here he's gone mooning around for months, and now he doesn't seem to mind at all."

"He's a strange sort of chap. But we Kaintocks are. You Creoles never understand us." He reached out, took Damita's hands, and drew her forward. "When can we be married? I may be a Kaintock, as you've often pointed out—just a rough fellow. But I love you."

"As soon as you wish. We've missed a lot of time."

"I guess it wasn't all lost," he said quietly. "We had to learn some things about ourselves, didn't we?"

Damita put her arms around him and laid her cheek on his chest. "I think we did, but we've found each other now."

⁓

"I still think you're leaving too soon. You need to rest a bit longer, Charissa," Damita said with concern. Charissa had rested for two days but was now dressing to leave, saying she needed to get back.

"I'll be all right, Damita."

"I have to tell you something, Charissa. It won't come as any surprise to you, but I'm the most selfish woman who ever lived. I don't do anything but take," she said quickly. "I took Yancy's help when I nearly died. I was so selfish with Jeff. I let him court me when I didn't care for him. And I took your help when I didn't deserve it." She reached out and took Charissa's hands. "I wish I could do something unselfish for you."

Charissa looked at Damita with shock. She saw that she had tears in her eyes and knew that this was not the same self-centered young woman she had served years before. "Why, don't cry," she said. But then the tears rolled down Damita's cheeks, and Charissa did something that, in previous years, would have been unthinkable.

Stepping forward, she embraced Damita and felt the tremors passing through her body as she wept silently. "I want you to forget the past, Damita. You've got a new life now. You serve the Lord God and Jesus. Let Him be your King. You've got a good man, and I forbid you to brood over what God has already forgiven."

She held the weeping young woman and thought, *What a miracle this is, that God can take what she was and make her into what she is now. And He did the same with me.*

⁓

Charissa stood beside Jeff, and as the new bride and groom passed by, they threw handfuls of rice. Charissa laughed as Yancy and Damita gave them a quick glance and waved, smiling.

They followed the crowd until the two were in a carriage and pulling away to the sounds of the crowd's cheers.

"Well," Jeff said, "they're married."

Charissa turned to look at him. "Are you sure you don't feel a little bit broken up about that?"

"Oh, no. I'm a hardheaded, rather stupid fellow, but it finally sank in. I know she's got the right man. Come on. Let's go get something to eat. Weddings make me hungry."

Charissa had watched Jeff carefully as the wedding day approached. He was such a transparent man, and as far as his emotions were concerned, she had been relieved to find that, indeed, he was over his infatuation.

"Excuse me, sir."

Jeff and Charissa turned to see a young man with dark hair and dark eyes beside them. He removed his hat and said, "You remember me, Miss Charissa?"

"Why, of course. Mr. Ransom, isn't it? We met at the hospital when you were visiting your cousin."

"Exactly right. I'm pleased you recall it. I understand you've been ill."

"I'm perfectly well now."

"I'm glad to hear it," Ransom said and smiled. "I would like to invite you to a party that I'm giving next Thursday night. Now that the fever's gone, people can begin to have lives again."

Charissa's mischievous streak arose. "Why, Mr. Ransom, you'll have to get my brother's permission."

"Oh, of course. I'd be—"

"I am not her brother. But no, she won't come."

Ransom drew up to his full height. He was still two inches shorter than Jeff, but he looked intimidating. "Are you trying to provoke me, sir? I'll be happy to give you satisfaction."

Charissa said, "Mr. Ransom, please go away. Dr. Whitman's been under a strain. I apologize for him. Come on, Doctor."

As they hurried away, Jeff growled, "Why, that insolent puppy! What does he mean, coming up in broad daylight, asking you to parties?"

"Would you rather he came sneaking around after dark? Don't be such a bear."

Charissa pulled him along firmly to the carriage, and when they got in, he was still mumbling about puppies.

Ever since Charissa had left the plantation, and it was clear that

Jeff was through with Damita, the young beauty expected him to show an interest in her. But he seemed preoccupied and troubled most of the time. She had grown impatient with him and devised a scheme. "Jeff," she said, "I'm going away for a while."

Jeff turned to stare at her. "What do you mean, 'going away'?"

"I'm going to take a vacation."

"I think that's good. Why don't you go over to Savannah. That's a nice—"

"No, I mean a long vacation. Maybe half a year."

"What are you talking about?"

"I've been thinking about going to England. You know, we talked about it before. I've decided to go."

Jeff sat silently, and when she snuck a glance at him, she saw that he was staring at his hands. She expected him to argue, but he said only, "If that's what you want to do."

"It is!" she said sharply. "I'll be going very soon. Next week, perhaps."

~

The next week was a strange one for Charissa. Since she had spoken to Jeff about her going to England, she had expected him to try to persuade her to stay home—or to offer to go with her, as they'd discussed some time ago. Instead, he had grown silent and sullen. *If he doesn't want me to go, why doesn't he say so?* she wondered impatiently. *He does nothing but mope.*

She purchased her passage on the *Orion,* a steam-driven ship, and had begun packing her things a little at a time. Jeff and Debakky both asked about her plans, but she was purposefully vague. "I'll decide when I get there" was all she would answer.

Two days before she was to leave, Jeff arrived home from the hospital whistling. He spoke to Charissa cheerfully and smiled, and that night he laughed a great deal, at least for him. He was very lively over the following two days. Charissa did not know what to make of him. *I thought he was sad at my leaving, but now he seems delighted.* This depressed her. She had no real wish to go to England; now she saw no way out. *I've got to go,* she decided. *Even though he's acting as if I were traveling around the block.*

"I'll go to your cabin with you, Charissa," Jeff said. "I'd like to see it."

"All right, Jeff." Charissa was downcast. She had lost all taste for a sea voyage.

Debakky had said good-bye, hugged her, and told her to enjoy herself. For some reason, his eyes had danced, and he had said, "It'll be the best thing in the world for you."

"You don't seem very sorry to see me go," she said reproachfully.

"A young woman needs to get away. You have a good time!"

Now, as they walked up the gangplank, Jeff was speaking rapid-fire about the voyage. "You'll love it," he said. "Beautiful weather for an ocean voyage. You'll stay out on the deck a lot, and get sunshine and exercise, and the food's wonderful."

"I'm sure it is," Charissa said shortly. She stepped on the deck, and Jeff asked a steward in a white coat how to find her room. Then he took her arm and led her down some stairs and into a corridor. "This is almost a brand-new ship. You're going to have a wonderful time."

Charissa glanced up at him. *He could at least act as if he's a little sad,* she thought.

"Here it is. Let's see if the key works. It does. Step inside, my dear."

Charissa did so, and Jeff followed her. "It's a small room, but then, you don't need a lot of space. You will be eating in the dining room, and I understand there are dances and things like that. You will have such a good time, Charissa."

"I worry about you, Jefferson," Charissa said, trying to turn the conversation to more personal matters. "You always work so hard."

"Oh, don't worry about me. I'll be fine." Jeff sat down and began to speak of England. "I brought you some maps and some books," he said, handing her the parcel he'd been carrying. "Here, let me show you. One place you should go is Cornwall. I've read a lot about Cornwall. It's where King Arthur was supposed to have been."

Charissa listened to him dully, and finally a whistle blew, and she said, "That's the warning for you to leave, I think." A voice cried out faintly, "All visitors ashore!" Charissa stood up and said, "Well, this is good-bye."

"These ships never leave on time. Sit down. I want to show you some other places. Now, Brighton—there's a place you must visit."

Charissa sat, and Jeff continued to open the maps and the books and chatter in an excited fashion. Twice she warned him about the ship's pulling out, but he said, "There's plenty of time."

She felt the ship move, and she said, "Jeff, the ship's leaving!"

He looked up at her and rose to his feet. "Is it, really? I believe you're right."

"Jeff, you've got to get off!"

"Oh, too late now for that."

"But, Jeff—"

"Come along, Charissa. There's something I want to show you."

Charissa stared at him. His eyes were sparkling with a spirit of joy, and he took her arm and led her back to the deck, then down another set of stairs and into a corridor. "It's right down here, I think."

"Jeff, the ship is leaving right now!"

"I know. Just this one thing."

She followed him until he came to a door, whipped a key out of his pocket, and unlocked it. "Step in here."

Charissa did so, and he followed her, shutting the door behind them. "How do you like this?"

The elegant cabin was three times as large as her own. It was furnished magnificently. Charissa demanded, "Jeff, why are you showing me this?"

"This is the honeymoon suite."

"The what?"

"It's used for newly married couples. That's what a honeymoon is." Jeff pulled her close and said, "I'm staying in it all the way to England, and I want you to stay in it with me."

Charissa could not understand what he was saying. She was aware of the motion of the ship, but she was far more aware of his arms holding her tightly. "I couldn't do a thing like that, Jefferson."

"Why not?"

"You know why not. Because it would be wrong."

"It would be wrong only if you didn't marry me."

Charissa stood perfectly still. She felt the blood leave her face, and she saw that he was now perfectly sober. "Jefferson, what are you talking about?"

"I've been talking to people. I talked to Debakky, and he said you loved me. And I talked to Rose. She told me you've loved me for a long time. And I got a letter from Olga. She called me a stupid oaf and said that you cared for me even back in those days at St. Louis. They all say it, Charissa: You love me."

"Jeff," Charissa began, her voice breaking.

His arms tightened around her, and he said, "When you were sick, and I thought you might die, I found out I couldn't do without you. All my fool talk about a sister! What idiocy! I love you, Charissa, as a man loves a woman."

Charissa felt warmth then coming to her face. She looked into his eyes, and he kissed her.

"I've loved you for so long," she whispered. "I thought you'd never care for me."

"I guess I couldn't get it in my head that you could love a big, awkward fellow like me." He squeezed her, kissed her thoroughly, and said, "The captain can marry us. Are you ready?"

Charissa smiled. "Yes, I'm ready."

"Let's go get married. We'll have a fine honeymoon, and when we return, we're going back to St. Louis. I've already made arrangements."

"Oh, Jeff, really?" Charissa cried.

"Yes. Come along. I'm in a hurry to get married."

Charissa took his face between her hands and cried, "So am I, Jefferson, so am I!"

About the authors

DR. GILBERT MORRIS is a retired English professor. He is the author of more than 170 novels, many of them bestsellers and several of them award winners. He has been married for fifty-three years to Johnny, and they have three children. His daughter, LYNN MORRIS, has coauthored many books with her father, including the *Cheney Duval, M.D.* series.

THE EXILES: A NOVEL

BOOK ONE OF THE CREOLES SERIES

The Exiles, the first book of The Creoles Series, introduces Chantel Fontaine. Readers follow Chantel through the streets and swamps of Louisiana as she falls in love, faces the loss of both her parents, and searches for the baby sister she thought was lost forever.

The culture of the citizens of nineteenth-century New Orleans was as varied and intriguing as their complexions—French, Spanish, African, and American. As the layers of these cultures intertwine, a rich, entertaining story of love and faith emerges. It is the early 1800s, and Chantel Fountaine has finished her education at the Ursuline Convent. But the trials and tragedies that preceded her graduation have put her Christian beliefs to the test.

From bestselling authors Gilbert and Lynn Morris, this captivating novel offers a unique perspective in a distinct cultural setting that comes alive in the minds and hearts of readers.

ISBN: 0-7852-7002-7

Look for Books Two and Three of The Creoles Series:

The Alchemy

The Tapestry

An excerpt from
book one of
The Creole Series,
The Exiles

HAVANA, CUBA, JULY 3, 1810

Aimee Fontaine looked out of the open carriage and immediately shut her eyes. She turned and threw her arms around her husband and cried, "Cretien, we'll all be killed!"

He held her tightly and said, "We won't be killed, darling. It's not far to the docks, and once we get on board the ship we'll be safe."

Opening her eyes, Aimee moved her head back far enough to get a good view of Cretien's face, and the very sight of it encouraged her. Faults her husband might have, but if Cretien Fontaine was a coward, no one had ever found out about it. His chestnut hair escaped the tall black top hat, and his brown eyes glowed as they always did when he was excited. He showed no fear whatsoever.

"They've gone crazy," she whispered, holding on to Cretien's arm.

"Revolutionaries are always crazy," Cretien said. He turned to the driver, saying, "Get in the back with Elise, Robert. I'll drive."

"But, sir—"

"Mind what I say!" Cretien's eyes flashed, and Robert got up awkwardly and fell into the back, where Elise Debon was crouched down, her large eyes frightened. Cretien took the lines and slapped them on the backs of the pair of bays, holding the horses firmly. "They're crazy fools! They don't even know what they're fighting for."

Others besides Cretien had made that remark concerning the uproar that had shaken Cuba to its very foundation. The countryside was alive with flames where men, apparently driven mad by the revolutionary fervor, had set fire to the homes of innocent people. The government had tottered and collapsed, and now Havana was packed with a mindless mass of humanity.

Darkness had fallen, but men carrying torches held them high, and the flickering red flames cast shadows over cruel faces loose with drink. The air was filled with drunken cries and screams of women who were being attacked regardless of their politics. Gunfire rattled, sounding a deadly punctuation.

"We'll never be able to get through this crowd, Cretien," Aimee whispered.

Indeed, it did look impossible, for the street that led to the docks was filled with milling people. Many of them were armed men, but some were the helpless victims of the revolutionaries.

Cretien pulled his hat down firmly, reached low, and pulled the whip from the socket. "Hold on, everybody!" he cried. He slashed the rumps of the horses furiously, and the bays lunged forward against their collars. "Get out of the way! Clear the way!" Cretien yelled. He stood to his feet and whipped at men who reached out to pull him from the carriage.

Once Aimee saw the whip strike a man right across the cheek and leave a bleeding cut. The man fell back with a scream and was seen no more.

Aimee hid her eyes, for the horses ran over anyone in their way, and the wheels bumped over the bodies that had fallen. The carriage careened wildly, and the shouts grew louder. A gunshot sounded clearly close to the carriage. Aimee's heart seemed to stop, but the marksman had missed.

"We'll be all right," Cretien said. He sat back down but kept the horses at a fast clip. "There's the ship, down there." A few moments later he pulled the horses up short, and they stood trembling and snorting under the light of the lanterns that hung from posts on the dock. *The Empress,* one of the new breed of steamships, loomed large and black against the ebony sky. "Robert, you see to the luggage. I'll take care of the women."

"Yes, sir!"

Aimee stood, and Cretien lifted her into his arms and set her down firmly on the dock. She clung to him for a moment, but he gave her a quick hug and said, "We're all right now. Don't worry. I'll get you and Elise on board, and then I'll come back to help Robert with the luggage."

Aimee gratefully leaned against her husband, but they had not gone three steps toward the gangplank when their way was blocked by a roughly dressed group of men. All had a wolfish look, and their eyes were wild with drink.

"Hold it there!" one of them said. "We'll take your money."

"That's right. He's an aristocrat." The speaker, who wore a crimson rag around his forehead, pulled a knife from his belt and laughed drunkenly. "His kind's gone forever. Give us what you've got, and maybe we'll let you go."

In one smooth motion, Cretien pulled a pistol from under his coat and aimed at the man bearing the knife. The shot struck the ruffian in the upper arm. The wounded man shouted, "That's the only shot he's got! Get him!"

The men moved forward, eyes glittering. Suddenly another shot rang out, and a short, stocky man staggered and grabbed his thigh.

"He got me!" he cried.

Robert, Cretien's manservant, stepped out and said, "The rest of you had better leave."

But the three were so drunk they could not think. They all drew knives and, screaming, surged ahead. Cretien reached into the carriage and produced a cane. He pulled a sword from the hollow container, and when one of the men came close he swung the blade in a circular motion. The tip of the sword cut a gash in the chest of the man.

"I'd advise you to leave before you are all dead," Cretien said tightly.

"Come on, let's get out of here!" the leader cried. Since three of the four had been wounded, his words were convincing. They all turned and made their way, cursing and holding their wounds.

"Come along, Aimee," Cretien said at once. His face was pale, and the violence had shaken him, for he was not a man of action. "And you, Elise, I'll get you on board. Robert, start loading the luggage. I'll be back to help you."